Trouble

amazon publishing

Aforke

ALSO BY ADRIANA LOCKE

The Exception Series

The Exception

The Connection: An Exception Novella

The Perception

The Exception Series Box Set

Landry Family Series

Sway

Swing

Switch

Swear

Swink

Sweet

The Landry Family Series: Part One

The Landry Family Series: Part Two

The Gibson Boys Series

Crank

Craft

Cross (a novella)

Crave

Crazy

Praise for Adriana Locke

"Adriana Locke creates magic with unforgettable romances and captivating characters. She's a go-to author if I want to escape into a great read."

—*New York Times* bestselling author S.L. Scott

"Adriana Locke writes the most delicious heroes and sassy heroines who bring them to their knees. Her books are funny, raw, and heartfelt. She also has a great smile, but that's beside the point."

—*USA Today* bestselling author L.J. Shen

"No one does blue collar, small town, 'everyman' (and woman!) romance like Adriana Locke. She masterfully creates truly epic love stories for characters who could be your neighbor, your best friend—you! Each one is more addictive and heart-stoppingly romantic than the last."

—Bestselling author Kennedy Ryan

"Adriana's sharp prose, witty dialogue, and flawless blend of humor and steam meld together to create unputdownable, up-all-night reads!"

—*Wall Street Journal* bestselling author Winter Renshaw

Dogwood Lane Series

Tumble
Tangle

Stand-Alone Novels

Sacrifice
Wherever It Leads
Written in the Scars
Battle of the Sexes
Lucky Number Eleven

ADRIANA LOCKE

This is a work of fiction. Names, characters, organizations, places, events, and incidents are either products of the author's imagination or are used fictitiously.

Published by Montlake, Seattle

www.apub.com

ISBN-13: 9781542018456
ISBN-10: 1542018455

Cover design by Letitia Hasser

Cover photography by Wander Aguiar Photography

Printed in the United States of America

To Mom and Dad:
You made me believe I could accomplish anything.
Thank you for that.
I love you.

CHAPTER ONE

Penn

"How hard is it, Penn?"

Dane's keys hit the table. They skid into the saltshaker, sending it rattling around the tabletop. He shoots a raised brow that is some kind of warning my direction before he turns and signals for a coffee.

"Well," I say as Claire approaches the table, "I probably shouldn't answer that. I am a gentleman, after all."

"You are not." Claire side-eyes me as she sets a mug down in front of Dane. "You and the word 'gentleman' should never be used in the same sentence."

"But you just did."

She rolls her eyes. "Want me to accidentally-on-purpose miss the cup and pour this piping-hot liquid on your lap?"

"You've tried that before. I'm too quick."

Claire snorts, her lips twisting into an amused smile. "I heard that about you."

My jaw drops in mock horror.

"Will you two stop it? You fight like brother and sister," Dane says.

"That would make Claire's dreams awkward."

Her gaze whips to mine, her eyes narrowed for my benefit. There's a comeback on the tip of her tongue. I lean forward as if I'm waiting on her reply. She laughs instead.

"I hate you," she says before turning to Dane. "Do you want anything to eat?"

"No. Thanks. Just trying to track this jackass down all morning." He jabs a thumb my way.

"Yeah, well, good luck now that you've found him. He's sat in here for hours, giving me hell," Claire says. "If *you* need anything else, let me know."

Claire walks away, swaying her hips a little for my benefit. It's appreciated. I'd much, *much* rather think about her hips than whatever it is Dane's going to rope me into.

He sips his coffee beside me like it's another morning at the Dogwood Café. The table of farmers by the door probably think it's just Madden Carpentry having some breakfast before we find Matt, my best friend and Dane's younger brother, and get to work.

But it's not.

Something is brewing, and I don't know what it is. What I do know is that Dane doesn't start blowing up my phone at six in the morning on an actual workday, let alone my first vacation day in two years.

Yeah. Something is up, and I'm not going to like it.

"So?" Dane asks finally. "Did you lose your phone last night or something?"

I tug it out of my pocket and slide it across the table. "Nope. It's right there."

The irritation on his face is satisfying.

"Then why aren't you answering it?" he asks.

"Do you answer calls when you don't want to talk to someone? No. The invention of caller ID makes ignoring people a breeze."

He sighs. "Penn."

"Dane," I mock, stretching my legs out in front of me. "What do you want so I can get on with my day?"

"I want to talk to you."

"Then talk."

The longer he takes to explain whatever it is that's going to ruin my day, the more my stomach twists. Visions of fishing and taking a nap while watching that show about shiplap slip away.

It's my turn to sigh. "I'm not going to be screwing off today, am I?"

"Depends how you're using the word 'screw.'"

Sitting up, I cross my arms on the table. My tattoos bend and flex as I move. My latest ink, a small triangle that isn't exactly straight because the guy who did it reeked of vodka, sits on my forearm like a permanent reminder of all the dumb shit I've ever done in my life—like this tattoo. And, most likely, whatever it is I'm about to agree to.

It's going to be terrible, or he wouldn't have bothered to dance around the topic. He would've just said it. Dane doesn't use lube.

"I have an appointment in ten minutes," I say, watching a car turn into the salon across the street from the café. "Whatever is so damn important that you chased me down while I was having breakfast—"

"You weren't having breakfast. You were flirting with Claire."

"For your information, I did have breakfast, and I was not flirting with Claire."

"You were totally flirting with me," Claire says as she walks by.

Dane waves a hand in my face, blocking the view of Claire's ass. "Let's bring your attention back here."

"Can I think about it?"

"No." His words are filled with equal amounts exasperation and irritation. "Look, as much as it pains me to say this, I need your help."

I knew it.

I pull my wallet from my pocket and lay a five-dollar bill on the table for Claire. Avoiding Dane's eyes isn't easy work, but I'm a pro.

"Penn?" he asks.

"Catch ya later, Dane." I get my phone and climb to my feet three seconds before he does. As I head to the front door, he's just a half step behind me.

The sunlight is warm against my face as I make my way outside. The cool breeze that held so much promise earlier is now a tease.

"Just hear me out," he insists as he catches up to me.

I stop on the edge of the patio and raise my chin toward the sun. "I really do have somewhere to be."

"She can wait."

"It's not a 'she.'"

"Sure it isn't."

Lowering my eyes to his, I grin. "While I really love the fact that you think I have chicks lined up at nine in the morning, it's not a 'she.' For real. The only thing on my to-do list today is getting a haircut at Harper's."

"Fine. Whatever you say. I'll talk fast."

"You do that," I say, letting the toes of my boots hang off the edge of the concrete.

Dane looks at me with a seriousness that tells me this won't be fun, and it won't be quick. He winces. "Meredith Kelly is—"

"Oh no." My head swings back and forth. "I'm out."

"Penn . . ."

I look at him with all the gravity I can muster. "The woman is nuts."

"She's *not* nuts."

I slow blink. "She has a spa for her dogs."

"So, she's . . . eccentric," he says, waving a hand in the air like that dissolves my point. "That doesn't mean she's nuts."

"I don't know what 'eccentric' means, but if it doesn't mean 'crazy,' you're wrong." With another shake of my head, I start down the sidewalk.

Memories of building Meredith Kelly's house—reading her instructions on paper that smelled like flowers and changing the shade of pink in various rooms time and time again—filter through my mind. She was as sweet as her perfume and would send us cookies from some ritzy bakery in Nashville, but still. If Dane thinks I want to voluntarily sign up to do anything else for this woman, he's lost his mind.

If she were single, that would be another story. But she's very much married. So I'm very much out.

"It's a kids' camp thing," he says, stumbling over the words.

"Oh, a 'kids' camp thing.' I know exactly what that means."

I stop and stretch my arms over my head. I yawn for good measure. Maybe Dane will take pity on me and let whatever this is go.

He frowns.

Maybe not.

"I know Meredith is quirky, which is what 'eccentric' means," he says like I'd care. "But she's also got a really good heart and a lot of money."

"Good for her. I don't have either."

Dane's laugh barrels through the air. "You do too. The heart, that is. You have the financial sense of a monkey."

"Don't tell anyone that, will ya?"

"What? That you can't manage money?"

"No," I say, making a sour face. "Everyone knows that. Don't go spreading around that I'm a nice guy. It'll give people expectations and shit."

He tries not to smile. "Fine. Now, back to the issue at hand—"

"I don't even like kids," I whine. "They're loud and they don't listen and they fuck shit up. Your kid is the only one I can tolerate . . ."

Shit. Dane's eyes light up at the opening I just handed him on a silver platter.

"And if you don't help me here," he says like I'm a child, "I won't be able to take my sweet little Mia to the land of giant mice and princesses.

Think how disappointed she'll be if I have to tell her that her buddy Penn won't help me out and is ruining her vacation."

"Low blow, Dane. Low blow."

"So, you'll do it?"

I stick out my bottom lip. "I don't want to. I'm supposed to be on vacation too. Doesn't anyone care about me?"

My play for sympathy falls on deaf ears. Instead of capitulating, he shifts his weight and digs in for the kill.

"This is going to get a ton of press, and we'll get paid without having to chase anyone down." He shoves his hands in his pockets and takes a deep breath. "The Kellys are going to be investing thousands of dollars in Dogwood Lane, Penn. We have a great opportunity here to secure a lot of work. They already trust us. We know they're going to pay well. And to be honest, we need to bank the money now so when winter comes and the projects slow down . . ."

I toe a rock with my boot and try to hold my ground. But as he continues to stand next to me, I feel myself start to give in.

Winters are hard on construction guys like us. The work slows, but bills still have to be paid. It's not that bad for me or Matt, because we're bachelors with basic rent and truck payments. For Dane, the guy with a family to take care of, it's worse.

I sigh. "Why can't Matt do it? Isn't he required by blood to be your right-hand man?"

"He would, but the doctor hasn't released him yet. He's got another week or something."

"He fell off a ladder," I deadpan.

"Until you get your MD and release him to work, there's not a lot I can do about it." Dane blows out a breath. The lines around his eyes gather, the stress of potentially having to turn this job down evident on his face. "It's just a week—two, tops. Basic framing and layout work at this point. If Mia didn't have her heart set on this trip, I'd do it myself. But I can't break her heart."

"Don't use Mia against me."

He grins. "She already has her bags packed. I bet she'd cry herself to sleep for two weeks if—"

"Fine," I say before I can take it back. "But you're an asshole for using your kid. Who does that? It's dirty, Dane. Real dirty."

His shoulders fall in relief. "Just get it started, and I'll take over when I'm back. And Neely said to tell you 'thank you' as soon as you caved."

"Yeah, yeah, yeah." I glance at my watch again. "You tell your fiancée this is going to cost her a pan of lasagna. And for the record, if Meredith even mentions the word 'spa,' I quit."

He beams. "Thanks, pal."

"Pal, my ass." I start across the street. "Call me later."

"Will ya answer?"

I look at him over my shoulder as I cross the centerline. "Probably not." I flip him the bird for good measure.

Two years. I just got suckered into giving up a vacation I've earned for *two freaking years*. Next time, I'm the one who is leaving town.

Early.

CHAPTER TWO

AVERY

"Are you trying to get yourself killed?"

Harper's voice rings through the small, sunlit room. I glance at her from atop a dilapidated ladder I found in the storage shed behind the salon. She's looking at me over a stack of towels, a concerned curiosity etched on her face.

"I'm hanging a speaker so I can bluetooth my phone to it," I tell her. "I like to dance while I work."

Her laugh, easy and free, fills the room. She sets the towels down on her chair. "Just a heads-up, party girl: most of our clientele are farmers and ladies that play bridge. The only dance they know is the two-step."

I turn back to the wall.

I didn't know the two-step was still a thing. Come to think of it, I don't know that much about life here in Tennessee in general. This is probably why experts tell people not to make big life decisions on a whim. Moving from Los Angeles to the smallest town I've ever imagined is definitely on the large side of the spectrum and probably not the wisest choice to make after two bottles of wine on a Wednesday. Even so, I feel pretty good about it.

When I told her my plan, Mom thought I'd lost my mind. Dad was sure I was on drugs. Who wouldn't want to live in LA, the daughter of a famous actress, and take advantage of all the perks of the situation?

Me. That's who. Mainly because the so-called "perks" make my skin crawl.

I just couldn't do it anymore. I couldn't wake up another day and pretend to love the life I was living. It wasn't even *my* life but more like roles in everyone else's lives. How it got to that point I don't know, but I was done.

I was tired of being the daughter who toes the line. The only relationships my parents cared about when it came to me were the ones I had with their associates. As long as I didn't embarrass Mom and Dad or hurt their connections—or want crazy things like family dinners—we were good.

Work was exhausting on a soul level. There are only so many times you can have a man sitting in your chair and know he just got a blow job from someone in the back room right before his wife walks in. It's maddening. But you have to keep those secrets or get blackballed . . . even when some of those secrets involve your friends.

More than anything, I was tired of trying to be happy. Every man I met was a smooth talker, a one-upper, someone trying to position himself to use me somehow. It was all so superficial, and I felt that. Deeply.

I didn't know what to do, but I knew who would: Aunt Harper.

"You're going to have culture shock today," she says. "When was the last time you charged fourteen dollars for a haircut?"

"Um, never. You're joking, right?"

"I'm afraid not." She laughs, clearly amused at my wide-eyed response.

"How do you even live on fourteen dollars a haircut?"

"The same way you're going to have to—cheaply."

I mock the speaker bracket up on the wall as I think about Harper's statement. Fourteen dollars a pop is a pittance compared with what

I got in LA, but I don't even care. I actually kind of like it in some weird way. It feels . . . honest. Good. Kind of like how driving through Dogwood Lane felt this morning.

There's something satisfying about being in a town and having people wave. People holding doors open for you, men standing in their overalls at the gas station, saying "Good morning, miss," and having the streets lined with mom-and-pop businesses and not chain stores with fancy signs out front.

Even though everyone I know—everyone except Harper—believes I'm nuts, I'm not. This isn't some wackadoodle choice like they think. For the first time in my life, I'm doing what feels right *for me*. It's glorious.

I hope this town will be the same landing spot it was when I ran here ten years ago. Of course, back then I was eighteen, and I ended up having sex with the sweetest, most delicious guy on the banks of Dogwood Lake. I felt so awful about it afterward, having given him a fake name and a bullshit backstory, but what was I supposed to tell him? That the woman on the cover of the rag mags at the grocery store was my mom? That she hadn't meant to let her nipple slip on the red carpet the week before (even though she had)?

Nope. I didn't want to be judged because of her, nor did I want to be fawned over due to her name. I wanted someone to like me for me, and I think he did that night, even if he thought my name was Abby. And so far in my three days in town this time, Dogwood Lane has been as sweet to me as it was then.

I hold a nail through the hole in the speaker bracket. "I can live cheaply. Who knows? Maybe I can bring some new styles to the people."

"When was the last time you gave a perm?"

"That was an eighties fad."

"Eh, not so much." She snickers. "I think the people here are going to bring you some new skills."

"Maybe," I say, patting my pockets with my free hand. "Where in the heck did I put the hammer?"

Harper sighs. She marches across the room, picks up the hammer from the floor, and holds it out to me. "Why don't you just let me get someone to help you?"

"Because I'm entirely capable of hanging a speaker." I raise a brow as I take the hammer. "Thank you. Now stand back and watch me work."

"What I'm gonna watch is you breaking your damn neck, and I have no idea what I'll tell your mother. She blames me for all your wild-child tendencies the way it is."

"Dyeing my hair black during my emo phase, not being a fan of no-carb diets, and vetoing the offer of breast implants to, and I quote, 'get ahead in the world' aren't exactly wild-child tendencies. But yeah, I get ya." I grip the hammer. "I never did tell her you sent me that hair dye. Or the condoms."

"You know, that was one time I wasn't exactly sure what to do. You were seventeen. You didn't need to be having sex."

"Like you weren't having sex at seventeen," I scoff. "Besides, I didn't end up sleeping with that guy."

I line the hammer up with the nail and give it a swift hit. The force shakes the ladder, and I yelp as Harper grabs my legs to hold me steady.

"You're going to fall," she says.

"I am not." I pause and look over my shoulder. "But if I do, just tell Mom something along the line that her daughter decided to perform manual labor for fun. Her reaction after she processes the words 'manual labor' should entertain you for a while."

Harper and I exchange a grin.

People have always said that I take after my aunt. We look alike with our rich dark hair and full, curvy figures. Our personalities are fairly similar, too, with penchants for romantic comedies and coconut rum. And we both chose to go to beauty school—a lowly service-oriented job, as my mother so kindly calls it.

Harper, though, is stronger than I've ever been. She knows what she wants, and she's not afraid to go after it. When she realized she couldn't take the LA life anymore, she literally threw a dart at a map on the wall and trucked it to Dogwood Lane the next day. She gave no thought to what anyone said. It took me years to get the balls to leave. Of course, she also felt the need, somewhat crazily, to marry the same man three times. But that's not the point.

"If I could just get steady, I could get this nail in here and be done with this thing," I say, widening my stance as far as I can on the little platform. "I just want music. Music makes me happy."

She flashes me a grin and walks to the window. Her smile grows wider as she peers out at the street below. "What else makes you happy, Avery?"

"Chocolate factories," I say, trying to figure out where the stud is in the wall. "Waterproof mascara that comes off without scrubbing my eyes until they bleed. Men with great shoulders and amazing hearts that actually want to do the work to get to know me instead of flashing me a killer smile and pickup line."

I realize that I'm just pressing aimlessly on the wall. Stud-finding, at least in the construction department, isn't something I know how to do. I didn't think it would be this hard.

"I'm not even sure those things exist," I say to Harper. "So maybe I'm bound for a happy-less life."

When she doesn't respond, I look at her over my shoulder. She's watching me with a slightly amused look.

"What?" I ask.

"I beg to differ."

"Oh, really? Do you know where there's a secret chocolate factory that we can break into and befriend the little orange men in white-and-green jumpsuits?"

She laughs as she flips over the sign indicating we're open for business. "Not what I was talking about. Now, are you ready for today?"

"Ready as I'm ever going to be."

"Good. Because here comes trouble."

"Great," I mumble, turning my attention back to the speaker.

No matter where I tap, the hollow thud of a studless wall echoes back. I'm trying to figure out what to do when the door squeaks behind me.

"Hey, Harp," someone says.

The voice is definitively male—the kind of sound that is both a delicious whisper and a heady scratch against your skin. The southern twang to the tone is the kind of thing that dreams are made of. A smile touches my lips as I revel in the idea of living in a place where voices can almost be foreplay.

"Hey," Harper chirps.

I roll my eyes at the giddiness of her tone. If there's a chink in Harper's armor, it's her love of men. Give her a pretty face or great abs and she's toast.

Moving the bracket a little to the right, I mock a nail up to the top hole. I give it a tap. Instead of going in the wall, the nail shoots sideways and drops to the floor with a ping.

"Damn it," I mutter.

"What are ya doing up there?" The caramelly voice rings from behind me as I take two nails out of my pocket.

"Trying to hang a speaker." I put one nail in between my lips and hold the other against the hole.

"Need some help?"

It's clear he's entertained. That only makes me more determined to show him I can do it by myself.

"Nope," I say, biting the nail a little too hard. "I got it. Thanks, though."

"I'm just going to stand here and make sure."

"You do that."

I mock up another nail. Before I swing the hammer, I ensure my weight is evenly distributed and the bracket is poised exactly where I think it might work. Now that I have an audience, I can't fail.

"You know, if you move that about two inches to the left, there's probably a stud," he says. "I mean, there's one behind you, too, but you probably aren't looking to nail the one with the great abs. Or are you?"

My eyes roll so hard it almost hurts. I blow out a breath in exasperation. "I've nailed a lot of great abs. Unfortunately, the abs are usually where the greatness stops."

Harper's laugh barrels across the room and mixes with my self-appointed supervisor's chuckle. If I weren't so focused on getting the speaker hung and mildly irritated at his confidence, I'd probably really enjoy the timbre of his voice.

"All jokes aside, there's an outlet by the floor underneath you. Outlets are always on a stud. So if you really want to hang that thing, move it over two inches like I said, and you'll be fine."

"I was doing just fine without you," I say. But as I think about the logic behind his remark, he's probably right. *Damn it.*

"Suit yourself."

I wait for him to move into my line of sight. He doesn't. He stays positioned perfectly behind me so I'd have to actually look over my shoulder to see him. The thought crosses my mind that he might be checking out my butt, and I'm thankful I wore my good jeans today.

I want to see him but don't want to turn around. That would be obvious. I also don't want to move this bracket two inches to the left and prove him right, but I have to.

Ugh.

Sliding the metal across the drywall, I hold my breath and wait for him to say something. I put the nail into the hole and wait again. Still nothing. Just as I draw the hammer back, he speaks.

"Are you new around here or what?" he asks.

My hands drop to my sides as I spin around. The bracket pings as it hits the floor. "Why do you ask so many quest . . . ions . . ."

It's like his gaze is waiting for me. It plucks mine out of the air and locks it in place. As soon as our eyes meet, an audible gasp escapes my lips.

Holy. Shit.

I've seen those eyes before. They were lit up by a makeshift fire beside Dogwood Lake as we dined on a bag of cheesy chips and a can of soda from a machine by the bait shop.

He's smiling up at me with the deepest, sexiest dimple that God ever gave a man. "You are definitely new around here. I'd remember seeing you."

My mouth opens to call bullshit, to tell him he's seen more of me than what he's looking at now, when I stop myself.

He doesn't recognize me.

Well, hell.

Nothing like a kick to the self-esteem when your one-night stand doesn't recognize you, even if it was ten years ago.

His brows pull together. "Are you all right?"

"Yes, I—ah!" I move too fast for the old ladder. It rocks beneath me, the stabilizing bars on the sides wobbling. Before I know it, my legs are going one way and my top half is going the other and I land

In.

His.

Arms.

My breath comes out in panicked huffs, my heart thundering in my chest. I take in a deep lungful of air that's tinged with a clean, masculine scent—a scent that is like electricity in my veins.

Holy freaking crap.

One of his thick, muscled arms is wrapped beneath my legs. The other is cushioned around my back. He holds me with no effort and looks down, completely pleased with himself.

"I'm sorry," I say, trying to ignore the way a ripple of goose bumps speckles my skin.

"That's okay. I'm used to women falling for me."

I pull my hand away from across his wide shoulders, letting my fingertips trail the back of his neck for only a split second. "Put me down," I say while I have the sense to say it. "Please."

"Sure thing." He grins as he sets me on my feet. "Want me to hang the speaker for you?"

"No, I do not," I say, my cheeks flushing. "I can do it." It takes everything I have to rip my eyes from his tattooed arms—the arms I was just cradled in—and look at Harper. "You were right."

My phone rings in my hand. My mother's number is displaying on the screen. Even though I generally just put her to voice mail to avoid a lecture on how I'm screwing up my life, her timing is perfect.

"I was right about what?" Harper asks.

I head to the door and pull it open. Before stepping outside, I glance at Penn. The bastard is smirking.

"He's trouble," I say, and step out into the morning sun.

CHAPTER THREE

Penn

"Are you just going to stand there drooling like a puppy dog, or are you gonna say something?" Harper elbows me in the side.

I drag my eyes from the doorway and look at her. "What do you want me to say? Who the fuck was that? Because that's all I can think about right now."

Harper laughs as she watches my reaction to the woman who just gave me an instant case of blue balls.

Tight T-shirt with an eighties band emblazoned across "more than her fair share" breasts.

Eyes that are so dark I can't even tell what color they are.

And a smile that is like crack to my veins—if I knew what doing crack was like.

"No, for real," I say. "Who is she, Harp?"

"Actually, she's my niece. Her name is Avery Perry."

I pivot to face her, my jaw dropping for her amusement. "You've been holding out on me?"

"I'm sorry. Am I supposed to give you a breakdown of all of the members of my family?"

"If they look like you, yeah." My jaw springs back to a more normal, less shocked position. "With pictures, if you can spare them."

"You're awful."

"Have I not always told you that you're a hottie?" I tease.

"I could be your mother. I'm . . . older than that, even. I'm ten years older than Avery's mother, who is my sister."

I plop in her chair. "Well, I have nothing against cougars. Just saying."

"I don't know what I'm going to do with you." Despite her best attempt at pretending she's not flattered, she is. Her cheeks give her away.

Swiveling back and forth in the chair because I know it drives her crazy, I wait. Harper has been cutting my hair for as long as I can remember. I've learned a thing or two about her over the years—one being that she likes to talk. A lot. If I give her enough time, she'll tell me everything I need to know about her niece without me even having to ask.

She busies herself organizing shampoos until, like clockwork, she can't take it anymore.

"She's single, you know. In case you care," she says with a practiced nonchalance.

Bingo!

"Of course I care. Did you see her ass?"

"Stop that," she says, trying to take a swat at me.

"Stop what? Stop acting like that's the finest ass I've ever seen? All round and juicy . . ." I adjust my cock. "But for real, I'm happy to hear she's single. I do have standards."

"And I'm happy to hear that."

"So, what else do I need to know? Don't hold out on me now."

"Well, she's from Los Angeles. She moved in with me a couple of days ago."

"Is she running from some ex-boyfriend or something?" I ask. "I've been itching for a good fight."

Harper laughs. "No. I'm pretty sure she could hold her own with just about anyone. I can't see her running from a boyfriend. She is my niece, you know."

"I'd like to go toe to toe with her, if you know what I mean," I say, wiggling my eyebrows.

She gives me a solid once-over, like she's grading me somehow. It makes me squirm. Finally, she nods.

"You know, if you play your cards right—like I know you can—I think she could be a good match for you, Penn."

I flinch. The way she says it, like she's dangling a carrot in front of me, gives me everything I need to know. "You're talking about monogamy, aren't you?"

"Penn . . ."

"I'm allergic."

"You are not allergic." She sighs. "But you're going to be alone for the rest of your life if you don't straighten up, and that would be such a waste."

I try my hardest not to laugh, but it eventually comes out in a half chuckle, half snort. "Trust me. I'm *never* alone. I don't really see that being an issue."

"Not having someone in bed with you and being alone are two different things."

"I disagree, buddy."

Harper throws her hands up in the air. "I quit. Let's talk about why you're actually on time instead."

"It turns out that I can't sleep in even when I'm on vacation. How fucked up is that?" I get up, take my hat off, and hang it on a hook by the door. My hand goes in my hair, which needed cutting last month. It's sticking up everywhere and half-glued to my head.

I glance at the doorway again. "Do you want to go ahead and get started?"

"You worried Avery will see you all out of whack?"

"Trust me. Women don't care what my hair looks like."

"Trust me. They do." She ignores my question and goes back to organizing the combs on her station. "So, what's this about a vacation?"

I mosey over to the other side of the room and pretend to be killing time. Rocking back on my heels, I try to get a glimpse out the window.

"Oh, I have a couple of weeks off," I say as I take a step to the side. I try to get a peek in again and fail. "Dane, um, you know, he's . . ."

"Will you stop?" Harper laughs. "You're going to break your neck. Besides, you can't see anything from there. You'd have to walk over to at least the chair."

I spin around, caught red-handed. "What? I wasn't trying to see anything." I try to keep a straight face but fail at that too. "She's hot as fuck," I whisper with all the emphasis I can get away with.

Harper motions for me to come her way. I oblige in the hope that she's going to give me the golden ticket I need to cash in on her niece.

"Where is Dane going on vacation?" she asks. She does it in the way my ma used to do when she knew I wasn't listening. It's a slow cadence, like you use with a baby.

"Flor-i-da," I say just as slowly back.

A towel is brandished my way. I duck it easily.

Harper laughs. "You're a little shit, you know that?"

"You act like this is new information. So," I say, lowering my voice, "what do you know about her? Give me some pointers so I have something to go on. *Please?*"

She sighs. "First of all, if you want a real shot at Avery, you're going to have to change your game."

"Meaning . . ."

"Meaning she's my niece, Penn. She's not going to mess with you if you start fiddling with her the way you usually do women."

"I do not fiddle with women," I insist. "Maybe I *enjoy* them. But I never *fiddle* with them. That makes it sound like I'm mean."

Her face softens. "You aren't mean. I don't think you have a mean bone in your body. If I thought you did, there's no way in Hell I'd let you even talk to her. But I've seen enough things from you that I think you and she could . . . get along."

"Define 'get along.'"

"Penn . . . ," she warns.

"If you're going where I think you're going, you can stop. I don't go that direction. You know this."

"But the direction you've been heading for, what, twenty-eight years now isn't really getting you anywhere, is it?"

I shrug. "I'm really doing fine. And right now, I want to be doing fine with her."

Harper shakes her head like she's got the upper hand. "You can want in one hand and wish in the other, but Avery isn't going to be interested in being in Penn Etling's harem."

"Ooh, Penn's harem. I like the sound of that."

She rolls her eyes. "Just think about what I've said."

The door behind me opens. A stream of midmorning sunlight fills the small room as Lorene comes in. Her silver hair shines on top of her head. She's out of breath, and for a woman close to a hundred years old, that's not a good thing.

I exchange a look with Harper.

"I'm sorry," Lorene says. "I'm late, aren't I?"

Her cheeks huff and puff like it's taken all her might to get up the stairs and to the door. There's a purplish mark on the top of her hand that is reminiscent of the one I got when I slammed mine with a hammer.

A purse dangles from her arm. It trembles as she leans against the door. "One of these days, I'm going to remember I'm ninety years old and not the spring chicken I think I am."

"What do you mean, that you're no spring chicken? You don't look a day over twenty." I toss her a wink as I take her arm and steady her. "You okay?"

She pats my arm. Her hands are cold, the veins a striking blue against her pale skin. "I'm better now. Thank you, Penn."

Harper wags a finger my way. "Don't you get any ideas with Lorene, Penn Etling."

Lorene downright beams. "You let him have all the ideas he wants." She adjusts her grip on my arm, squeezing it tighter as she gazes up at me. "Would you help me get over to the chair?"

"Absolutely."

I guide her across the room and ease her into Harper's chair. She groans as she gets situated with her little green purse on her lap. Harper's eyes meet mine over the top of Lorene's head.

"Oh, dear," Lorene says, squinting to see the calendar on the wall. "I think I have the wrong day. It's not Wednesday, is it? I'm all messed up." She raises a shaky hand to her temple. "Dogwood Day isn't this week, either, is it?"

"No. It's in a couple of weeks," Harper says gently. "We all get a little mixed up sometimes. It's okay."

"I got in a hurry this morning for nothing," Lorene says.

"Not true," I say. "I think Harper just had a cancellation. You just sit back and get pampered a little bit. I bet that'll clear your head right up."

Harper mouths a thank-you and motions for me to follow her. "I'll be right back, Lorene," she says.

We walk to the side near where she keeps her supplies. That's also by the mini fridge, where I happen to know she keeps the best Popsicles for her younger clientele . . . and me. She even keeps extra grape ones for me, I think.

"Look at you being all chivalrous," Harper whispers.

"I'm a sucker for old ladies. What can I say?"

A bright smile inches across her face. Her head cocks to the side. "If you want to reschedule, we can. Or you could ask Avery to cut your hair."

I perk up. "Harper, you're a fucking genius."

"It's been said."

My head whips to the doorway only milliseconds before Avery walks through it. Her eyes instantly meet mine. My jaw goes slack again. I'm well aware of it before Harper's elbow digs into my ribs.

Avery gathers her dark locks and piles them on top of her head. As she twists a rubber band around her hair, she never drops her eyes from mine. I don't look away. I'm not sure I could even if I wanted to—and I don't. I really fucking don't.

I shift in my sneakers, trying to subtly adjust myself without her noticing. A smile tickles the side of her lips—full, kissable, cherry-tinted lips that I have all sorts of ideas how to occupy. As if she can read my mind, she laughs.

"Avery?" Harper calls out. "Is there any way you can fit Penn in right now?"

"I can make it fit—*ouch!*" I mumble under my breath as I take yet another elbow from Harper.

Avery looks at Harper, then at me for a lingering second, and then back to her boss. "It's my first day. Clearly, I have an opening."

"I—"

"Don't you dare," Harper whispers. She clears her throat. "Great. Thanks. It'll help me out."

Avery casts me a glance that tells me she thinks I put Harper up to this. I'm relieved to see she doesn't look pissed about that possibility, because even though it's not true, I'm not mad about it. Not even a little bit. In fact, I might owe Harper a favor for this one.

"Is this because of me?" Lorene asks. "I don't want to mess up your schedule—"

"Lorene," I say, "trust me when I say this is working out just like it's supposed to."

"Well, all right then," Lorene says. "I won't worry about it."

Avery raises a brow.

I grin.

She rolls her eyes and picks up her apron. It slips around her slim neck. Like she knows I'm an ass man, she turns away and ties the apron around her waist. The tie drops on top of a perfect, peach-shaped behind.

Harper laughs as she walks my way. She doesn't say anything until she's right beside me, where only I can hear her. "Penn Etling is flustered. What will Matt say about this?"

I square my shoulders, making a concerted effort to keep my voice low. "I'm *not* flustered. So don't go beauty-shop gossiping this around town. I have a reputation to uphold."

"Yeah. God forbid anyone think you might actually be interested in someone for real."

I lean forward and grin. "Oh, I'm interested in that, all right. I couldn't be more interested."

"You behave. She's a professional."

"Dear God, I hope so."

Harper smacks me in the stomach. I bend at the waist, mostly to hide my laugh. She hisses something about behaving again, but I don't hear her. I'm too preoccupied with watching Avery clean a comb.

Her lips are redder than they were earlier. And maybe it's just the shift in the sunlight coming through the windows, or maybe it's the fact that I've had a few more minutes to admire—ogle—the beauty before me. But there's one thing that needs no clarification or second-guessing: I'm in lust. Pure unadulterated lust.

Avery has captivated my attention. I don't know what that fucking means, but I'm here for it.

"You ready?" she asks with her hands on her hips.

"Definitely."

"Come grab a seat."

Yes, ma'am.

CHAPTER FOUR

Avery

I swivel the chair in his direction.

The room is warmer than it was a few minutes ago. I wonder if there's a thermostat I could adjust, but the closer Penn gets to me, the more I wonder if it's not just him.

He has the "boy next door" thing going on that I remember so clearly from before. It's a friendly, "you can trust me" output of energy that makes me relax. But now it's mixed with a swagger, a smoldering vibe that's not even fair.

His long legs stretch out in front of him after he settles in my chair. The jeans he's wearing are dark with scratches in the denim. There's not a damn thing about them that should make my mouth water, but it does.

"You ready to get this?" he asks cheekily. His pun is ill disguised, thanks to the grin that sinks deeper into his cheeks.

I raise a brow as I fight to keep from smiling.

"What?" he asks.

"You're absolutely right," I say. "Let's get to the inevitable."

"Sounds perfect." He digs his fingers into the vinyl chair. "What exactly are you thinking? I'm up for anything, just so you know."

I want to laugh, to ask him if this methodology works for him with other women. This overt offer to basically hook up. Something tells me it does.

Something also tells me it's not going to work for him this time.

As I take a step back and let my eyes run up and down his body, I kind of wish it would. He looks like *a lot* of fun. And it would be interesting to see how much he's changed from the uncertain, not-super-skilled teenager I was with the last time. But smooth talkers with killer smiles don't do it for me anymore.

I hope.

"I'm thinking you'll go pretty short on the sides and a little longer on top," I say.

"Um, that's not what I was getting at."

I smile sweetly. "I know." Grabbing my clippers, I turn to face him again. I try to figure out what height the blades should be adjusted to. "You're a two, right?"

It takes a split second for him to realize my own little play on words. Once he gets it, he settles back in his chair like he's getting cozy for the long haul.

"Most women call me a ten," he says with a tinge of pride.

"I bet they do."

"No, they do," he insists, stone-faced. "Sometimes it's even an eleven, but that's usually when they factor in more than just my looks."

"I bet they do," I repeat. "They probably take into account your personality, too, huh?"

"Sometimes. Sometimes it's . . . other stuff." He leans forward and lowers his voice. "We aren't alone right now, and I try to be discreet when I can."

"Of course."

Harper and Lorene are a few feet away, beside us. Their voices ring through the salon, but they may as well be a mile away. Penn watches me, his hand running through his wild hair, as both of us try not to let our grins turn into smiles.

This is fun, even though I wish it weren't.

"So, a two?" I ask again.

"Definitely an eight," he says. "But a *real* eight. Not the eight guys say they are when they're really a four." When I don't look impressed, he gives a little more assurance. "I'm a carpenter, so I use a tape measure all day. I know eight inches. I'm not just talking out my ass."

"You know, most guys that talk that much about their *tape measure* are trying to distract you from the fact that they can't use it. It's just another tool they play with." I cross my arms, the clippers still in my hand. "I talk to a lot of people. I know how it works."

A smirk touches his lips. "Well, I talk to a lot of people, too, and I guarantee you I know how it works. It works *great*."

That does it. The apples of my cheeks heat. I can't take it. I have to move. The energy coursing through my veins has to go somewhere.

"Sit still. This won't take long," I say, turning on the device in my hand.

"That's nothing a guy ever wants to hear."

I roll my eyes and get to work on his dark, silky locks. Whiffs of his cologne filter through the air like a genie in a bottle, luring me into his world. I fight the urge to touch his neck and the side of his face, which is peppered with last night's stubble.

It crosses my mind what his reaction might be if I tell him who I am. Would he even remember what I was talking about? In his defense, I look different now. Dark-brown hair and fairer skin, thanks to a fear about tanning that a magazine article drove home in my early twenties. I also am in better shape, and the acne that plagued me after high school is long gone.

I can't blame him for not realizing I'm the girl named Abby. But that doesn't mean my pride isn't a bit injured.

He moves in the seat, making it hard to cut his hair.

"Stop moving." I take a step back and try to get a good look at my work. "You're so fidgety."

"Sorry. I had a lot of coffee this morning."

"Well . . . have less before you get a haircut," I offer.

"Harper never minds."

"I'd smack you," she says, shaking her scissors Penn's direction.

"You're not in this conversation," he tells her.

She laughs before going back to Lorene.

I move him around so he's facing the mirror. His gaze is heavy on me through the reflection, and I ignore it the best I can.

"So, you're a carpenter. Do you work for someone or for yourself?" I ask, trying to take up the weird stillness between us.

"I work for a guy named Dane and his brother, Matt. Good guys, both of them." He looks up at me. "But they're kind of dickheads, so stay away from them."

I can tell he's kidding, so I bump his shoulder with my hip. "I'm going to hunt them down now, just to say hi."

"Dane's getting married, and Matt is a pussy. Just warning you."

I trade the clippers for a pair of scissors. "I like a good man who's in touch with his feelings."

"You'd like me, then," Penn says. "I know all of my feelings. Want me to tell you what I'm feeling now?"

A laugh comes out before I can stop it. "No. Thanks. You can keep your feelings to yourself."

"Look—if you're gonna tell me you're a woman who likes to skip feelings and get right to the good stuff, I might marry you right fucking now."

I narrow my eyes as I measure his hair in between two fingers and snip off the ends. "There's no need to run off to the jeweler, my friend, because I'm all about the feelings."

"Damn it."

I laugh again. "I didn't figure you'd go for that."

"I think you figure a lot of things about me."

"Do you figure I'm right?"

He shrugs. "Maybe. Maybe not. I think the only way for us to see if you're right is to have dinner. Which would be a real date because it's doing something with you in public."

"Gee, thanks, but no." I move to the other side, making a concerted effort not to touch him anywhere but his hair. "Nice offer, though."

"Claire over at the café explained to me this morning that a real date is dinner or a movie or a picnic or something. I didn't know that." He pauses. "Did you?"

"Well, I'm not a child, so, yeah, I knew that."

He doesn't seem fazed. He just watches me in the mirror as I work on his hair.

The feeling of having his attention so concentrated is heady. Almost intoxicating. I'd forgotten what it was like to be desired just the way I am.

I'm not sure Penn minds the curve of my hip. And if he's noticed the slight bunch at my waistline, he hasn't shown it.

I move so I'm in front of him. My breath catches in my throat as our bodies border on contact. His leg next to mine. His hand near my waist. My chest *this close* to his face. Sure, it was a hell of a lot closer than that ten years ago, but I can't think about that now.

How is it fair that he's more handsome now than he was then?

"Crazy question," he says, his tone huskier than before. "Do I know you?"

My hand stills. "Do you think you know me?"

I glance down at him. His thick, dark lashes frame the blues of his eyes, which are so light that they're almost clear.

He studies me for a long minute as I try to remember to breathe.

"I don't know," he says finally.

"Then I guess you don't."

I spin his chair around so he can't see my reaction. I'm partially relieved, but there's a piece of me that's disappointed too. That night meant a lot to me. It was the first time I really ranted about my parents and was honest about how I felt with someone other than Harper. Despite going by an alias, I felt so free, and it would be nice to think that it was memorable for him too.

But it wasn't. Obviously.

"Everybody knows everybody around here," Lorene cuts in. "Sometimes that's a good thing. Sometimes it's not." She brings the bruised hand to her mouth as she stifles a yawn. "It's how life in little places like this works."

"Is your hand okay, Lorene?" Penn asks. "What happened?"

"I fell on the steps at home," she says. "That second step has been giving me fits all spring, and it finally tripped me today." She looks at the back of her hand. "I propped it up with a brick, though. Should be fine now."

"Oh, that sounds safe," Harper chimes in.

"I survived the Great Depression," Lorene says. "Pretty sure I can survive a broken stair."

Thankful for Lorene's distraction, I work quickly. Penn's hair falls to the floor, the strands gliding through my fingers. I listen to him sweetly banter with Lorene and my aunt, and in record time, I brush off the back of his neck and remove his cape.

"There you go. All done." I turn him toward the mirror. "What do you think?"

He doesn't look at his reflection or touch his hair. He just looks at me through the mirror.

"I still don't think I'm a two," he says, making me smile. He seems to ponder his next question for a long moment before asking it. "Are you liking Dogwood Lane?"

"Yup."

I grab the broom from the corner and start sweeping up the dark tresses. Finally, I look back up at him.

"What?" I ask.

"That's it? 'Yup'?"

"Yup."

"Aren't cosmetologists supposed to be big gossips? Or chatty? Or something? Harper never shuts up."

"I'm not a gossip," I say, thinking of all the magazine headlines I've seen in my life. "I don't believe anything I don't see or hear for myself. I am chatty, though, I guess. Just with the right people."

"How does one get to be the right people?"

I refuse to make eye contact even as he follows me in a circle in his chair. Before long, there's no hair left to sweep.

"How do you get to be one of the right people?" I ask, repeating his question. "Well, there's a checklist, and it's ridiculously hard to meet all the requirements."

"You know, I'm really good at checklists. Dane gives me one every morning, and I nail it. I'm also an expert at nailing stuff."

A soft snort comes out of my mouth. "I bet you are."

"I am. Want me to show you?"

He grins like the cat that caught the canary. It's a dimple-displaying, shit-eating, "I can be as naughty as you want me to be" grin that leaves me grabbing for the edge of the workstation.

"No. I just want your fourteen dollars," I say.

Instead of getting up, he stays planted in the seat. The grin slips away into a look of confusion. "So, um, want me to pick you up tonight? Or tomorrow? Whatever works best for you."

"So, um, no. I just want fourteen dollars. Thanks." When he doesn't move, I laugh. "Do you get told no often?"

He smiles weakly. "That's what this is? We're done here?"

"Yes. I cut your hair. I dusted your neck. I made small talk. What more do you want?" I hold out a hand as his lips part. "Don't answer that. I walked right into it."

"What more do I want?" he asks. "Well, how about a date—proof of nailing abilities optional."

He flashes me a smile that I'm certain usually gets him whatever he wants. Unfortunately for him, I've seen smiles and heard promises all my life. Smiles that drip with sugary-sweet deception. Promises that are hollow because there's no intention of them being honored. *I'm done with that.*

Still, if this were a different time and a different place—like LA a few months ago—I totally would've taken him up on his offer. It would've been my *pleasure*. But once you have an epiphany and promise yourself you'll do better, you have to at least try.

I can't give in to the first hot guy who asks me out. It would be unfair to myself to throw away the hard choices I've made recently and be coaxed by a sexy smile . . . even if it's with a guy whose pheromones seem to be specifically made to lure me in.

Damn it.

"I'm sorry," I say. "I'm busy."

"I can be free whenever."

"I'm busy then too." I motion at the sign on the wall. "I take cash and checks. No credit cards yet because my swipe-box thing hasn't come in the mail."

He looks at me warily as he lifts out of his chair. Grabbing his wallet, he takes out a twenty and hands it to me. "Here you go. Keep the change."

"Thank you," I say.

Our hands touch as I take the money. My lips part as I pull away, my skin burning like it's been buzzed with a shock of electricity.

"No, thank *you*," he says. He gives me a long glance before turning around. "You need me to wait and help you to the car, Lorene?"

"I'll help her," Harper says, glancing at me before looking back at him. "You probably need to recover from being turned down, anyway, don't ya, Penn?"

He chuckles, shoving his hands in his pockets. "I don't think that qualifies as being turned down." He looks at me over his shoulder. "She'll cave eventually."

"Good luck with that," I call out.

"No luck needed." He has the audacity to wink.

"You're right. Luck will do you no good," I say, crossing my arms over my chest.

It's more of a defensive posture than anything else, a way of putting a barrier of some sort between the two of us. His energy knows no bounds, though, and pummels me right through my limbs until he pulls his gaze away.

"So, you're getting Ms. Lorene to her car when she's done?" he asks Harper, obviously stalling.

"Yes, for the second time," Harper says with a laugh. "Still in the process of making Lorene even more beautiful."

"I don't know how that's possible," he says.

Lorene holds out her hand. It trembles in the air as Penn takes it in his. "You're a good boy, Penn."

"Take care of yourself." He presses a kiss to her cheek.

I watch the gentleness with which he treats Lorene, and I want to kick myself for turning him down. But I have to. I know it.

"See ya, Harp," Penn says.

He opens the door. Sunshine and fresh air fill the room. My body pulls in that direction, wanting a final glimpse of him before he disappears outside. My brain tells me to fight the urge, that giving in is a signal I'm desperate. That's not accurate or pretty.

Still, at the last second, I turn around. Penn is watching me.

"If you need help with that speaker, give me a call," he teases. "I know how to handle a tool."

His eyes light up. "Glad to hear it."

"I bet you are."

He grins. "I really am an eight."

Laughter topples out of my mouth.

"Get out of here, Penn," Harper says.

"I'm going. I'm going." He starts to leave but stops again. "See ya around, Avery."

"I . . ."

The rest of the sentence doesn't come out before the door closes. It's just as well. What I was about to say—that I hope he doesn't see me around—would've been a lie.

I hope I see Penn Etling around. I just hope even more that I can control myself, because for the first time in years, being around a man felt . . . good. Easy. Enjoyable on a totally organic level. If I can keep my wits about me, I'll be fine. If not, it's a mess waiting to happen.

Trouble. I smile to myself. *That boy is definitely trouble.*

CHAPTER FIVE

Penn

I tap the wooden plank with my boot. There's no give, no wobble, and that godforsaken brick that Lorene had stuck under it is gone.

"That should do it," I say, admiring my handiwork.

A bead of sweat trickles down my forehead. I catch it with the back of my hand as I bend to pick up my tools.

The step was a quick repair. I didn't ask Lorene before I fixed it because she would've told me that her solution was fine. It was more *not fine* than I'd even imagined.

Tossing the tools in the bag, I let my mind drift. It snaps to Avery Perry.

A grin tickles my lips at the memory of her telling me no. I swear she got off on it. The way she dismissed me like I was some random guy at the post office asking for her number didn't quite jibe with the coy smile when she didn't think I was looking. Besides, there's no doubt she wants me. Everyone wants me.

And I want her.

Excitement begins to bubble in my stomach as I consider how to play my cards. I can't play them too fast, because something tells me there's a slight chance she'd back away. But if I play them too slow, there might be an opening for some other prick to get his foot in the door.

Or worse.

My teeth grind together.

The idea of her saying yes to someone else before she says yes to me is mildly irritating. As I ponder the vision of another guy's hand wrapped around her waist—before me or not—my jaw clenches harder.

The realization is uncomfortable.

"Let's calm down," I tell myself. "No need to get all out of whack because a girl is playing hard to get."

The words sound so easy when I say them aloud. The feeling doesn't translate into my body. My brain offers possibility after possibility as to how I can see her again. My body constantly moves—to the stairs, to my truck, to the little bed of flowers near Lorene's door—as if it's staying limber for some kind of pursuit. My fingers itch to dig into something . . . that's not the phone ringing in my pocket.

With a frustrated sigh, I grab it and bring it to my ear. "Hello?"

"Where are ya at?" Matt asks.

"Lorene's."

"Lorene? Like Lorene from the Dogwood Inn? How'd that happen?"

I grab a seat on a step. My leg bounces as I stare off across the field. "I ran into her this morning at Harper's. She said she fell because her step was busted, so I thought I'd run by and fix it."

"You taking side jobs already?" he jokes.

"Nah. It's just if I didn't come fix it, she would've fallen again, and I would've blamed myself. Plus, I didn't have a lot to do today."

Matt makes a noise like he understands. "How old is she these days? She has to be almost a hundred."

"She said she was ninety. But she still drives herself around and tried to repair this damn step with a brick, so she's doing okay."

"Does she still run that inn alone?" he asks. "I was thinking her family lives out of state or something. She can't possibly do all that on her own, can she?"

"What do I look like? Lorene's historian? I just saw her at Harper's and heard her step was broken. That's all I know."

Matt starts to say something but stops. He takes a breath and starts again. "You know, I've always wanted to own that place. Ever since I was a little kid. I'd—"

"Hey," I say, cutting him off. "This is pillow talk or some shit, and we aren't fucking."

Matt laughs. "You're a jerk."

"No, I'm not. I just don't want to hear about your hopes and dreams. Go tell 'em to whoever you're fucking these days." I pause. I rack my brain as to whom Matt has been spending his time with but come up empty-handed. "Who *are* you fucking these days, anyway?"

The phone rustles on the other side. Matt coughs and then grumbles before the phone rustles again.

"No one, really," he says finally. "I was supposed to take Brittney Blevins out last weekend, but with my busted spleen and all . . ."

"I still can't believe you are *that* injured," I deadpan.

"Penn, I fell off a fucking ladder."

I can't help but grin. "A ladder that was four foot high. I mean, come on, Matt. You—"

"I landed on a sawhorse. I'm lucky I didn't die."

"Pussy," I tease.

"I was pissing blood, Etling."

It's true, and I almost feel bad for giving him shit. But if I didn't, he'd think something was wrong. And . . . it *was* four foot high. I told him to rub some dirt on it and call it a day, but Dane hauled him to the hospital instead. It's one of the times in my life that I'm glad no one listened to me.

"For the record, I'm glad you didn't die," I say, getting to my feet.

He chuckles. "Gee, thanks. But I would be a lot more touched by your sentiments if I thought it was for my well-being and not just so you didn't have to pick up the slack at work."

"Can you imagine if Dane hired someone to replace you? I couldn't work with anyone else."

"Because no one else would put up with your shit."

"True. Now, did you call me for anything in particular, or am I good to get on with my life?"

"Yes, actually. I did call for a reason."

I flick a piece of wood off my jeans. "Which was . . ."

"I'm bored. Want to meet me at Mucker's tonight?"

I grin at the opening he just handed me.

We meet at Mucker's more nights of the week than we don't. It's a routine, a habit we've grown accustomed to over the years. Matt has bowed out a lot recently due to his "injury," but giving me the heads-up that he's ready to enjoy a beer green-lights me to get some help where I need it.

"Sure," I say, "if you want to help with The Meredith Project."

Matt chuckles. "I heard you already committed. I'd hate to take that away from you."

"Oh, you would not."

"Eh, true. But I feel like getting out of this job of hers is God's gift to me for the pain of slicing my spleen."

My gaze drifts across the fields surrounding the inn again. It's peaceful and reminds me of the forts Matt and I used to build behind his house when we were little. We'd get so busy creating our castles that his dad would have to come looking for us with a flashlight after dark.

As much hell as I give Matt Madden, he gets equal amounts of respect. I don't know a nicer guy. No one is more loyal, and despite the truth about not wanting to even have to try and fill in for him on our three-man crew, I'd miss him if something happened to him.

I'd never tell him that, though.

"You feeling good enough for a beer?" I ask. "If you feel good enough for Mucker's at night, you feel good enough for work in the morning."

"You sound like my dad."

"Kill me now."

I pick up the rest of my tools. There's always a bit of pride when I look at them and think about it. I'm a carpenter. A taxpaying, work-every-day, responsible guy—even though Dane may disagree about that since I left the cutoff saw out in the rain last week. Regardless of my fuckups, I didn't turn out like my pops, even though everyone said I would.

Matt laughs again. "Dad's getting soft in his old age. He's in his backyard right now, digging another koi pond because Mia wants a few more and there's no room in the current one."

"For the record, I will never go soft. Ever. Too much testosterone in this blood."

I lean against my truck and look up at the sky. The blue is so bright, the breeze so perfectly warm that it reminds me of being out on a boat with not a worry in the world—exactly what I had planned for my vacation.

I close my eyes and breathe in the fresh air . . . and as soon as my mind relaxes, I see her face again.

Avery.

Shit.

"Ugh," I say, pushing off the truck.

"What?"

I shouldn't bring her up. There's no reason to. She's just another gorgeous, witty girl that I'll get my fill of. I know this. But I want to talk about her. To say her name out loud.

"Matt, do you know a girl named Avery?" I say it quickly, probably too quickly, and cringe as soon as the words are out of my mouth.

"Um, not that I know of. Why? Should I?"

I kick a rock. There's some satisfaction when it bangs into the lattice under Lorene's porch. "No. Probably not."

He laughs. "Is it finally catching up with you?"

"Is what catching up with me?"

"Are you finally confusing all the women in your life?"

"First of all," I say, "I don't have *women in my life*."

He snorts. "Bullshit. You have more women in your life than anyone I've ever fucking met. Period."

This is a point I could argue, although I typically don't. My reputation is that of a man who gets women by the boatloads, and it's not inaccurate. I generally don't have a problem finding someone to spend time with, to put it nicely. But at this point, I think my exploits have become a little exaggerated.

There was definitely a time when I lost track of whom I was seeing here and there. Lately, that's not been the case. There are a few numbers I can call if I want to fuck. But what single person in their late twenties doesn't have that?

"The problem I have with that whole thing is the 'in my life' part," I say. "That makes it sound like I'm spending time with them doing things other than getting off."

Matt chuckles. "It never ceases to amaze me how crude you can be and women still like you."

"I could explain that."

"Please don't."

I lift my toolbox and toss it into the back of my truck. It hits with a loud thud as Matt goes into a spiel about how I need to settle down and date one woman at a time. I roll my eyes as I pretend to listen.

The Saint Christopher's medal that's hung around my neck since I was nine catches the sunlight. I take it in my palm and feel the warmth radiate into my hand.

My grandmother promised me on the day she gave me my grandfather's pendant that as long as I wore it around my neck, I would be blessed with safe travels. I thought she was crazy. I still think she might be crazy. But I wear it, anyway.

"You listening to me?" Matt asks.

"Yup."

"Liar."

"I heard everything you said, and I still disagree," I say, hoping I'm as much of an expert on Matt's rambling as I think I am. "Here's the thing—I can't remember my own shit, let alone anniversaries and birthdays and favorite colors and . . . dog names. Ain't for me, man. Ain't for me."

"It must really suck to be so messed up that you don't want to have an in-depth conversation with a woman."

A few weeds are growing through Lorene's mulch. I walk over and rip them out. "I talk to plenty of women, thank you."

"I mean more than, 'Do you want it in your mouth first?'"

"Shut up."

He laughs, which makes me laugh.

"You do realize there's more to a relationship than dates and details, right?" he asks.

"Yup. That's why I opt out." I blow out a breath. "If you start talking to people, you end up knowing shit about them that they expect you to remember. I'm okay with that on some . . . trivial level. Like, I know you prefer diesel engines over gasoline. I know that. Why I know that, I don't know, but I do. And here's the thing: you don't expect me to know that. You aren't pissed if I don't."

"Because we aren't dating."

"Exactly."

I wait for his response, but he's silent. I think he thinks he proved his point. A part of me thinks I should explain how his "Because we aren't dating" actually proves mine, but I let it go.

"I'm trying to decide if you have daddy issues or mommy issues," he says cheekily.

"I have both. Clearly. You've met my parents."

"I have, and I still like you. What's that say about me?" he asks.

"That you're dumb. We already knew that."

"Possibly so. But at least I keep my dates straight."

Just like that, Avery's plump lips pop back into my mind. "So, you have nothing on an Avery?"

He sighs. "No. I don't. Where's this coming from, anyway?"

"I met a girl this morning at Harper's when I went to get my hair cut. She's Harper's niece. She's working there now, I guess, and . . . I feel like I know her."

I think back to her eyes and how familiar they are. And how her smile put me at ease like only my closest friends can do. There's also the zing to her touch and the way it feels so . . . right. Like a piece to a puzzle has been snapped into place, but I can't figure out why. It's so weird.

"Do you?" he asks. "Do you know her?"

I pause. *"Do you think you know me?"* The way she asked me that has stuck with me, but I don't know what it means. I can't place her for the life of me.

"If I did, I wouldn't be wondering, genius," I say.

The words are gruffer than I intend for them to be, and Matt picks up on it. It's one of the nice things about being friends with someone for as long as you can remember—they know stuff, and unlike me, he wants to remember it.

"Maybe you do," he offers. "Maybe you just need some time to think about it."

I think back to her hands in my hair. I remember her smile and the way the sun made her dark hair look like it was glowing. The way her eyes were intelligent and assessing with a hint of playfulness that drew me in like a hook. It sends a burst of energy through my veins again. It's exciting . . . probably because I don't know her.

"No," I admit. "It's probably just because she's new, you know? That, or she's reminding me of someone else."

Matt takes a deep breath. "Okay, I'm going to give you a piece of advice, and then I'm going."

"Fine. Shoot."

"Don't tell her you think you know her. She'll think you're really thinking about someone else, and that's never, ever a good idea."

I pop open my truck door and climb inside the cab. "For a dumbass, you're pretty smart."

"Thanks. I think."

I grin. "Mucker's at six?"

"Yup."

"See ya there."

CHAPTER SIX

Avery

"Well, what did you think?" Harper flops onto the sofa. Fresh from a shower, her hair is twisted up in a towel, and her body is clad in a set of pajamas.

I'm no better. I came home—Harper's, for the time being—and changed into a pair of fleece pants and a T-shirt.

"Today was actually really good," I say from the recliner. "Do you know how long it's been since I actually enjoyed a day at work? A long damn time."

It was enjoyable. It's a novel concept to wake up and go about a day and not hate everything about it. My work was fun and low drama; getting to and from the shop was effortless. And the people—they were amazing.

Everyone was so incredibly *nice*. I was invited to more get-togethers, Sunday dinners, and church services than I can keep straight. I know what to order at the Dogwood Café and Mucker's—the only two places where you can get food in this town—and to never buy the coffee at the gas station. Someone even gave me a casserole recipe.

It's amazing how different life can be if you aren't surrounded by hedonists. I'm a fan.

"I'll admit that I was shocked at how busy we were," I say. "I expected about half that."

"Yeah, well, most days it is about half that." She yawns. "You just might be the shot of energy Hometown Hair needed."

She closes her eyes. Her hand stills on her stomach, and I'm not sure if she's asleep.

I flip off the television. Silence descends on us immediately.

Sitting on the edge of town, Harper's little white house is about a half mile from her closest neighbor. There are ferns in hanging baskets on the front porch and a whiskey barrel that catches the water from the downspout on the side of the house. The only thing missing from making it the ideal home is the lack of cookies baking in the kitchen because, like me, Harper doesn't cook.

It couldn't be more opposite of the living conditions I had in the city. For five years, I had the same neighbors—ones whose names I never knew but whose routines I had memorized by the sounds blaring from their apartments.

"We haven't really gotten a chance to talk about what you want to do here," Harper says with her eyes still closed. "Besides working for me, obviously."

Even though she can't see me, I shrug. "I don't really know. Everything happened so fast. I guess I didn't plan far enough out."

She opens one eye. "You did good, Avery."

"I know," I say, trying to quell the bubble of uncertainty threatening to pop in my gut. "I'm happy I'm here. Honest. But what kind of adult decides to move across the country on a Wednesday and has her stuff in the car by Friday, with virtually no plan at all?"

Reality takes a swipe my way. My heartbeat quickens as a miniscule amount of panic begins to grow. I did this. I'm here. Fish out of water with no real plan to find a new sea.

"The kind that has an awesome aunt like me that has only begged you to come here for the last, what? Five years? You had to get out before

Hollywood ate your soul." She sits up and yawns again. "But to answer your question seriously, the kind of person that does something like that is someone that's learning to identify what's right for her. That's hard for anyone to do, let alone someone that's the child of *your* mother."

It's my turn to close my eyes.

My mother's face wastes no time popping into my mind, chastising me for ruining my life. The little caricature reams me for taking all the advantages she worked so hard to give me and throwing them away. She'll never understand that I prefer conversations and family holidays and peace in my heart.

My stomach knots.

"We're going to have to find something to occupy your time," Harper says. "Otherwise, you're going to sit here and overthink everything."

I look at her. She grimaces.

"I'm not overthinking anything," I say. "I'm just . . . thinking. Without the 'over.'"

"I'll bet."

"I am. Promise." I push the button on the side of the recliner. It sits me up with a ping. "Not that I plan on being a social butterfly, but what is there to do in this town? Anything?"

She laughs. "Not much. Most people hang out at Mucker's at night. If you want a fancier meal, you have to go to Rockery. They have a steakhouse and seafood shop over there, a couple of bars, that kind of thing."

"But what do people do to kill time? Is there somewhere to shop? Outdoor music? A cute tennis pro that gives lessons at the club?"

"What club?" Harper laughs. "You need to remember where you are, girlfriend. The only club this place has is the bowling club on Thursday nights, and I have a feeling that's not what you're looking for."

I slow blink. "People still have bowling clubs?"

"Shocker, I know." She gets to her feet and stretches. "We'll find you something to do. What do you like to do? Have any hobbies?"

"Well, let's see . . ." I think back to all the things I've done and wonder how much of it would be useful here. "I like animals. I worked in a pet shop once. Tons of fun until your favorite animals get adopted, and then you cry because you'll never see them again."

"That would be me," Harper says. "What else?"

"I like to lie on the beach, which will do no good here. It actually didn't do me any good in California, either, come to think of it," I note. "What else? Let's see . . . I like to sew a little, but I'm not very good at it. I sat with the costume department during an entire movie production when I was twelve, and they taught me the basics. It was the most fun I ever had on a set."

"I tried to sew once. Sewed my finger to a pair of pants. Never tried it again."

I laugh. "You sound like my mom."

Harper's face twists in horror. "That's blasphemy."

I laugh harder. "Sorry."

She nods, letting my comparison go. "So animals and beaches and sewing. Anything else?"

"Well, I like to paint."

"Like paint-by-numbers, paint houses, paint portraits?"

I tilt my head back and close my eyes. Vivid colors stream through my mind as I remember the little painting nook I had at my apartment in Los Angeles. The walls were lavender and the flooring a warm oak. When the early-morning sunlight would fill the room, it was perfect . . . until my last boyfriend decided he needed that space for his office. He sweet-talked me into giving it up.

I've always regretted that. It wasn't about losing my space per se, but about losing a part of me and what makes me happy. Losing my voice. Giving things up way too easily because of some smooth-talking man.

"I just like to paint," I say, holding up my hands. "I haven't had official classes or anything. But I did well in art class in high school, and the art teacher knew a group leader at one of the local latchkey clubs. So she hooked me up, and I painted murals over some graffiti they had on the outside wall. That parlayed into teaching painting one summer to the kids, and that rolled into teaching a class for women that really just liked to drink and paint by number."

Harper laughs. "Drinking and painting by number doesn't sound bad, actually."

"I know. We should totally get a group together and do a paint night at the salon. It would be so much fun."

"Once you get settled in, we're doing it. Consider it done."

I smile. "Perfect."

"Any other hidden talents I didn't know about?"

I rack my brain for anything helpful but come up with nothing. "That's all I'm good at. And I'm not sure I'm even *good* at that."

"Stop that."

"What?" I ask.

"Stop playing down your strengths." She narrows her eyes.

"I didn't mean it like that."

"I don't care how you mean it, Avery. That kind of mental rhetoric is poison, and you do it all the time. It's a common problem, especially with women, and I hate it. Be proud of the things you can do, sweet pea."

Her words filter into my soul. I think about all the times little lines like that have slipped from my mouth or from someone else's. Do I believe those few things are all I have to offer the world? No. Not really. I know I'm capable of things, and I'm not a bad painter, even if I am untrained. So why do I think like that?

Because I've allowed people to make me feel that way.

"You're right," I tell her. "I'm a decent painter. Maybe even better than decent some days."

Harper smiles. “And even more important, you’re resilient and courageous. Look at what you’re doing right now—switching up everything in your life to find what makes you happy. That’s huge.”

I grin. “I don’t know about huge, but it’s pretty good.”

She laughs. “It’s pretty good, all right.” She sits up. As she angles toward me, her eyes glisten with trouble. “So what did you really think of today?”

“Um . . .” I try to smile, but it ends up like a cringe. “I already answered that. What are you getting at?”

Her smile turns mischievous. “What did you think of Penn Etling?”

Penn Etling.

I want to tell her that he’s one of the best-looking men I’ve ever seen. That I didn’t want to stop cutting his hair because I liked the way I felt when he looked at me. I nearly mention that although his off-the-cuff antics were ego-driven and irritating, they were somehow still charming.

And I don’t mention, either, that I’d like to give him a redo of the night we spent together, but that would require a rewind of the last week of my life. It would be the whole “one step forward, three steps back” kind of thing . . . if I could stop at three with him. I’m not sure I could.

It’s clear what Penn wants: a booty call. An adventure. A new woman to entertain him for a bit, and that’s perfectly okay. Hell, that kind of thing is even fun. But at this point in my life, I want something less superficial. I want more. I’ve gone my whole life without it, and I want it.

Still, it’s impossible not to think of him and be curious as to what he’s like now. I hate it that I even wonder. It’s like sniffing the kryptonite.

“Avery?” Harper asks, trying to draw me out of my haze.

“Huh?”

“Penn? What did you think of him?”

"Penn? Oh, he's pretty cute," I say, hoping it's realistic enough to satisfy her and vague enough to make her drop it.

"Cute?" She blatantly avoids my cue. "He's not *cute*. He's downright gorgeous. And an eligible bachelor. Just saying."

"Well, bachelors are eligible for a reason, Harper," I say, looking back at her. "Although let me clarify that if I do hook up with anyone, it will be someone single. For the record."

"Well, Penn is single. And I'm sure there's a reason for that, but I'm also sure there's a remedy that some woman will find. And that woman, whoever she ends up being, will be lucky." She narrows her eyes. "I've known that boy for a long time, and there's so much good in him. He just needs to be polished up a bit."

"Good for him. But I'm only interested in polishing up myself, whatever that means. I just . . ." I rest my head against the chair. "I guess I feel like a relationship shouldn't be so much work. I mean, I get that you have to put in effort and compromise and all that, and I'm okay with it. I want to do those things. I just don't want to have to expend so much energy *polishing up* someone else that I'm on the back burner. Again."

Harper walks to the fireplace mantel and picks up a little bell. She turns it upside down and then back around again.

"I'm always in the mind-set that you have to do what works for you," she says. "Always. No matter what. Your grandparents hated the fact that I didn't want anything to do with show business. Your mother thinks I'm a lunatic for living here and doing what I do. But you know what? I love it."

"I know you do, and I can see why. It's lovely here. I think I can be happy here too."

She smiles. "You're a lot like me. You coming here shows that. But along with power and self-confidence can come something else—a predisposition to close doors. We can rule things in or out too quickly.

It's important to make sure we don't make snap judgments. Sometimes that will close the doors we need to walk through."

I raise my brows. "So we're referring to Penn as a door now?"

"Maybe."

"Maybe, my butt," I say with a laugh.

"I heard you turn him down today." She leans against the couch and looks amused. "I doubt that's ever happened to him in his entire life."

I certainly didn't turn him down the first time he asked.

My cheeks heat. "Well, I guess there's a first time for everything, right?"

"I guess."

The air between us gets heavy, and I know she's waiting on more from me. I get it. Most girls would have loved to have been pursued by Penn. But most girls aren't in my shoes, either, trying my hardest to move beyond guys like Penn. Although the men in LA sometimes wanted something else—a good word put in with a director or a meeting with an agent—it was always *something*. And it's a singular "something" with Penn too.

I can't blame Harper for being curious, but I can't blame me for not wanting to go into it. Not when I'd have to mention sleeping with him.

"He's really not my type," I lie.

"If you aren't attracted to that boy, what on earth are you looking for?"

She can't be serious.

"Harper. For real. I'm nearing thirty years old. Am I sexually attracted to him? Yes. I'm not blind, and pheromones are a real thing. But I'm over that. I've had sex with the bad boy. I've given in to a sexy smirk and played the cat-and-mouse game. Done it. Won it. The prize isn't so great." I blow out a breath. "I have dreams of having a life where I feel . . . fulfilled. I want to go to sleep at night feeling valued, like what I bring to my relationships and to the world I live in is important and cherished. Things that aren't based on my last name or exemplary business dinner manners or skills in the sack."

"Of course you want those things," she says, nodding like crazy. "You should want those things. But the fun part of life is that you don't know where you're going to find that fulfillment."

"I don't think it's from your boy Penn."

Harper cocks her head to the side. "It might be. Who knows? I know he comes across as a playboy, and he has been one—don't get me wrong. But there's more to him than meets the eye. That's all I'm saying."

"Maybe that's true," I say, shaking a finger her way this time. "But I'm not wading through the one-liners and innuendos until *he* realizes that."

"Fair enough."

She heads into the kitchen, and I follow her. The remnants of a chocolate cupcake sit on the counter next to an empty glass of milk. Harper cleans it up as I pull out a chair at the table.

"I'm going out tonight with a couple of my friends to Mucker's," she says. "Do you want to come?"

I consider it. It would probably be fun, and I do need to meet people. But the adrenaline that got me through my first workday has evaporated, and my bones feel tired. The more I think about getting dressed again, the more I don't want to put on a bra.

"Nah," I say. "I think I'll stick around here. If I change my mind, I'll come later."

"Suit yourself." She tosses a sponge into the sink. "We always sit on the patio if you come. The dining room will be packed, so just try to slip outside."

"Will do."

She pats me on the shoulder as she walks toward her bedroom.

I pick up a saltshaker and spin it between my hands. The silence sinks around me. My phone is quiet in the other room. There's not a single text or phone call from any of my so-called friends from California, and while I didn't expect them to really care, I can't help but be a smidgen disappointed that not one of them does.

"It's for the best," I say out loud. "It'll make this transition even easier."

I start to get up, but a blue label from a jar on the counter catches my attention. The blue is bright, and the way it touches the dark syrup makes me think of blue eyes and dark hair.

I sink back in the chair and recall the way my body buzzed when it was near Penn's. How he leaned into my hands and looked at me with a warmth that was hard to ignore. That's hard to forget.

It's unfortunate that I've experienced enough hedonism in my life before now. It's unlucky for me that I know what it's like to cave to a cad with boatloads of charm. If I didn't know those things, I could've explored what Penn has to offer.

It's just too bad I learned my lesson before I saw him again.

He *might've* been the best bout of trouble I ever got myself into.

I get up from the table and head to the bathroom. There are few things a hot bath won't fix. Hopefully, being unable to wipe Penn Etling from my mind is one of them.

CHAPTER SEVEN

Avery

I pull my car into an empty spot next to the door. A sign reading **Mucker's** hangs next to a basket of flowers. Harper's car is parked on the other end of the lot, which is lit up by the dining room lights streaming from the windows.

"This place looks cute," I say as I shut off the engine.

I've driven by Mucker's every evening that I've been in town. The parking lot is always full. As I kept going down the road, because I wasn't about to walk into a place that was already bursting at the seams alone, I wondered if the food was good or if it's packed because it's the only place to go.

Tonight, I'm going to find out because my bath earlier this evening failed me.

I expected my best bubble bath and thriller novel would help redirect my thoughts away from Penn. But when I got out and dried off and realized I hadn't read a word and was still thinking about his stupid smile, I decided I needed another tactic. One with people, food, and a new energy.

Bolstered by the kindness shown to me at the salon this week, and the loneliness at Harper's with her gone, I grab my purse. Once my feet are on the pavement, a sweet nighttime air greets me. It's filled with laughter and the twinkle of lights from a small outdoor patio that's attached to the building.

The ambiance reminds me of college.

A bright-eyed woman about my age is exiting as I reach the front of the restaurant. She holds the door open.

"Thank you," I say.

"You're welcome," she says, her red curls springing around her shoulders. She waits until I step inside before releasing the door.

I don't hear it shut. From the television blaring a baseball game on the wall to the patrons shoulder to shoulder in the tight dining area to the heavy scent of oregano, it's sensory overload. As I look for a clear path through the crowd, I spy a woman at the end of the counter.

"You heading to the patio?" she calls out.

"I'm trying to," I say.

She motions for me. "Come this way and then scoot along the wall." She points to her left as I get closer. "There was a town council meeting tonight. It brings them in like flies."

I nod, not bothering to reply because her attention is already redirected to the kitchen. After saying "excuse me" several times and sucking in my stomach to get behind a high chair holding an adorable little girl, I make it to the door.

My foot hits the brick pavers outside just before I look up . . . and stop.

The sweet scent in the air is now kissed by a cool, crisp cologne that I recognize immediately. It takes only a quick glance to my right to ensure I'm correct.

Penn Etling.

Naturally, he's here.

He's leaning against a table that's outfitted to look like a tiki bar. A beer in his hand, his hair a sexy, rumpled mess, he's the nightmare of my dreams. And while the idea of feasting my eyes on him while I feast on a burger doesn't seem like a terrible plan in theory, when he looks my way and a smirk settles on his stupidly kissable lips, that idea is less appetizing.

Because damn it if I don't want him, even when I know I shouldn't.

He sets his beer on the bar. With a swagger that should be illegal, he moseys my way. "When I said I'd be seeing ya, I'll admit I thought I was going to have to work harder to make that happen."

"Just pointing out the fact that you didn't have to put *any* work into making it happen."

"Yeah. I know. It's fate."

"No," I say with a laugh. "It's called 'Mucker's is the only place open.'"

He frowns. "You know, I didn't have you pegged as a fun-sucker. But here we are."

I can't help but chuckle. His words are playful, his tone smooth and unassuming. But the heat in his eyes, the mischief lurking right behind his lashes, is anything but.

My chest rises and falls much quicker than I'd like, but there's not a lot I can do. Every cell in my body tugs toward the man in front of me, and it takes all the restraint I can muster to stay cool.

"I'm a good sucker of fun . . . Don't you say a word," I say, wagging a finger his way. My cheeks heat at the opening I just gave him.

"I have no idea what you're talking about."

"Don't play innocent with me. I saw your eyes light up like Christmas trees."

A slow grin slips across his lips. "Oh, did you think hearing you say the words 'fun' and 'suck' was going to have an effect on me?" He shifts his weight, crossing his muscled arms in front of him. "You're damn right it did."

The other patrons' gazes are shifting my way. I can't even care. I'm too busy trying to figure out how to navigate being around Penn.

Diverting my gaze away from him, I spy Harper and give her a wave. "What are you doing here, anyway?" I ask.

"I'm having a beer with my buddy Matt. What about you?" His eyes twinkle with anticipation.

"I'm meeting Harper."

"Just the two of you?"

"I think she's meeting a friend or something," I say. "I'm just here as the third wheel. Or fifth. Or whatever it ends up being."

He sticks his tongue in his cheek. "I can't say I'm sorry to hear that."

I try to flash him a disapproving look, but he makes it impossible. The overt sexiness that seeps from his pores is mixed with a playful energy that makes it virtually impossible to not be entertained by his antics.

"You're a handful," I tell him.

"Two handfuls, thank you very much. Now come on and meet Matt."

My heart skips a beat as I realize the toe I thought I was dipping into the deep end is suddenly my whole foot. And if I don't watch it, I'll slide right into that pool and drown faster than I can ask for help.

This is how it happens. One minute, you're vulnerable to a smile. The next, you're meeting his friends. Five minutes later, you're in his bed, having the orgasm of your life.

I've gotta slow my roll.

Taking a step back, I shake my head. "No. It was nice seeing you, but—"

"Come on, Avery," he singsongs. "I can't have you walk in here and not introduce you. What kind of a gentleman would I be if I did that?"

I raise a brow. "You're a gentleman?"

"Uh, yeah."

"Uh, no."

His blue eyes are bottomless, and he knows it. He uses his long lashes and heavy brows to lure me in.

My gaze is held by his, almost *caressed*, and I feel it *everywhere*. The zip of his touch earlier today is still so fresh in my mind that I'm tempted to brush against him just to feel it again.

I watch the edge of his shirt ride up as he stretches, giving me a hint of the muscles lying beneath the light fabric of his shirt. The heat of his gaze puts me into a spot that's as comfortable as it is not, and in lieu of fanning my face in the middle of Mucker's patio, I blow out a breath.

I can't take the bait.

"Are you coming or not?" he asks, lowering his voice. "You know you want to."

Before I can come up with a response, a polite way of saying no, another man joins us.

"Who do you have here?" he asks before tipping back a beer. A headful of sandy-brown hair flops off his forehead as he moves.

"This is Avery," Penn says.

There's a hint of something in his voice that doesn't go unnoticed. Penn's friend raises his brows and holds back a grin.

"Avery," Penn says, oblivious to our catch, "this is Matt Madden. Matt, this is Avery."

"Nice to meet you," I say, offering a hand.

"Penn's told me a lot about you," Matt says, taking my hand and giving it a gentle shake. There's a smugness to his tone that makes me curious.

I look at Penn out of the corner of my eye. "Is that right?"

"I didn't say a lot about you. Matt is being a dick."

"I beg to differ," Matt says.

"How would that even be possible?" Penn asks me. "You didn't tell me jack shit about you, even when I asked. So how would I know anything to even say? You didn't even shake my hand, like you just did his. Just thought I'd point that out. Not that I care."

I open my mouth to tell him exactly what I did with him when I first met him, to remind him of the ant bites on our legs as we tried to lie on a jacket he had in his truck. I shut it as quickly as I opened it.

"If I could take back the fact that I fell off a ladder and shake your hand instead, I would," I say.

"Whoa," Matt interrupts. "Did you say you 'fell off a ladder'?"

"Sadly," I admit.

"I think we are destined to be friends," Matt says.

His smile is easy and open, his posture relaxed. I like him immediately.

"I'd love to be your friend," I say.

Matt clamps a hand on Penn's shoulder, releasing a hearty laugh. "Guess she likes me, big guy."

"She just met you," Penn says. "She doesn't know if she likes you yet."

"Um, I just met you too," I say. "So who knows? Maybe I like Matt better than you. He has said a number of sentences to me without propositioning me."

"I can tell you right now that I definitely like you better than him," Matt cracks.

Penn's jaw drops. He looks between the two of us like he's shocked. As we laugh, Penn shoves Matt. Matt winces as he loses his balance and grabs the edge of a nearby table.

"Fuck you," Matt groans, clutching his side.

"I forgot. Honest," Penn says.

Matt looks up at me. There's pain written across his handsome face. "I injured my spleen. Sympathy is appreciated."

"He fell off a kiddie ladder. One lower than yours, even," Penn interjects. "Don't feel sorry for him. He's just trying to capitalize on you saying you might like him more than me."

"Penn! He's in pain." I make a face at him before turning to Matt. "You poor thing. You fell off a ladder. I did that today, and I know how terrifying it is." I hold out a hand. "Let me help you."

"Are we really doing this?" Penn asks, straight-faced.

"Doesn't look like *you* are doing anything," Matt says.

Penn quirks a brow. "I'm warning you . . ."

"You are too easy to rile up, Etling," Matt says.

"And you are too easy to injure. Remember that," Penn tells him.

I roll my eyes as I realize my hand is still dangling in the air. Matt takes it just to annoy Penn. I help him stand and dust off his shirt.

"There you go. You feel okay?" I ask.

It's hard to keep a straight face when Penn is this close and my interest in Matt is clearly bothering him. It's even harder when Matt plays along.

"I think so," Matt says, making a show of holding his side. "It's hard to get anyone to take me seriously around here."

"I'll take you seriously." I toss him a wink.

Penn moves so he's standing closer to me. It's like he knows his testosterone permeates the air and makes my head foggy. I turn to look at him in time to see a waitress sidling up to him. She's petite with long blonde hair and a pretty smile.

"Need another drink, Penn?" She looks up at him as if he could ask for anything and she'd get it, or do it, right there.

My gaze whips to Penn. He's looking at me. I can't help but feel a little bit satisfied.

"Nah," he says. "What about you, Avery?"

The waitress follows Penn's line of sight to me. "I'm sorry," she says. "I didn't see you come in. It's been crazy here. Can I get you something?"

"I was going to grab dinner but haven't seen a menu. Maybe a burger? I heard they were great," I suggest.

"We have great burgers and tenderloins, and breaded mushrooms to die for. Let me grab you a menu so you can make an informed decision." She pauses. "My name is Alexis. Don't listen to anything these punks tell you about me."

I laugh. "Deal."

She turns to go. Penn's head turns to follow her.

My stomach tightens as I watch him watch her. His expression is mostly neutral . . . until he catches me watching him. He runs a hand through the hair I just cut, the dimple in his left cheek shining.

"What?" he asks.

"Nothing." I tuck a strand of hair behind my ear. "I'm going to go grab a seat with Harper. It was good seeing you, Penn. Nice to meet you, Matt."

"Oh no," Matt says. He shakes his head from side to side. "Uh-uh. That's not gonna fly."

"What are you talking about?" I ask.

He quirks a brow. "You have to sit with us. We're friends now."

The two of them stand shoulder to shoulder like two linebackers protecting the end zone. Only in this case, the end zone is my self-restraint.

A warmth spreads in my stomach as they silently challenge me. For some unexplained reason, though our interaction can be measured in minutes, I feel like I've known them forever and better than I know all my old friends in California. It's so odd. Alarm bells should be going off. But they're not.

"Maybe I like sitting with Harper," I say.

"She looks like she's on a date," Matt says. "But I could be wrong. What do I know?"

"Then I'll take it to go," I suggest. "I'm perfectly happy eating at home."

"Just, um, really quick—you would be at home alone, right?" Penn asks. "I mean, there's no one there waiting on you?"

I try to ignore the way his lips twist to hide a grin. "How smart would it be for me to tell you if I'll be at home alone?"

"It wouldn't," Matt says quickly. "Trust me. Bad idea."

Penn glares at him before turning his attention back to me. "It would be super smart. What if something happened to you and you didn't know who to call? Come to think of it, I should totally give you my number too."

"Nine-one-one is pretty convenient. I think I'll be okay."

"Ooh, she doesn't want your number," Matt jokes. "Let's write this one down in the record books, boys."

"Will you shut the hell up?" Penn sighs. "Give the girl some time. It's probably pretty overwhelming to meet me." He turns slowly, his eyes full of salaciousness. "I'll give you some time. No worries."

I roll my eyes to distract him from the goose bumps breaking out across my skin.

"You can give me all the time you want," I say. "It won't make a difference."

Instead of being dissuaded, his position solidifies. The look on his face threatens to dissolve me where I'm standing. It's heady, a mixture of alpha and beta. A combination of sweet and sexy that's so intoxicating that I feel like I've already had a drink. But I'm not going to entertain that reaction.

I need to find out who I am, not who wants to sleep with me, and I have little faith that giving in to Penn will somehow become an epiphany about my life.

Epiphanies over orgasms. I need that on a shirt.

"Do you really believe that?" He raises a brow.

"Absolutely." I rip my gaze away from him and flip it to Matt. "Where's the bathroom around here?"

He points across the patio to a door behind the makeshift tiki bar. There's no hiding his amusement with Penn and me. "Want me to show you?"

"I can find it. Thanks." I start to step that way but stop. "If the waitress comes back, will you tell her I'll just have a bacon cheeseburger, no onion? And to take it to Harper's table?"

Matt grins smugly. "Will do."

My eyes drag over Penn as I focus once again on the bathroom.

The jerk is smirking.

I flash him my sassiest smile and walk away.

CHAPTER EIGHT

AVERY

The bathroom is clearly marked and also thankfully unoccupied. I dart inside, my mind racing, and fiddle with the lock. A screw is missing, and it takes forever to get it latched. Once I do, I collapse against the wall and breathe.

There's a little sink with a mirror hanging above it that looks like it was put there before I was born. The toilet is obscured from view by a wall. The room definitely leaves a bit to be desired but is somehow still charming.

I close my eyes and inhale a deep lungful of air.

"Look at me, walking away," I say out loud.

A dose of pride washes over me because that wasn't easy. But I did it. I didn't cave.

Laughter drifts through the crack between the door and the floor, and I find myself listening for Penn's voice. It doesn't take long until the friendly timbre makes its way to me.

Even if I could actually avoid him in this town of nine-hundred-or-so people, I don't know that I'd want to. He's funny and friendly, and everyone who knows him seems to like him, even Harper. And the way he talked to Lorene today at the salon was downright adorable.

"But that's the problem. He's everything I like. He's just everything I don't trust too," I whisper to myself.

My mind projects the next six months like a home movie. There are two potential end results if I give in to Penn.

The first is that we hook up and then move on. That wouldn't be terrible if it weren't a complete waste of time. Also, it has me repeating the same behavior I've had my whole life: giving in to what other people want when it's not what I want.

Not that I don't want to sleep with Penn. I do. So much. *So, so much.* But it's a one-night stand—a week at most—and I'm not in the market for that. I don't want to be.

The second potential outcome is that we somehow finagle things into a semblance of a relationship. But would it even be a relationship I wanted to be in? Or just a relationship that has an expiration date on it from the get-go?

I sigh. "You are not even thinking about this," I tell myself. "You promised yourself you'd find someone that truly wants *you*. That's probably not Penn. No, that's definitely not Penn."

This is true, regardless of what Harper says. Case in point: he doesn't even remember me. While he's not to blame, it is a red flag for future interactions.

An awkward lump takes root in my stomach. For the first time since that night so long ago, I kind of regret sleeping with him.

Penn was so sweet when I stumbled upon him by the lake. He distracted me with fishing stories and tales of small-town life and then listened as I ranted about my problems. We laughed and commiserated, and as the sun set and the stars came out, I found myself in his arms.

By the time the sun kissed the horizon on its way back up, I had walked to my car, grabbed my things from Harper's, and was at the airport.

I never saw him again, and I've always been okay with that. It's been this special moment that was just for me. No one knew about it. No one could taint it for me. There wasn't a soul in the world who could guilt me for my actions or tell me he was desperate—or worse, that I was.

I've never wished that night to be any different.

Until now.

"I could tell him he knew me before," I think aloud. Even as the words leave my mouth, I know there's no way I can. The lump grows in my stomach and turns into a rock. It grows heavier as I imagine mentioning our history—and that he forgot and I clearly didn't—and trying to wash over it all with some kind of silly laugh.

Embarrassment creeps up my cheeks.

"Yeah, no thanks."

Walking across the room, I look at myself in the mirror. My face is a bit flushed, my pupils large, black dots.

I take my hair down from a ponytail and smooth it out. I wonder how many calls I've missed from my friends in Los Angeles. *Probably none. They've moved on by now.*

My fingers go through my tresses as I think about my old crowd. They love the ladder-climbing lifestyle. Running into and with celebrities, hitting the hot locales, taking the perfect snaps for social media at the right spots—that is their life. It was never truly mine. The older I got, the more I felt like I was let into their circle because of my mother. There's little doubt they've filled my spot in their circle with someone else who can bring something to the table.

I pause and look at my reflection. My eyes are so clear, like a weight has been lifted from my shoulders, and I realize that I feel that way. Lighter. Intuitively happier.

My hair goes back up again as I smile to myself. I check myself out from all sides, making sure I don't have little fins of hair sticking every which way. Even though I roll my eyes at my antics, I don't stop.

"You just go back out there and pretend like he's another guy," I say to my reflection. "You can flirt. Flirting with cute boys isn't against the law and is great for the ego. Just remember he's not for you." I twist my lips. "Or he would've remembered the first time."

After giving my hands a quick wash and dry, I take a piece of paper towel to the door. I use it to unlatch the lock and twist the knob before throwing it away.

The music is mellow, a pop song from the nineties, as I hesitate behind the little bar. It's his laugh that makes a beeline to my ears. Despite the oregano in the air and odor of spilled beer, it's Penn's cologne I gravitate toward.

I need a drink.

"Hey, Avery."

I jump at the sound of Harper's voice. My hand clutches my chest. "You scared the crap out of me," I tell her.

She laughs. "I see that. You okay?"

"Yeah. Just zoned out a little, I guess."

Harper bites her bottom lip and eyes me suspiciously. "Are you joining us, or are you hanging out with Penn and Matt?"

"I'll be joining you. Thanks."

"Well, if something happens and you end up with the boys, don't worry about me. And if you get back to the house and I'm not there—again, don't worry about me." She shimmies her hips. "I'm working on a little dessert, if you know what I mean."

I laugh. "Well, good luck to you. With the cleavage you're toting tonight, I have a hard time believing you'll get turned down."

She cups her breasts and squeezes them together. "I'm quite proud of these babies."

"I can tell."

"Now, you go out there and make friends. Just try not to burn the place down with all the heat between you and Penn."

"Harper, please," I hiss. "Stop it."

"I know sparks when I see them."

I blow out a breath and ensure she catches my annoyance. "There's no smoke. No fire. There's not anything to make a big deal about. He's not even my type," I add. "I told you that."

There's not a piece of her that believes me. She just stands there in her billowy blue dress and waits for me to laugh or say I'm kidding.

"I'm not joking, Harper."

She rests a hand on my shoulder. Her whiskey-colored eyes offer a soft spot for mine to land. "Listen, I don't care who you date or don't date. It's no skin off my back. I just . . . Penn's a nice guy. You're a great girl. When I see you two together, I get this feeling right here." She pats her chest.

"I think that's heartburn."

She snorts. "No, I think it's called a gut feeling, thank you very much."

I back away slowly with a grin. "Keep your feelings to yourself."

She laughs. "Will do. Now, if you'll excuse me, I gotta pee." She flashes me a wave before disappearing into the restroom.

The air grows thicker as I stand alone. I brush back a few blades of fake tiki grass and, like a complete creeper, find Matt and Penn. They're sitting at a table with a giant pizza placed between them.

"They're just two guys," I say, rearranging the grass. "Maybe you can be friends with them."

I walk around the end of the bar as I finish my pep talk. Penn's eyes hit me before the thought fully launches into the universe. My flush must be obvious, because he winks.

Damn it.

I force a swallow as I approach them. There are four chairs around the small rectangular table, two on one side and two on the other.

Matt points to a plate in the middle of the table. "Your burger was delivered here."

"Why does that not surprise me?" I ask.

Matt grins as he motions toward a pink-and-orange drink next to Penn. "We also ordered you a Rocket Razzle."

"A Rocket what?" I laugh. "What's in that thing?"

"It's a rum-and-something," Penn says. "If you don't drink or don't like rum, I'll drink it. No worries."

"No, I love rum. I just have an aversion to tequila." I shrug. "Long night. Cheap tequila. Longer next day as I puked up everything I've ever consumed. I can't stand the smell of it now."

"Sounds like a good story," Matt says. He pulls out the chair beside him. "Grab a seat."

I look between the two empty chairs—one by Matt and another by Penn. My body wants me to take the seat next to Penn. My brain is screaming at me to be intentional about this decision and make the smart choice, meaning the one by Matt.

Before I can sort out the internal dilemma, the redhead who opened the door for me comes bouncing our way.

"Hey, guys!" The bracelets adorning her wrist jingle as she comes to a stop. "I can't believe I left the stupid grill on at the café. Who am I these days?"

"Claire Collins, the same girl that called me last week because she left her car running all night and ran it out of gas," Penn says.

She slides into the chair by Matt. "You're an asshole, Penn."

"Why?" he says. "Because I speak the truth?"

"Because you're you." She looks up and notices me for the first time. She points a finger my direction as she thinks. "Didn't I just meet you?"

"Claire, this is Avery. Avery, this is Claire." Penn motions between us but looks at me. "Wanna sit?"

"Um . . ." I was going to, but for some reason, I'm not sure now. "I should probably go sit with Harper," I say awkwardly.

Penn drags the chair next to him against the brick pavers. "Sit." He looks at me with a raised brow. "Claire will be offended if you leave now."

Claire snorts. "Don't use me to woo her."

"He's not wooing me," I say.

Her eyes light up. She sits back in her chair and looks at Matt. "Where did you find her? Because I like her already."

"Right? She's turned him down a couple of times, and I just met her," Matt says. "She's a fucking unicorn."

"I'd fuck a unicorn." Penn looks around the table. "What? I would."

"Color me not surprised," Claire mumbles. "Anyway, Avery, if you'd like to sit with us, please do. I could use some estrogen to balance the testosterone around here."

I look around the patio. There are open tables and a chair next to Harper, who looks cozy next to a guy in a leather jacket. But then I consider Claire and what she had to say. She's not wrong. Two women would make it much easier to defuse this craziness with Penn, and if I'm staying here, I need to make friends. Given she just called Penn an asshole, I might get along with her just fine.

"You sure?" I ask, lowering myself slowly next to Penn.

Penn leans forward, his elbows resting on the table. "I'm sure," he says, his voice low and gravelly. The tone sinks all kinds of ideas into my head. Ideas that don't belong there.

"Great," I say as neutrally as I can.

Claire takes a slice of pizza and pops it onto a paper plate. "Want a piece?" She offers it to me.

My shoulders relax as I'm tugged away from Penn's attention. "I have a burger. But thanks."

Matt slides the plate my way. "I hope it's right. Penn ordered you the drink, and we started arguing over whether you said no tomato or no onion and that turned into a conversation that I don't want to get into, so, short answer—it might be wrong, and if it is, it's Penn's fault."

"Thanks. It'll be fine, whatever it is," I say.

"I'm guessing you're new here?" Claire asks before chomping off the end of her slice of pizza.

I take the Rocket Razzle and let the cool glass bleed into my palms. Penn moves beside me, his thigh nearly brushing mine. I hold my breath until he stills again. Only then do I look back up at Claire. She's grinning.

"I just moved here from Los Angeles," I tell her.

"I've always wanted to see LA," she says. "I'm sad to admit it, but I've only been out of Tennessee three times. What kind of life is that?"

"California is amazing. You have the desert down south, Lake Tahoe in the north. There's redwood trees and beaches and everything in between. It's pretty stunning, really."

She nods, wiping a drop of grease off her chin. "I saw a travel show about San Francisco last week. It looked amazing."

"It is," I gush. "It really has its own vibe."

"It's on my bucket list," Claire says.

I take a sip of the Rocket Razzle. The rum is smooth, and what I'm guessing is pineapple juice is sweet and heavenly. I take another drink for good measure.

"You guys doing all right?" Alexis asks, coming back to the table. "Anyone need another drink?"

"We're good. Thanks," Claire says.

Alexis smiles and then looks down at Penn. Her hand rests on the top of his chair. "We still on for Friday night?"

I grip my glass and prepare myself.

The truth of the matter is that I don't know Penn. As much as he flirts with me, guys like him flirt with *everyone*. Besides, it's not like he didn't have a social calendar before I showed up today, and I bet his calendar is full. This is the second red flag for me to stay away.

"I didn't know we had something on Friday," he says to her.

"Well, we don't," Alexis says. "I was just hoping . . ."

He leans back in his chair. His arm rests across the rail of my seat, making his biceps inches away from the back of my neck.

My breathing hitches in my throat as the feeling of being surrounded on two sides by Penn overtakes me. His lips part as he looks at me, spreading into a wide, roguish grin.

I take a bite of my burger in the hope that it'll occupy my mouth and distract me from his.

"I'm taking Avery out on Friday night," he says with a cool confidence that makes me want to smack him. "I'm sorry, Alexis."

"That's okay." Alexis takes an empty beer bottle off the end of the table. "Maybe next time." She walks away with a side-eye aimed toward Penn.

I wait until she's out of earshot before I turn to him.

"You're what?" I ask. I feel Matt's and Claire's eyes on me as I search Penn's for an answer to this craziness.

"I'm taking you out on Friday."

The words are so concrete, so matter of fact, that I wonder if I somehow agreed to this and just don't remember.

As Matt laughs across from me and the corners of Penn's lips begin to upturn, I shake my head.

"You are not," I tell him.

"She just told him no," Claire gasps. "Matt. Did you hear that?"

"Shh . . . ," Matt says. "Let's watch and see what it looks like when Penn gets turned down."

Claire's giggle pierces the air as she reaches for a napkin.

Penn shifts in his seat. His arm flexes behind me. "Thursday, then?" His voice drops. "Or I can be free on Saturday?"

"How about no," I say.

He cocks his head to the side. He's so intently focused on me that I'm not even sure he hears the ribbing from Matt and Claire.

There's no way for him to know that my life in LA has prepared me for invitations like this and that I've heard it all before. It'll take more than an assumption that I'm like the other girls he sees to break me.

"Don't you need someone to show you around?" he asks.

"Nah, I'm good. Thanks."

"I'm sure you are." His eyes narrow, the tip of his tongue sliding across his lower lip. It's enough to wake me up.

"You would know if you remembered," I say before I can think about it. My knuckles turn white as I hold on to the chair with all my might. I swallow hard. My brain tries to come up with something to distract him from that stupid, stupid little statement, but I come up with nothing.

His eyebrows furrow. "What's that mean?"

"It means . . . ," I say, swallowing again. "It just means that if you remembered what I said at the salon, you'd know I have a checklist."

I'm in trouble.

He leans in so close that I feel his breath on my cheek. The anticipation of what he's about to say has me struggling for oxygen.

When I was cutting his hair, I was in charge. The playing field is much more level here, and the only thing I can use as a barrier is a glass of Rocket Razzle.

I need to pull away. I need to stop this before he does something stupid like kiss me, and I do something stupid like kiss him back.

"Avery?" he whispers in my ear.

"Yeah?"

My heart beats in my throat. I shiver as the proximity of his lips becomes so deliciously obvious. If one of us moves even a muscle, his mouth will be touching me.

"You have a pickle on your shirt," he says softly.

I look down to see a bright-green pickle right between my boobs. Penn pulls back, but not before I swat his shoulder.

"We are not friends," I tell him, grabbing a napkin from the holder in the center of the table.

"We're friends, though, right?" Matt asks.

"Definitely." I look across the table. "You can even be my new best friend."

"Wanna fight?" Penn looks at Matt. "I'll fight you right here."

Matt takes a long drink of his beer as Claire jumps into the fray with a tale of Penn and Matt in an actual fight in high school. In the midst of the heckling and storytelling and pickle plucking, I find myself laughing easily with them.

The longer we sit, the more normal this feels. We eat our meals lazily and get our drinks refilled again and again. There's no rush, no subtle hustle to an underlying agenda from any of them. They genuinely like each other's company. And mine, I think.

I grab the water glass I traded for my Rocket Razzle an hour ago and settle back in my seat. Matt segues into a story about a dog named Blue. As they continue on, asking me about my life and filling me in on theirs like we're long-lost friends, an overwhelming sense of comfort washes over me.

These three people might just be my first true, "like me for me" friends. Even though they've had years together to really build their friendship, we just seem to click. Best of all, I don't have to be someone I'm not to fit in.

The breeze filters through the patio, ruffling the covers on the tiki huts. It reminds me of sitting on the beach by my apartment in California, the only place I ever felt free from that world. I'm starting to feel free here in the midst of people who might just be *my people*.

The thought makes me smile.

As the breeze settles and Claire finishes her story about a doughnut, Penn's knee brushes against mine. A flurry of goose bumps breaks out across my skin because even if I can't play in that pool, he's gorgeous. He glances at me with a sinful grin.

Penn might be a lot of things. Persistent. Likable. Dreamy, even. But as I watch his eyes hood and read between the lines, one thing becomes clear: he won't be my lover.

CHAPTER NINE

PENN

"And that's how I ended up with the name 'Happy' tattooed on my body." Claire tips the end of her beer bottle toward Avery. "I told you that I always find the dandies."

"I think I'm going to have to agree with you," Avery says with a laugh. "Remind me never to let you pick my dates."

Alexis comes by and drops off the leftover pizza she boxed up for Matt. She doesn't say anything to me. She hasn't said a word my way since I told her I had a date with Avery. I don't really care because despite Alexis's easygoing smile, she's a vulture. She smelled a new woman and was trying to stake a claim.

I watch Avery swirl a straw around her drink as she talks about her last date. The guy sounds like a douche. At least I'll give her a good story to tell when we have our date, because we will. I just need more time.

The fact that I need more time has me more turned on than I've been in a while.

She's sat beside me all night, driving me freaking crazy. Her skin is soft as she bumps my arm, and I can't even tell if she's doing it on purpose. Her laugh is contagious. I've smiled more tonight than I might ever have, and that's concerning.

I'm going to look like the Joker if I don't get out of here.

But getting out of here means not being with her while I can. While I'm not the smartest guy in the world, I'm smart enough to know that math doesn't add up.

"Are you staying in town forever? Or are you just here for a job or something?" Claire asks. "Most people don't move here out of the blue. Most people don't even know that Dogwood Lane exists. It's not like we have anything here to attract people."

"Except me," I cut in.

"Here we go," Matt mumbles.

Claire rolls her eyes. "I was being serious."

"Me too," I say. "Take Avery, for example. I met her this morning, and she tracked me down tonight. I attract people."

"Clearly," Avery scoffs, resting her chin in her hands. She looks up at me and bats her eyelashes. "So that's why when you asked me out two, maybe three, times today, I've told you no? Because I'm just so attracted to you?"

"No, but I'd like to know what kind of game you're playing with that whole 'I'm not attracted to you' thing. I've never seen it before. I'm not sure how it works."

Her cheeks are tinted pink, her lips slightly pouty, from the rum. The knot of hair on top of her head is wild, and I wonder if that's what it looks like when she wakes up in the morning.

The lighting from the dining area of Mucker's clicks off, indicating it's closing time. The string lights around the patio area seem a bit hazier without the glow from the restaurant and create an almost halo effect around Avery's head.

"It's pretty straightforward," she says. "It means I'm not interested in spending time with you."

"But you are right now."

"Alone, then," she amends.

"So you're an exhibitionist? I can get down with that, Ave." I flash her a grin as she struggles to remain unaffected by me.

She raises a brow. "'Ave'?"

"Yeah. Since we're friends and all, I thought you needed a nickname. You have a problem with it?"

"Maybe."

"Good." I twist in my seat to face Matt. It kills me not to look at her, but I have to show some self-control—even if I have to fake it. "You about ready to go, Madden?"

He downs the rest of his beer and then adds some bills to the stack in the center for Alexis. "Yup."

I pile my trash on top of my plate and do my best to avoid Avery. I figured she'd give in more tonight, but she didn't. And I'm not sure what to do about that. She happily conveyed details of her life to Claire—the ones she wouldn't give me earlier.

She's from LA. She has a sister. She likes the color purple . . . *I remember things about her.*

Shit.

I drop my wallet. My chair scratches the pavers as I scoot back to grab it.

"You okay, Penn?" Matt asks.

Nope.

"Yeah. Yup. I'm great," I say, scooping up the black leather and shoving it in my pocket.

I get to my feet as Harper comes by our table and stops.

"Closing the place down tonight, kids?" she asks.

"Just showing Avery how we do it," Matt says. "How ya been, Harper?"

"Good. How's the injury? I read about that in the paper," she says.

"I'm healing up, but it hurt like hell."

"He's healing up so well that he's going to work with me tomorrow, aren't ya, bud?" I ask.

Harper shifts her bag on her shoulder. "What are you guys doing?"

"Fuck if I know," I say. "Something for kids that I'm sure will be as clear as mud. The last time I had a job like this, I had to buy paint colors called Blush and Bashful. Those are pink, if you didn't know."

"Oh, I know," Harper says. "I think I know what project you're talking about, actually. I heard something about it at the café this morning." She taps her chin with a long fingernail. "Anyway, I'll be home later, Avery. Don't wait up." She tosses her niece a wink and heads toward the door.

Avery stands and gathers her things from the table. I don't stare at her ass. I want to point that out, to make sure people see what a good job I'm doing, but I keep it to myself.

Claire says goodbye and walks out with Harper. Matt, catching my pointed glare at the last minute, stands at attention.

"Avery," he says, "it was nice meeting you. I'll see you later, Etling."

"By 'later,' you mean tomorrow morning, right?" I ask.

"Maybe."

He knows he has me in a bind. If I argue with him, he'll still be here to walk Avery out. If I let him go, I'll have her all to myself for a few precious minutes.

As she looks at her phone, I motion my head toward the door. Matt chuckles.

"I'm going," he mouths. "See ya, Avery."

She looks up at him and smiles. "It was nice meeting you."

"Same. Catch ya later, you two." He grabs the pizza box and heads for the gate. I don't miss the shake of his head or quiet snickering.

The music that's played all evening stops, and the string lights flicker off. The squeak of the gate as Matt leaves indicates Avery and I are alone.

I take a deep breath.

This should be easy enough. I've been alone with more than my fair share of women. But as she looks at me with a grin that's a little less confident than before, I feel myself pussying out for the first time in my life.

My heart thumps, my knees bounce, and my fucking lips won't stop smiling. It's reminiscent of the night I found myself alone with Michele Santos when I was twelve. We were playing a massive game of hide-and-seek in the park at dusk. Somehow, we both ended up behind a statue memorializing a Civil War battle and left as newly cemented kissers.

"You ready?" she asks. I almost get the feeling she wants me to say no. But as she steps toward the gate, I figure it's just wishful thinking.

"Sure." I make sure to get ahead of her in time to open the gate. "Here you go."

She dips her chin as she walks out. "Thanks."

I get the gate latched and find the padlock hidden behind a giant pot that holds prickly red flowers. Through the gate it goes before I slam it shut.

Avery laughs. "I didn't even see the gate when I pulled up. I went through the dining room and all those people for nothing."

"They just installed it a few months ago. It's hard to see if you're not looking for it," I tell her. I give the lock a jerk to make sure it's fastened. "There we go. All done."

"Is there a reason you're the one locking up?"

Her eyes shine under the moonlight. There's a softness to her features that I haven't seen before, yet it feels familiar.

"It's kind of a thing around here," I tell her. "Most of the regulars just lock it if we're the last to leave. Small-town stuff, I guess."

"I like it."

I know she means the small-town life, but I pop my collar, anyway. "Thanks."

She laughs. "I didn't mean you."

"Uh, yeah. I think you did."

She rolls her eyes and turns toward her car. "You're pretty confident for a guy that keeps getting told no."

"Let's talk about that. Why are you playing hard to get, anyway?"

"I'm not playing, Penn."

"So, you're just hard to get?" I stand a few feet away as she opens her car door and tosses her purse into the passenger seat. "I kind of like that in a woman. I'm not mad about it."

She leans against the doorframe. She brushes a lock of hair out of her eyes as she chooses her words.

"I've rendered you speechless, huh?" I say, hoping to make her laugh.

It works. The sound dances over me and makes me feel some way—a way I'm not sure how to identify. I just know I like it.

"Has anyone ever told you that you're a piece of work?" she asks.

"It's usually a piece of meat, but I like work too."

She shakes her head. "Thank you for walking me to my car, even though I didn't ask you to."

"I'm attentive to every need, Ave, and can help with all kinds of things without being told or asked to. Just remember that."

Her pupils are dilated, her throat constricted as she forces a swallow. She crosses her arms and then uncrosses them, and for a woman who's trying to act like she's not attracted to me . . .

She fails.

Hard.

That makes both of us.

"Do you have any family here besides Harper? It's an honest question," I add before she can interject. "I'm being serious."

"No. I don't. My family is all back in Los Angeles, which is fine. Trust me. They're . . . a lot."

"I know you're going to think this is a pickup line, and if you want it to be, then it *so is*." I grin. "But if you don't, it's just me trying to be a nice guy."

"What?"

"If you want my number, I'll give it to you," I offer.

Her head falls back and she laughs. "That's an awful pickup line."

"It wasn't one."

"Yes, it was."

"I assure you, Ave, it wasn't," I insist. "My game isn't that weak."

She starts to talk and then stops. Her arms cross her chest again, and she takes a deep breath. "Then give me your best shot."

I laugh. "What? My best shot? What does that even mean?"

"Give me your best pickup line."

I blink a couple of times. She's issued me a challenge—one I wasn't expecting. I scramble to come up with something, but I need time.

"You've put me on the spot," I say.

She grins, proud of herself. "You talk a lot of smack. I want you to work for it."

Whether she means to or not, she chooses this exact moment to lick her lips. And I don't mean to, but I almost whimper.

"Does this mean I win a prize if I woo you?" I ask, trying to delay. My brain searches every mental file I have for a pickup line.

"You can't woo me."

"That sounds like a dare."

She presses off the car. There's heat in her eyes that I can feel in my blood.

"It's not a dare. It's a fact," she says. "You can't woo me. I'm un-woo-able."

"Is that so?"

"Absolutely."

"I'm about to woo you."

My mind starts racing again. It's like I'm totally unprepared for a very important test.

"When, exactly, does the wooing commence?" It's a tease, a nod to the fact that she thinks she's already won. "Because I don't have all night."

"Before I start, what do I win?"

If I weren't looking as closely as I am, I wouldn't notice the uptick in her breathing. The way her chest rises and falls like she's preparing for . . . *something.* And dear Lord, how I'd like to give her all of my *something.*

"If you win, which you won't, I'll give you a haircut for free," she offers.

"I can get them for free from Harper all day long."

"She doesn't charge you?"

"Yeah, but if I didn't have the money, she wouldn't make me pay. Ever wonder why she's operating out of a she shed? It's because she's too nice."

She nods. "Fine. If you win . . ."

"If I woo you," I say, taking a step toward her, "then you owe me a favor."

"And if you don't, you owe me."

"As long as it's sexual."

She smacks my chest. I capture her hand before it can retreat and hold it against me.

Her breathing all but stops. Mine gets jagged. All I can feel is her small palm lying like a ton of bricks against my shirt. I hear nothing but the tiny sips of breath she manages to take.

A car drives by and honks. I don't even look up to see who it is. I'm not sure that Avery hears it at all. She stretches her fingers over the fabric of my shirt. With every movement, my heart pounds harder.

I force a swallow as our eyes lock. There's an invitation in her eyes, a breakdown of the woman-not-interested persona she's put on all day.

With more care than I've ever put into a kiss, I lean down slowly. Her eyes widen as her chin lifts toward mine.

I shift my feet so I'm closer to her body. Her free hand touches me lightly on the hip. My insides are on fire as I near her lips, which are partially closed and waiting for me.

"Penn," she whispers.

"Yeah?"

"You have pizza sauce on your face."

My head jerks up to see her smiling at me. I drop her hand and bring mine to my face, dabbing at my mouth. When she laughs, I realize what she's done.

"That's not even funny," I say as she laughs harder. Adrenaline leaves me sluggish and defeated. "I can't believe you just did that."

She shrugs. "You owe me."

"You were wooed," I say.

"Hardly."

"I saw you," I tell her. "You wanted that kiss."

She climbs in her car and sticks the keys in the ignition. "If I wanted that kiss, your tongue would be in my mouth right now."

"Stop talking foreplay," I groan, adjusting myself.

The car starts. She closes the door but rolls the window down. "Seriously, though. Thanks for inviting me to sit with you guys tonight. It was fun."

"Anytime." I take another step backward. "Feel free to call that favor due whenever. I can give you a list of my specialties."

She puts the car in reverse and waves. "Bye, Penn." A wicked laugh slips out the window, and I find myself smiling in response.

"You *were* wooed," I call after her.

I watch her drive off into the night. Standing way too long in the parking lot, my hands jammed in my pockets, I take in the weird twinge in my chest. Couple it with the smile on my face and two things are certain.

She was wooed, and I am screwed.

CHAPTER TEN

AVERY

Good morning, sweet pea." Harper flounces into the salon, looking fresh as lettuce. Her hair is curled into amazing beach waves and her pineapple-print maxi dress is adorable. "I stayed at my friend's last night," she says, wiggling her eyebrows, "and got here early. I just ran over to the café for a cup of coffee and a doughnut."

I yawn.

"Glad you're chipper this morning." She sets her cup on her station. "Late night?"

"Kind of," I say. "I forgot a spoon for my yogurt so I'm kind of cranky."

"Out all night with Penn?"

"No." I give my one-word answer as much emphasis as I can in the hope that she leaves that specific topic be.

"But you wanted to be, huh?"

"Wanted to be what?"

"That's a yes." She chuckles to herself as she picks her coffee back up again. "It's okay, Avery. He's cute. Things happen with cute guys."

Things don't always happen with cute guys, and I can thank a mosquito for that. If it hadn't been for that blood-sucking insect biting my calf when it did, I'd have been bitten by Penn instead.

His playful yet provocative methods of trying to win my favor worked. I wasn't able to think about much other than that non-kiss all night. I even thought about it while I got dressed this morning.

I hate to admit it, but I was kind of wooed.

Damn it.

I just wonder what kind of a kisser he is now. Does he run his hands through your hair? Cup the sides of your face with his calloused fingers? Does he kiss sweetly or aggressively? Does he use his tongue on the first go at it, or does he hold back?

Things I'd like to know, true. But I'm better off not having a clue.

I avoid her eyes. "Yes. He is. There's no denying that. But he's . . . And I'm . . . And we . . . just can't," I say. "We can't. That's all."

"Oh, I'm sure he could."

"But *I* can't." I spring to my feet in a sudden urge to move. "He's exactly what I moved here to get away from, Harper. I would be an idiot to get sucked back into . . . that."

She sits in her chair and crosses her legs. She's completely unrushed, like she has all the time in the world to have this conversation. "Like what? What is *that*?"

"Gorgeous. Funny. A little bit cocky. A smooth talker with a predisposition to use innuendo as an actual language."

I pace in front of the fake tree in the corner. While I'm aware I probably look like a crazy person, I don't care, nor do I stop. Moving feels good, much better than lying in bed all night, replaying every word he said yesterday and trying to find something horrible in it so I can stop thinking about him.

Ugh.

"You know how oil is great on its own? And water is an essential element of life?" I stop walking and face her. "Put them together, and they just don't work. Like toothpaste and orange juice or black socks and brown shoes."

"Go on . . ." She sticks her tongue in her cheek while she waits.

"Penn and I wouldn't work out, Harper. It's just that simple."

She sighs. "Let me get this straight. You and Penn wouldn't work because he's cute, makes you laugh, and knows it?"

"Correct."

"You do see how nuts you sound, right?"

I collapse back into my chair. She's right. I do sound nuts, but I'm not wrong.

On paper—heck, in person—Penn looks pretty great. But I know from past experience that guys like him are great in the role they want to play, and Penn's made it perfectly clear what role that is.

But at the end of the day, this isn't about him. I can't let it be about him. It has to be about me and what I want, and I'm not even sure what that is right now. I just know that if I say "To hell with it" and give in, I should've stayed in LA.

"Well, you do you," she says.

"I am doing me, Harper. That's what I'm trying to say."

She takes a sip of her coffee and watches me over the brim. When she sets the cup back on the counter, she sighs.

"When I first started doing hair, I had this woman come in that wanted her hair dyed red. I had a terrible feeling about it. I mean, I even tried to talk her out of it."

"Why?" I ask.

"I don't know. Maybe because I ate a red crayon as a child and puked it up. Anyway, that was the worst color job I've ever done, and in retrospect, a part of me thinks I convinced myself it would be bad before it ever started. I had a phobia about red dyes for years."

I laugh. "That's tragic."

"It is. But you know what's more tragic?"

My face falls. I brace myself for whatever truth she's readying to hurl my way. And no matter what it is, I have to listen because Harper wouldn't waste her time with nonsensical advice.

"What's more tragic is when we do that to people, when we decide someone is difficult or bad or a rogue without giving them a chance."

I roll my eyes.

If I were to somehow convince myself that Penn was worth pursuing, then I'd have to broach the "we fucked" subject, and I'm not feeling that. And it's not really about that, anyway.

"Look," I say with a frustrated breath. "I'm not judging Penn for being the consummate flirt he is. I actually like his attention. But at no point last night did Penn want anything to do with me outside of a hookup. I've had that for years, Harp. Just, the men before wanted my parents' connections or to gain credibility because of my last name. Penn just wants to get off."

Harper forces a swallow. "I get that. That was a mildly disturbing way to put it, but okay."

I sigh. "I just . . . I don't want to get married. I'm not looking for something serious, even. But I do want to have some sort of relationship with a guy who doesn't want to flirt with everyone. A guy who asks me questions because he wants to know *me* and not just my family or my vagina."

"Okay, I hear you," Harper says. "I do. And I'm going to let it go."

"Thank you."

"For now, anyway," she says.

I swivel from side to side in the chair. This is entirely too heavy for this early. "How busy will we be today?"

She stands and picks up her purse. It drops into the chair with a thud. "We won't be that busy. So I did you a favor."

"Why does that concern me on some level?"

She digs through her giant black bag. "Because you know me well," she mumbles. "Got it." She extends her hand. A business card sticks out between her fingers. "Here. Take this."

I do. It's on light-pink cardstock and smells faintly of roses. "What's this?"

"You said you like to paint, right?"

"Yeah. I mean, I'm no Picasso, but I enjoy it. Why?"

"I found you a side hustle." She moves the purse out of her way and sits again. "I had a little aha moment last night and made some calls. I found you something that I think will fill your soul and pad your pockets a little."

"What is it?" I ask.

"I'm not totally sure, to be honest. But Haley—have you met her? She runs Buds and Branches."

"The flower shop?"

"Yes."

"No, I haven't been in there, but it looks so cute from the outside."

Harper nods. "It is. And she's just as cute. You'd love her. Anyway, her boyfriend, Trevor, and his family are a bunch of wealthy do-gooders around here. Great people. They're doing something with kids down at the old library, and I thought you could help out. Meredith, that's Trevor's stepmom and the brains and moneybags behind the project, said they need an artist."

I laugh. "I'm not an artist."

"You'll do fine. She said it would just take a couple of weeks—no big deal. I told her I'd send you her way this morning if you were interested. You could just meet her and see what she's doing. I didn't commit you to anything."

I curl a leg up under me and watch Harper mess with a broken fingernail. This time yesterday, Penn was walking through the door. *"Here comes trouble,"* Harper said.

She doesn't even know how right she was.

I yawn again. "What's she like?"

"Who? Meredith?"

"Yeah."

"She's married to a retired, big-shot attorney from Nashville. They bought some land up here a couple of years ago and built a huge, and I mean *huge*, house on top of the hill out there. In the fall when the leaves drop, you can see it. It's pretty incredible."

"I think I know the spot," I say. "I was trying to get to the lake yesterday . . . Anyway, long story. But the point is, I think I turned around in their driveway, because I can't imagine two houses here that are that big."

Harper laughs and goes back to her fingernail. "That was probably it. You know, Penn, Matt, and Dane built that . . ."

She lets her voice trail off to create an opening for me to poke around. When I don't, she looks up at me.

"What?" I ask.

"Oh, nothing. Anyway, Meredith is nice. You'll like her. She has a lot of energy."

I glance up at the clock. We've been open for ten minutes, and not a soul has called or come in. It's so odd to me. The old salon I worked at would've been swamped already.

While the idea of hanging out here with Harper and cutting a walk-in or two really doesn't bother me, I need to not take this laid-back lifestyle too far.

"Should I go now?" I ask. "Or wait until lunch, or what?"

"Just go now. I have a couple of appointments this morning. If anyone walks in, they can wait."

"You sure?"

"Absolutely."

"Okay." I grab my purse and the container of yogurt I brought for breakfast. "Where do I go?"

"The old library. Do you know where that is? Down past Buds on the right. The Kellys bought the building after the city closed down the library." She laughs at the memory. "Then they bought the flower shop and combined it with the library. Told you she was energetic."

I laugh. "Sounds like it." My purse goes over my shoulder. "If you need me, just call or text. I can be right back."

"I got this covered."

"Thanks for the hookup," I say.

Harper's eyes sparkle. It causes my stomach to rattle around.

"What are you not telling me?" I ask.

She shrugs. "I don't know. That you look pretty today?"

"You're up to something. I feel it."

"Oh, I know!" Harper gets up and heads to the cabinets by the mini fridge. A spoon comes sailing my way. "Take this so you don't wear that yogurt."

I snag the spoon out of the air. "You don't have enough faith in me."

"I think I have more faith in you than you do."

I pull a face that makes her laugh. "I'll be back once I meet Meredith and see what this thing is all about." Turning toward the door, I stop. A flutter kicks up in my stomach. I look over my shoulder to see Harper grinning. "Why are you smiling?"

She plays dumb.

"Harper . . . ," I warn.

"Go. Shoo. Tell Meredith I said hi."

I furrow my brow and turn to the door again.

"Tell Penn hi, too, if you happen to see him," she calls out.

I turn around, launch the spoon at her, much to her delight, and then leave.

CHAPTER ELEVEN

Penn

"I'm pulling up right now." I steer my truck into the parking lot of the old library. "You owe me for this, you know."

"I know," Dane says on the other end of the phone. "I really do. Here, Mia wants to say something to you."

The phone gets scratchy as he passes it to his daughter. I pop the truck into park and rest back against the seat.

The brick building that once housed the Dogwood Lane Library sits in front of me. There are a couple of cars in the mostly vacant parking lot, and the front door is propped open with an overturned bucket.

"Penn," Mia singsongs. The static makes me think we're on speakerphone. "You are my hero."

I grin. "How are ya, Mia?"

"Good. On our way to Florida. Have you ever been there?"

"Once the year after I graduated high school. It was a good time—"

"That's enough," Dane shouts. "Move this conversation along."

Chuckling, I rest my hand on the top of the steering wheel. "You're gonna love it, Mia."

"I'm so excited. Dad said we almost weren't able to go, but you did a job so we could. So thanks, Penn. You are the best."

"Of course. I couldn't let my buddy get her vacation canceled, could I?"

"No," she says with a giggle. "Neely wants to say hi."

"Hi, Penn," Dane's fiancée calls out.

"What's up?"

"Can you go make sure we closed the garage door? Dane swears he did, but I think it's open," she says.

Dane sighs. "It's closed."

As they debate the status of the garage door, I spy Meredith pulling up. She gets out of her cream-colored Range Rover with a white dog tucked under her arm. By the skirt she's wearing, she's not planning on doing any manual labor today.

She pauses on the doorstep and looks over at me, then sends a small wave my way. I wave back and contemplate throwing the truck in reverse and getting the hell out of Dodge.

It's Mia's voice that stops me.

"We're stopping to pee. Talk to you later, Penn," she says. "Thank you again. You are my favoritest person in the world."

"You're welcome. See ya, Mia."

The phone snaps off speakerphone.

"You'll check the door?" Dane asks. "Humor my girl, will ya?"

"I expect a raise for all this, just so you know," I joke. "And your brother better be here today, or I'm going after his pansy ass."

Dane laughs. A dinging sound rings through the phone before a series of car doors slam shut.

"I talked to him a bit ago. Not sure if Matt's coming or not, but I brought it up. That's all I can do," he says.

"I'm just saying—if the roles were reversed and I was quote-unquote 'injured' like Matt, you'd have my balls if I didn't show up."

"It's because I can count on you," Dane says.

I laugh as I flip off my engine and then climb out of my truck. "I don't know if I'm more insulted that you're lying or that you're pandering to me."

"I am pandering to you a little bit, but you aren't *completely* unreliable. You did show up this morning."

The early-morning air that I thought I'd be spending with a fishing pole winds through the parking lot. The sun is bright but not hot, the air warm but not humid. It's a perfect day . . . and I'm spending it here. With Meredith.

Fuck my life.

A truck revs up and coasts in beside mine. Matt gives me the biggest, fakest smile ever before he hops out.

"Dane, I gotta go," I say.

"Is that Matt?" he asks.

"Yup."

He sighs. "Good. I feel better, then."

"You just said I was reliable," I point out. "Make up your mind."

Dane laughs as Mia shouts something in the background. "Okay, I'm going. Don't forget to check the garage door, please. And thank you. All jokes aside, I appreciate this, Penn."

"Yeah, yeah, yeah. Goodbye."

I end the call and shove the phone in my pocket as Matt comes around the front of his truck.

"You feeling better this morning, princess?" I tease.

He scoffs. "That's a better question for you. Did you wake up and wonder if you were living in some kind of twilight zone when you realized you actually got shut down last night?" He grins happily. "That might be in my top ten best nights of all time."

I don't fire a comeback his way. Instead, I kick at my front tire and let my mind float back to Avery.

When I went to bed last night, I figured I'd wake up and feel different about her. Not as . . . interested. Less curious. *Something.* I certainly didn't think I'd find myself wanting to see her again.

I'm Penn Etling, for fuck's sake.

But here I am, Penn Etling. Trying to scramble to see Avery again without looking desperate.

"Anything remarkable happen after I left?" he asks.

"Nah."

"Did you at least get her number?"

I consider telling him I did.

"You didn't, did you?" Matt's face fills with humor. "She held out. Good for her."

"She wants me," I say.

"Eh, I think maybe she doesn't, actually."

"Yes. She does. I can tell. She's just fucking with me, that's all. Making me work for it."

Making me woo her.

I take off my hat and scratch the top of my head. I did woo her. I'm sure of it. But maybe I need to woo her harder—and not the way that sounds when I say it in my head. Sadly.

I sigh and look at Matt. "How do you . . . How do I say it? How do you . . ."

I pace a circle. Slamming my hat back on my head, I try to think of a word other than *woo*. I'd never live that down.

"I want to win her over," I say. "And she wants to be won over. I just have to, I don't know, show her I want to win her over, I guess. Does that make any sense?"

Matt stands in front of me with a smile on his face.

"What?" I ask.

"You actually like her."

I flinch for both our benefits.

He says the words "like her" as if I'm trying to date her. The concept in itself makes me ill. My face screws up like I've sucked on a lemon, and that only amuses Matt more.

"I don't *like her*. Not like how you said it," I say, slightly offended.

"How'd I say it?"

"Like I *like her* like her. Like I *have lost my balls* like her. Like I *want to attach myself to her* like her." I shake my head. "It's not like that."

"What's it like, then?"

"I don't know . . ." I take my hat off again. My fingers slip through my hair as I try to figure out what I'm thinking. "She's a challenge, I guess. She asked me to give it my best shot last night. To give her my best pickup line."

Matt leans on his truck with one ankle crossed over the other. He looks too damn comfortable for this conversation.

"I'm intrigued," he says.

"Why?"

"I'm dying to know how you responded to that."

"Probably like anyone else would've," I say. "I mean, what do you do when someone says that and they have their clothes on?"

Matt bursts out in laughter. His delight in my frustration doesn't help. It only makes me more irritated.

"Matt, seriously. Shut up or help me here."

He shoves off the truck, a shine in his eyes. "Is *the* Penn Etling asking for my help on how to win over a girl?"

"No," I protest. "That's not what I was saying."

"Sounds like it to me."

I put my hat back on. "I was just a little thrown off, okay? Put on the spot. Guys like me don't have pickup lines shoved in our back pockets. We don't need them."

"I think Avery proves that's not quite true," Matt says, patting my shoulder as he walks by. "But I like your confidence."

I walk beside him as he heads toward the front door. He watches me out of the corner of his eye, waiting to see where I direct this conversation. The truth is, I don't know where to take it.

Do I need help getting Avery to admit she wants me? No. I can manage that just fine. It just might take longer than I want it to. But would I feel a little better if Matt would just tell me this is all normal? Fuck yeah.

"It's okay to like someone, you know," Matt offers. "It doesn't make you weak or anything."

We stop a few feet short of the door. He turns his body to face mine.

"Yeah, I know," I say, blowing him off. "It's just fucking with me because she didn't give in. That's all."

Matt opens his mouth and then shuts it. He sticks a hand in his pocket as the wheels turn in his brain.

"Can I ask you something?" he asks.

"I guess."

"If you did like her, would you tell me?"

What the fuck?

"Why? Do you like her or something?" My blood begins to heat as the idea of seeing Matt and Avery together washes over me. When Matt laughs at my reaction, I narrow my eyes. "This isn't funny."

"No, I don't like her, caveman. Settle down. Damn."

"I'm not unsettled."

He smacks his lips together as his chest bounces with a quiet laugh. "One of these days, you're going to have to realize that you're a mortal just like the rest of us."

"Nah. That's a rumor."

He snorts. "Look, Penn. You're a giant pain in my ass. You waste more of my time than any other human being in the world. You've gotten me in more trouble than anyone I know. You make me do all the trim at work, and you still haven't paid me back for demolishing my bumper."

"Take it up with the deer that jumped out in front of me. Or with your brother, who just had to have treated posts on the jobsite when he got there the next morning."

"Or you could've taken them the evening before like you were supposed to."

I grin. "I had plans."

Matt sighs, shaking his head.

We stand around, feeling each other out. This isn't a conversation we have often. Or ever. Matt doesn't date a bunch, and when he does, he's not talking about it much with me. I'm never asking him for advice or needing to talk shit out. This is new ground for us. I don't think either of us particularly knows how to get where he wants to go.

"Look," he says after mulling it over for a while. "You've made a career out of not settling down. I get it. No problems with it." He makes a face. "I kind of admire it in a really weird, kind of sick way."

"Hey, thanks," I say, appreciating the compliment.

He laughs. "That wasn't meant to be taken the way you just took it. Anyway, you've managed to avoid getting to the root of your antirelationship strategy for a long time. Maybe now's a good time to think about it and fix it."

"And why would I do something like that?"

"So you can be happy."

"I'm happy. I've never not been happy. I'm the happiest motherfucker on the planet."

"But you could be happier."

I blink. "I just said I'm the happiest motherfucker on the planet. Did you not hear me?"

He looks at me like I'm certifiable, like there's a padded cell somewhere with a person in a white coat on standby.

He's wrong. I'm not crazy. I might joke around about it and have a few different excuses just so I don't have to talk about it honestly, but I know exactly why I don't want a relationship. It comes from the most logical, uncrazy part of my brain.

Matt takes a deep breath. "What if you managed to convince Avery to give you a shot? She's a nice girl, Penn. You two could have something together."

"The only thing I want with her are orgasms."

He looks at the sky like it's somehow going to change my mind.

"I'm just not that guy," I say. "Never have been. Never will. It's just not in my DNA."

"I think your DNA is what's to blame."

His head lowers and he faces me again. I know what he's thinking. I can see it in the way he holds his mouth—a firm, tight line.

Matt's never said it, but he thinks my lack of wanting to couple up with someone is because of my father. He thinks that because my dad made our household a living Hell, loving my mom and me one minute and then not really giving a flying fuck the next, I've shut myself off from allowing anyone that kind of closeness with me again.

Matt would be right.

I, however, will not admit it. Saying it out loud would make me feel like I need the white-coat guy.

It's not that Matt wouldn't understand it. Hell, he gets it without my admission. But in his "rose-colored glasses" view of the world, he'd try to rationalize the irrational. He would try to explain away my parents' behaviors and prove to me that there's more out there for me.

There's not. I'm okay with it. I'm not sure Matt would be, though. It might ruin his view of the world, and who am I to do that?

I wrap my arm around his neck and start walking toward the door. "For the record, if you were a girl, I'd totally date you."

He shoves me off him, toward the brick wall. "You're a prick, Etling."

I laugh as I follow him inside.

CHAPTER TWELVE

Penn

Meredith's perfume, the tapping of her heels, the yapping of her dog all make their way to us before she does.

"Hello, Penn. Hi, Matt," she says. "It's so good to see you guys again."

Meredith's tone is way too high for this time of day. Or any time of day. *Why does anyone ever need to be that chirpy?*

"Hey, Meredith," I say, trying not to wince.

The poodle in her arms has a yellow collar with rhinestones wrapped around it. I swear the dog assesses me and labels me unworthy to breathe the same air it does.

"How have you been?" Matt asks her.

She waves a hand through the air. The diamonds catch the light. She's a real-life version of one of those princesses in the movies Mia watches. If she busts out a tiara, I won't even blink.

"Oh, good. Busy. You know how it goes. We got the house decorated finally. My interior designer got behind schedule because her . . . Well, you guys probably don't care." She laughs. "I'm rambling. Just let me say that I'm really happy you could come out today and discuss my new project."

Matt takes the lead, as I knew he would, and relays part of a conversation he had with Dane. I check out mentally. I only want to know what I need to know, and what Dane said about the subcontractor insurance doesn't mean jack to me.

I don't plan on falling off any kiddie ladders, unlike some people.

Instead, I take in the large, mostly vacant room.

The bookshelves that used to line the walls are gone. Everything looks clean and ready to go.

Besides the main room, there are a couple of offices and two meeting rooms down the hall to the right that we used to use for banquets and parties when I was growing up. It's odd to see it so blank, but it should be fun, watching it transform into something new.

"I got the building permit this morning," Meredith says, her heels clicking against the concrete floor. "They expedited it for me. It's nice to have friends in high places."

"I bet it is," I say.

"My stepsons are supposed to come by this morning with the renovation plans. Jake drew them up for me based on a conversation we had last week, and Trevor created a budget." Her eyes sparkle. "But you know how I am with budgets."

"Yup. You pretty much ignore them," I deadpan. "I think we quadrupled the budget for your house in paint alone."

She points at me. "But I'll have you know it was worth every penny. Bashful was the perfect choice for the sitting room. My husband agrees. It's just so fun."

"We're glad you like it," Matt says, casting me a warning to stay quiet about the ridiculousness of the same two shades of pink. "So what are we doing in here?"

She sets the dog down. Its claws mimic the sound of her heels as it races around the room, yapping at dust bunnies in the corners. When she stands, she presses her manicured nails together in front of her like she's praying.

"This town has a lot of sports activities for kids, but there's nothing for children that just want to be kids. Not every kid is athletic or wants to be an athlete," she says.

"You mean you weren't a soccer star?" I joke.

She laughs. "No. And I know you're shocked." She brushes a strand of hair out of her face. "There's no community pool. The park is a wreck. And while I'm not a fan of arcades or pool halls or things of that nature, Dogwood Lane has none, anyway. So we're going to fix that." She walks to the far side of the room near the big, bright windows I hope she plans on keeping. "I know we have to do this in stages. Rome wasn't built in a day, after all. But I want to really create the foundation of something truly special for the youth here."

"Like a kids' club or something?" Matt asks.

"Exactly." She smiles wide. "The first phase will include framing up some of this giant room to be more intimate. Jake will have more information on that later today. He said he projects it will take about two weeks to get this part done. I'm not sure about the mural. That might take longer. Have I told you about the mural?"

"No," I say.

"Oh, let me tell you all about it," she almost squeals.

"Yay."

Matt shoves my shoulder as we follow Meredith to the back wall.

"I have big ideas for this space," she says. "I'm seeing something that screams quaint and community, something vibrant and fun. There's supposed to be an artist coming by today to take a look at this and tell me what she can do. I . . ." She slides her phone out of her pocket. "I know this is rude, but I do need to take this. Can you two hold on?"

"Sure," Matt says.

"It's her world," I mutter as she walks away. "We just live in it."

Matt chuckles. He moseys around the room, surveying the space, as Meredith click-clacks her way out the front door with her puppy in her arms.

I follow a few steps behind Matt, trying to get an idea of how much work this thing is going to take. From what I can tell, two weeks sounds like plenty of time as long as some artist doesn't come in and screw up our mojo.

I turn to tell Matt that I'm taking my time on this project just so it won't be done when Dane gets back. Before I can get the words out, the hair on the back of my neck stands up. I whip around to see an empty room behind me.

"What's wrong?" Matt asks.

"Nothing. I just felt like someone was standing there."

"Maybe it's a ghost. Are you going to be scared if you're in here all alone?"

"I . . ." My voice trails off as Avery walks in. She slips a pair of sunglasses off her face and lets her eyes fall on me. "I've never been scared of ghosts that look like that."

My heart skips a beat as I instinctively start toward her. Whether she knows it or not, she moves my direction too.

"Damn Harper," she says, fighting a grin.

"You've second-guessed the end to our night all morning, haven't you?" I ask. "Just had to come find me."

"What would make you say that?"

"Well, why else would you be here?"

She laughs, sticking her sunglasses in her purse. "I love how you think that every single thing revolves around you."

"I don't think *everything* revolves around me. But I also know a spade is a spade, if you catch my drift."

The yellow V-neck shirt she's wearing makes her skin glow. Her hair is in this half-up, half-down thing that draws attention to her face. And cleavage. Definitely to her cleavage.

"I'll have you know," she says, "that I didn't know you were here. Harper sent me over to see about a painting job." She looks around the room. "Hey, Matt."

He waves.

"Am I in the right spot?" Avery asks. "Harper said it was the old library, and I swear that's what the sign said outside."

"This is it."

Matt comes up beside me. "One question: How bad was Penn's pickup line last night?"

Avery readjusts her purse on her arm and looks at me with a cocked brow. "You told Matt you attempted a pickup line last night? Because if I remember correctly, you couldn't even think of one."

Matt cackles until I threaten to jab him in the spleen.

"I was more than a little disappointed," she says.

"I couldn't think of one, *Ave*, because guys like me don't need them." I cross my arms over my chest. "I do love that you were disappointed. That means you wanted an excuse to cave."

I'm confident with this explanation. It's self-evident. She knows it's true. Still, she doesn't back down.

"First of all, I don't need an excuse to cave. If I want to cave, I'll cave."

"Feel free," I say with a grin.

"I'm good. Thanks." She lifts a brow. "Second, if you don't need pickup lines, what do you use?"

"For what?"

She rolls her eyes. "To win over women."

"Easy." I grin. "My charm."

She doesn't look impressed.

"And my abs."

"Oh, please," Matt says.

"Fine." I ensure my features are as smooth as silk as I bore my eyes into Avery's. "My cock."

Matt howls with laughter, but Avery doesn't. A grin tickles her lips as her cheeks turn a shade of pink I'd call Bashful.

My body lights up at her reaction. I can feel her blush in my veins, the heat of it blazing from my head to my toes.

Damn this girl.

"Good thing I'm unimpressed with charm and abs then," she says.

"But you still like cock, huh?" I crack. "Good to know."

She moves as if her body can't bear to stand in place. It's as if she has as much energy coursing through her as I do.

My chest rises and falls at a quickened pace as I hold my breath and wonder if she's going to do what I think she is: talk about cock. If she does, heaven help me, I may lose it right here.

"I do like cock," she says, watching me closely. "I'm just tired of mediocre cock."

I'm dead.

My hands ball into fists at my side as I restrain myself from reacting to the influx of testosterone flooding me—from the idea of her and my cock and . . . *I can't.*

I press a hard swallow down my throat. "May I remind you that I'm a solid eight inches?"

"May I remind you that it doesn't impress me?"

If this were anyone else, I'd toss her a smart-ass line and walk away because I'd know she'd chase after me. But Avery? She might not. I'm fairly sure she wouldn't, actually. Worst of all is that I'd want her to.

I narrow my eyes. "Fair enough. What impresses you, then?"

Matt stays quiet. There's undoubtedly a remark on the tip of his tongue. I can tell by the way he shifts his weight. I'm usually out the door if a woman gives me this much trouble, and I know Matt is eating it up that I'm still standing here and sparring with her. I'm just glad he keeps his mouth shut this time.

Avery considers my question. She nibbles on the end of her nail as the wheels turn in her pretty little head. Finally, after what feels like an eternity, she drops her hand.

"Sustainability," she says. "That's what's impressive."

"How very green of you," I say.

She sighs. "I mean it in terms of a relationship. It's easy to have nice abs or to tell a woman what they want to hear. It's harder to want to create a connection with someone that's mutually beneficial. To build something sustainable. *That* desire? It would impress me."

Gross.

"Well, you haven't seen my abs or cock, so I have faith either would work," I say.

Matt snorts. Avery's lips part to reply when she's silenced by the walking hurricane that is Meredith Kelly.

"Okay, guys," Meredith calls out as she prances into the room. "Let's go ahead and get this ball rolling. I'm trying to figure out how we can incorporate a pet rescue into this whole dynamic because wouldn't that be amazing? Children helping displaced animals feel loved, and animals helping children cope with the trials of life in this day and age? Apparently, that's a bit of a permit and insurance issue."

I turn to Matt. "It's gonna take a lot of vodka for me to cope with this circus."

Meredith stops and places her dog on the floor. She runs a hand down its back before it skedaddles across the room, yelping at a moth.

"Where was I?" She pauses when she sees Avery. "I'm sorry. I didn't see you come in."

"I'm Avery Perry. Harper sent me over about a painting job."

"Yes," Meredith almost squeals. "I have so many ideas that I can't wait to get your opinion on."

Avery pulls out her phone and taps on the screen. "I have some examples of my work, if you'd like to see."

"Oh, I trust Harper's judgment."

"Well, that's great and all, but Harper has only seen me cut hair. She's never seen my painting projects."

Meredith squints as she considers this. Matt and I look at one another. I wonder if I should say something and vouch for Avery just to keep her around when Meredith smacks her lips together.

"I just have a good feeling about you," she says. "I'm not usually wrong about people. So if you want the job, you're hired."

"Just like that?" Avery asks. She gives me a bewildered look before turning back to Meredith. "I mean, absolutely, and thank you, but I won't be offended if you want to get some references or something."

Meredith gazes around the room with a dreamy look in her eye. Her dress flutters in the breeze coming in through the open front door. The perfume she used to spray on our work orders floats on the air, and I wonder if I should give Avery some kind of warning about what she's getting into here. Then I think better of it.

If I warn her, she might take off. If I don't, she'll be stuck here with me.

Easiest decision I've ever made.

"I like to surround myself with good people," Meredith says finally. "That's more important to me than anything. When I get a vision, it becomes a part of my heart, and I want people I love and enjoy helping me bring my dreams into reality." She smiles at Avery. "I like you. You have a yellow aura."

"She has a what?" I ask.

"An aura," Meredith says with a laugh. "She has a yellow energy that surrounds her."

"And that means . . ."

"It means she's creative and inspired and intelligent." Meredith glances at Matt. "You're very blue. Very cool, calm, and collected."

"That's me. Mr. Reliable," Matt says.

Avery clears her throat. We all look at her as she smoothens her features. "So," she begins. "What's Penn's aura?"

"Orange." The answer is out of Meredith's mouth quickly, as if she's already considered the question.

"And that means . . ." Avery raises a brow.

Meredith grins. "I'll just say this: it's associated with one's reproductive organs."

"Really?" Matt responds immediately. "Did he pay you to say that?" He looks at me. "You did, didn't you?"

"I did no such thing," I say, quite pleased with this bit of information. "I can't help it that my aura shows my prowess."

Meredith laughs. "Just be careful. People with orange auras have a hard time holding on to them." She fires a grin my way before pulling out her phone again. "Trevor is out front. Would one of you come with me and talk construction with him so I don't relay things incorrectly?"

Matt side-eyes me. "I'll go. I don't want to be punched."

"Perfect. If you two could take a look around and see if you get inspired by anything, I'd love that." Meredith smiles wide. "This is going to be great. I know it."

"Yeah, great," Matt mumbles as he follows her to the door. "Gonna be splendid."

Once they're out of earshot, I turn to Avery. She's toying with the hem of her shirt.

"Guess that leaves us all alone," I say. "You and my orange aura."

"Lord help me." She shakes her head, and then her ass as she walks away.

I watch her study the mural wall as if she already envisions something there. She bites her bottom lip as she takes it all in from different angles. I want to ask her what she sees or what she's thinking, but I don't.

"Inspired already?" I ask.

"Actually, yes. I am."

"It's my aura, huh?"

She looks at me over her shoulder and rolls her eyes. "Yeah. Definitely your aura. How did you ever guess?"

The sarcasm is thick and plentiful, but the look on her face makes it so worth it. The light comes in the window and highlights her cheekbones and the copper highlights in her hair. I'll take her mockery if it gives me a view like this.

She turns back to the wall. I imagine a paintbrush in her hand and find myself curious about a lot of things. How talented is she? What else does she like to do? What is she good at?

Is she the ultimate package? I don't know. But I'd sure as fuck like to give her mine.

CHAPTER THIRTEEN

Avery

I don't turn around to see if Penn follows me. Even if I couldn't hear his footsteps against the floor or smell his cologne teasing me as he pursues me from behind, I'd still feel the overwhelming sensation of having him this close.

I'm an adult, and I have control over what I say and think and do. Acknowledging I have a problem, a super slight, possible crush, is the first step to recovery.

I look over my shoulder.

Lord have mercy.

He's leaning against the wall, a dimple nestled in his cheek. The glimmer in his eyes tells me that he knows exactly what I'm thinking, what I'm struggling with over here, and he's ready to counterattack.

"If this wall were bright, it'd really lighten up this whole space." I press my hand against a crack in the drywall. "I think we need a repair here first, though."

"I can do that."

I wait for the sexual innuendo, for the comment that has nothing to do with construction at all. Nothing comes.

"What's back here?" I ask.

Walking away from Penn, I continue through the building. A hallway extends off the main room. There's a bathroom and a meeting room across from a small office. At the end of the hallway is a closed door. I pop it open and peek inside.

Oversize bay windows are centered on a long wall. The area is bright and spacious with only a table that's been shoved into a corner.

"I love this," I say as I take in the antique molding around the ceiling. "What kind of thing is Meredith doing here?"

"Something about kids and animals." His voice envelops me, wrapping around me like a warm sweater. "That's all I got."

"Kids and animals, huh? That's super specific."

I turn around to see him watching me.

He grins. "Kids and animals aren't my specialty. I tuned out when I heard that."

"Funny. I had you pegged to be someone that would love kids and animals."

He shrugs. "I probably like animals better than kids, but I'm not really a fan of either."

"No pets, then?"

"I had a goldfish once," he says. "I won him at Dogwood Day. His name was Floater, and he committed the fish version of hara-kiri by diving onto the floor of the kitchen. I figured that was some kind of sign. What about you?"

"None at the moment." I hop onto the table by the wall. "Maybe someday."

"I'm good with not having any. I'd probably forget to feed them."

My feet swing back and forth. I wonder if he's truly irresponsible, or if he just plays that card. Most guys I know, especially ones in his league of looks, are content with someone doing everything for them. Yet Penn seems like he might be different. That, or my hormones are trying to convince me otherwise. It's happened before.

Penn walks around the room and surveys the space. "I was in this club when I was a little kid. We had these hats and vests and shit. We'd go into the woods and learn how to start a fire and survive if, for some reason, we were left alone in the forest."

"Was that a concern of yours growing up?" I ask with a laugh.

"Nah, my ma loved me. Most of the time, anyway."

"Is she around?"

"No." A frown drifts across his face. "She died a couple of years ago."

He turns away. His shoulders slump a tiny bit, and I wonder what happened.

My heart sinks as he rolls his shoulder around like he's trying to free himself from the memory. I wish I knew what to say. I want to hug him, to wrap my arms around his waist and pull him against me. But I don't. I don't know him well enough to do either of those things.

The thought makes me sad.

"I'm sorry, Penn."

"Yeah. Me too." He looks at the floor for a brief second. When he turns around, he tries to smile. "She was a cool lady. I mean, she had to be to be my mom, right?"

"Absolutely."

We exchange a grin that feels more intimate than anything we've ever shared. Not that we've shared much, but something passes between us in that moment that hasn't before.

He meanders through the room. Occasionally he stops and inspects a piece of trim or knocks on a wall. Mostly, though, he's quiet. As the seconds pass, I watch the somberness of the conversation before it evaporates into thin air. In its place is the cool confidence I've come to expect from him.

Even when he's quiet, he oozes it. Every movement he makes is filled with a self-assuredness that's magnetic. And despite the delicious outside package, *that's* the biggest turn-on. *That* is my Achilles' heel in a nutshell: the man who can handle anything.

And Penn definitely looks like he can handle *anything*.

As I think of him handling me, I shiver.

He stretches his muscled arms over his head. The white T-shirt pulled across his body has me wondering what he looks like without it. The hem lifts just enough to give me a glimpse of his tanned stomach, and I have to look away or else run the risk of losing all control.

"Anyway," he says through a yawn, "the last time I was in this room was to get a badge for first aid."

He gazes at me as I lower my chin. Looking at him through my lashes, I laugh.

"Is there a joke coming about mouth-to-mouth?" I ask.

He grins, dropping his arms to his sides. "No. But I love that your mind went there."

"It's just what I've come to expect from you."

"I do know CPR. Want me to demonstrate?"

Yes. "No," I say with all the confidence I can muster. "I don't. That's not what I was saying."

He pretends to study me. He works his bottom lip between his teeth as he narrows his eyes and scans me from head to toe. Finally, his lip pops free.

"Nah, I think it was," he insists.

"No, it wasn't."

He lays his head to the side as he takes me in. "You know what I really think?"

"Bet you're going to tell me."

A slow smile spreads across his face. There's something carnal, almost lascivious about it. My feet stop swinging.

My palms are slick, threatening to slide off the edge of the table as I deal with being in his sights. His gaze is heavy, invested, even, and it's the most delicious discomfort, having his attention on me. Because it's all right here, squarely on my shoulders. There's no doubt he's thinking only about me.

Holy shit.

He takes a step toward me. "I think you *want* me to make a joke about mouth-to-mouth."

"I do not."

The air fills with his scent, the temperature rising out of nowhere. The back of my neck prickles with excitement as he takes another step toward me.

"I think you do, Ave. And I think I did woo you last night, even though you're denying it."

My mouth goes dry as he gets closer. "You didn't woo me. Not even close."

My heart skips a beat. Then two. The grin on his face tells me he's unfazed by my refusal to admit my attraction. The fire in my belly tells me I'm unfazed by it too.

I'm lying. We both know it. And if he doesn't keep his distance, I don't know how long I can keep it up.

"Fine," he says. "I didn't. But you wanted me to." He stands just inches away from me, armed with a killer smile. "Come to think of it, I think you wanted me to do a lot more than that."

My lips part. My brain shoots a laundry list of things to fire his way. It's a list brimming with words like "no" and "ha" and "you wish." Instead, I find myself wishing he'd reach out and touch me.

What would it hurt? My legs spread apart as he comes even closer. Any logic I might've had is marred by the anticipation of feeling his hands on my body.

He grins a devilish smile, his eyes hooded as he watches me from above. He plants his large hands on either side of me.

Memories of the night we shared, details I thought I'd forgotten, come buzzing back. The feeling of his weight on me. The softness of his lips against the side of my neck. The roughness of his voice as he growled my name.

"Are you tired of pretending you don't want me?" he asks.

"No."

"Come on, Avery."

It's less of a plea and more of a taunt—a lure from a man who knows exactly what he does to me.

Because he does it to everyone. And I don't want to be another notch, even for Penn.

I force a swallow. "I don't want you, Penn."

"Fine," he says. His eyes bore into me. "How about this, then? I'll call my favor due."

"First of all, you didn't win."

"Bullshit."

I swallow again. "You didn't. And if we're going to work around each other here, we're going to have to stop this."

"Stop what?"

"Stop . . . this, whatever it is." I shift, careful not to bump his arms, which are caging me in. "You thinking I want you."

He rocks back, his fingertips sliding to the edge of the table. His eyes are the color of the sky on a clear summer day.

My fingers itch to touch the stubble dotting his jawline. My lips swell at the thought of touching his. A part of me wishes he'd just kiss me and get it over with.

Maybe if I just kiss him, he'll stop this, and I can go on about my life.

He leans in again, and I think I pant.

What's one kiss, anyway?

My head spins as the air between us heats. He fixes his eyes on mine with a seriousness that tightens the knot in my stomach.

"Double or nothing," he says.

"I don't know what you mean."

He looks at me like I'm the only thing in the world, like he wants to completely devour me right here. A grin so seductive, a smile that's so full of everything I'd like him to do to me, jets my way.

While I can't let him do all those things, I could let him kiss me. And if I did that, maybe it would put out some of the fire between us.

One kiss. I can totally handle one kiss.

It would be a means to an end. The only way I can figure to stop this nonsense.

"If your panties aren't soaked right now, you win. I'll leave you alone."

Fuck it.

I grab his face in my hands, startling him for a moment. The roughness of his cheeks prickles my fingertips.

His eyes go wide as I stare straight into them and lower his lips to mine. Just before they touch, he gasps the slightest breath.

White noise pours through my ears, muting everything except my thundering heart.

He moves until his body is against the table and his powerful thighs are situated in between my own. Otherwise, there's no movement from him as he lets me take control of the contact.

I reach up and gently press my lips to his. My eyes flutter closed as the warmth of Penn spills into me. I fully intend on pulling back but am caught in an intoxicating state of wanting more.

Craving more.

Needing more.

His lips part, and I take advantage. As I slide my tongue into his mouth, the heat of his body filters into mine. His erection presses into the inside of my leg, and I whimper.

My hands go to his hair. The silky strands run through my fingers as his hands find my ass. He yanks me forward so that I'm against his body.

He's a wall built of muscle and desire. My back arches, my chest pressing into his; his tongue wraps around mine and makes it hard to tell where he starts and I stop.

His fingers find the hem of my shirt and dip beneath it. The small of my back is electrified by his touch.

I breathe him in. I taste the sweetness of his lips. I feel the steadiness of the man who wants me as bad as I want him.

A low growl erupts from the base of his throat. And that does it. I'm jostled by my reality and the precipice on which I stand. I can keep going, keep kissing him, and get so much more. Or I can stop and not ruin the next six months of my life.

I press a final kiss to his mouth, committing the taste of peppermint gum to my memory, and pull away.

Our breathing is ragged as he searches my face. He rests his hands on my thighs as he steps back, giving me space to get myself sorted.

"Avery . . ." He chuckles as he licks his lips.

I could reach up and pull him back to me, knot his shirt in my fist, and spend the rest of the day doing all the dirty things I can imagine doing with him. But as I start to wonder how different this time will be from last, I'm reminded of the fact that he doesn't even know this will be round two.

I press against his chest before hopping off the table. My heart still clamoring, I adjust my shirt.

"Glad we got that over with," I say.

"I . . . What?" He looks at me like I'm crazy. "Got what over with?"

"You won. Happy now?"

"Oh, that makes me happy, all right. But that's . . . you know . . . not what I wanted." He looks at the ground, his Adam's apple bobbing as he swallows.

I hold my breath, hoping stupidly that he'll say something more—something that will prove me wrong. That he's not the cad, the player, the guy who will lose interest in two weeks flat.

Instead, he just shrugs. When he looks back up, it's with a resolution that makes my heart sink.

"You're probably right," he says. "Better stop there."

I clear my throat. "Exactly."

"Penn? Avery? Where did you go?" Meredith's voice rings down the hallway.

I give Penn a final chance to say something, anything, but he doesn't. He runs a hand through his hair and heads to the doorway.

"We're coming," I shout.

As I follow him out, I touch my lips. They sting from being pressed against his. My mouth tastes of peppermint and heat, and I find myself wishing I could rewind time. But I'm unsure if I'd kiss him again or avoid the situation altogether.

He looks at me over his shoulder. His features are blank, completely void of any indication as to what he's feeling. My stomach twists into a tight knot as I realize he's probably not feeling anything. That kiss that just rocked my socks probably just checked a box and turned his attention elsewhere. All I managed to do with that little slipup is make things awkward with one of my three friends here.

It takes everything I have to ignore the pounding of my heart. I lift my chin, refusing to feel defeated.

It's all right. I'm not here for Penn. I'm here for me.

Yet as we turn into the main room and Matt shouts something our way, the levity between the three of us is gone. Penn flips him the middle finger. Matt looks at me with confusion written all over his face.

"I need to talk to Meredith," I say. I give Matt the realest smile I can manage. "If you'll excuse me . . ."

Before I walk out, I pause and hope Penn will say something. He just looks at the floor.

"Suit yourself," I mutter and head for the door.

CHAPTER FOURTEEN

PENN

"*Better stop there.*"

The final words I said to Avery after she kissed me ring through my mind.

I cast my fishing line back into the water. The lure hits the top of the lake with a plop before I tighten the line and begin to reel it in slowly. Each smooth spin of the rod and reel helps me focus.

"Happy now?"

My jaw tightens as I squat near the water's edge. Am I happy now? Is she freaking kidding me?

For the first time in my life, I have no clue what to do.

She kissed *me*. In the sexiest, most in-charge move I've ever seen a woman make, she kissed me. And it wasn't because she thought I wanted it or to prove some kind of point, like she wanted me to fuck her . . . No. She kissed me because she wanted to.

Eyes don't lie. You can always tell what someone is feeling when you look into their eyes. She stared into mine as she held my face in her hands and touched our lips together.

So why did she act like it was a one-and-done?

"Glad we got that over with."

I jerk the line out of the water and cast it again. It goes out farther this time, sailing across Dogwood Lake. The early-evening sun shoots its final rays across the sky. The blue is met with purples and pinks and bright oranges. It looks like a painting.

I wonder if Avery can paint things like that.

The thought makes me smile.

I wonder what else she can do. And when I realize I'm thinking beyond sexual arenas, I laugh out loud.

"What the hell is wrong with me?" I wonder aloud.

Who am I to get all screwed up just from kissing someone? What even is this bullshit?

I rub my temples, trying to bring some clarity to my mind. All it does is bring her question—*"Happy now?"*—back to the forefront.

"No, Avery. I'm not happy now."

I'm actually less happy than I usually am, and I'm a happy guy. Shit doesn't bother me. My father can hate me. Dane can ride my ass. A woman can think I'm a jerk for not seeing her exclusively, and I don't really care. It's life. It's not roses. But the way Avery looked at me today, like I somehow made her sad, bothers me. The fact that I'm bothered bothers me.

"I'm a bothered man."

I swear a flock of birds laughs at me from the treetops. Hell, I have half a notion to laugh at my damn self.

If only I could figure out why this whole thing is under my skin. Is it because she's rejecting me, even when I know she doesn't mean it? Because she can't possibly mean it. She's not dumb. Or blind. Or a lesbian.

No, it can't be that. So what is it?

I throw the line in the water once again. A breeze rolls off the lake and whispers across my face. Inhaling a lungful of crisp air, I close my eyes and try to relax.

"I'm *not* fucking bothered," I say to myself. "I'll figure this out."

I think. I'm kind of out of my wheelhouse here.

Standing tall, stretching my legs out as I reel in my line, I listen to the crickets. This spot on the lake is always empty. My grandfather showed it to me when I was thirteen, months before he died.

"This is my honey hole," he said as he led me on the trail to the water.

"But you're never supposed to share your honey holes. Especially with me," I said, looking up at him and grinning. *"I'll catch all the fish, and it won't be your honey hole anymore."*

Grandpa laughed. *"Fish isn't all this honey hole is about, Penn. This is where I get all my good thinking done."*

"Um, I'm just here for the fish."

"That's all right," he said. We stood under the giant oak that hangs over the lake. Grandpa put his hand on my shoulder as he gazed across the water. *"But one of these days, I won't be around. And you'll want to think about things. Life gets harder as you get older, boy."*

I thought about my life then. My hand went up to my eye and patted at the residual swelling from my dad's fist.

"You'll be okay. You're strong," he said. *"But you'll need this spot. Trust me."*

"But what if I can't get here? Then what?"

He grinned. *"Then you think about me, and I'll help you."*

I kick a rock into the water and smile. He was right, as he always was. I've found myself drawn to this spot hundreds of times over my life already. It's so quiet, so peaceful. And only once has anyone else ever shown up here. It's like no one knows this exists.

As I glance under the oak tree, my mind drifts back to a night filled with cheesy chips and ant bites. I chuckle.

"Kinda did more than just thinking that night, Grandpa. But she was fun. Different. *Memorable.*"

I've thought about that raven-haired enigma several times over the years, always with a smile on my face. *"Gotta roll with it,"* she said that night after we commiserated about our lives. I've rolled with it ever since.

"I'm going to have to figure this one out," I say, tearing my eyes off the tree. "I'll be seeing her at Meredith's, and I don't want it to be weird. I have to fix this fuckup."

I don't want things to be awkward. I don't want to lose the way things are—*were*—over a stupid kiss. Even if she's not lying somehow and doesn't want anything else from me, I don't want to lose the fun energy between us. I like her laugh and her stories and the way she's so easy to be around. There's no point in ruining that over a sexy-as-fuck kiss.

It's a kiss, after all. I'll have many more over my lifetime with many other women. No sense in getting fucked up about this one. Besides, she doesn't have anyone here, and Matt and Claire really like her. I would be a complete dick if she stayed away from our group because of a stupid kiss.

Damn it.

Yanking my line out of the water, I get it reeled in. It slides easily into the bed of my truck. I grab my phone out of the cup holder and fish through my contacts and ignore the texts from Alexis. I wasn't all that into her to start with. Now? She doesn't feel interesting at all. I scroll until I find Harper's name.

My thumb hits the "Call" button before I can think too much about it.

"Well, look who it is," she says. "What are you up to? And if you need bail money, call someone else. I'm broke."

"You're two people down the call list for bail. No need to worry for a while," I joke.

"Good to know. So what's up?"

Suddenly, I'm not sure what to say. My mouth goes dry as different words attempt to make their way past my lips.

"Penn?" Harper laughs. "You okay?"

"Oh, yeah," I say, forcing a swallow. "I just, um, wanted to check on Avery. She doing okay?"

"Yeah. Why?"

"No reason. She, um, just came by the library today, and you know how Meredith can be."

The laugh that topples out of my mouth is so fake that there's no covering it. I cringe.

"Well, I tell you what," Harper says. "I haven't seen Avery this evening. She popped into the salon after she met with you all, and we had lunch from the café. Then she went home, and I had a date, which I'm still on, by the way. So that shows you where you rank in my life."

"I'm sorry, Harp."

"Nah, don't be. He conveniently didn't have condoms, which he wasn't all that upset about. Surprise, surprise."

"Ditch him. He sounds like a total asshole."

"I probably will," she says. "He went to get them now, but I'm getting less and less inclined to wait around here. Anyway, what do you want? For real?"

I kick at a rock, look at the sky, and listen to the crickets again. None of them give me the words I need to explain what I want.

"Well . . ." I take a breath. "I want to sort of do something nice for Avery. Like, not buy her flowers or some lame thing like that. It's not like that, anyway," I say hurriedly. "I just think since we're going to be working together that maybe I need to, you know, make some kind of gesture so she knows it's cool between us."

"Why wouldn't it be?" She gasps. "Did you sleep with her already?"

"No. No, no, no. I mean, I wish, but no. I just . . . help me."

It's funny how you can know someone is smiling on the other end of a phone. There's no sound, really, and you sure as heck can't see them. But sometimes, you just know. And I know Harper is grinning like a loon.

"Harp . . ."

"Penn, I am proud of you."

"For what?"

"For being so sweet."

My eyes bug out. "I'm not sweet."

"Yes, you are. And I know it's hard for you."

"I'm not sweet," I say again. "And I think you're making too big a deal out of this. I just want her to feel comfortable, you know? She's a nice person. And I don't really know what I'm supposed to do right now."

Harper's voice softens. "You're doing it."

"Rambling like a moron?"

"Yes." She laughs. "Think about what's happening right now. You're going out of your way to make a woman happy, and it has nothing to do with you. You aren't asking me for tips to get someone to date you or, God forbid, advice on lube."

"I only did that once," I say quickly. "And it was halfway a joke."

She doesn't care. She just laughs. "I like this side of you, Penn."

"Yeah, well, this side of me feels like a pussy."

I walk in a circle as Harper tells me to get a grip. That being thoughtful, which is what she's classified me as being right now, isn't weak. Or lame. She lies and lies to me because I know the truth. The problem is, I don't really care about the truth. It's secondary right now. First up is making sure all is right between Avery and me.

"I'll tell you what," she says. "Let me call Avery and see where she is. If she's not busy, maybe you could swing by and say hello."

"I don't have to take flowers, right?"

"No."

"Okay. Good. What about chocolate or something?"

Harper laughs again. "Are you taking her on a date?"

"No," I hiss, making a face.

I don't know what to say. I don't even know what I'm thinking. I just don't want that kiss, the one I'll think about all damn night and again every time I look at her, to screw things up between us.

And, truthfully, I want more than one kiss too.

Fuck.

No, I don't.

Do I?

"It's okay," Harper says. "I think I get what you're saying. Let me call her. I'll send you a text and let you know where she's at and if it's a go." She pauses, as if considering whether she should say more. "And Penn?"

"Yeah?"

"Relax."

"Yeah."

She sighs. "I'll text you in a few."

"Okay," I say, my throat burning.

I end the call. Walking back to the water's edge, I watch the colors in the sky. They drift together easily, melting into each other in a smooth dance.

I've watched this same view many evenings over my life. It never fails to occur to me that I'm not one of those colors. I can't flow into someone else like that. Not like Dane does Neely or Haley has done with Trevor. I'm like the clouds above them, alone in my race across the sky.

Why is that? I'm glad my friends can. I see how happy it makes them. Maybe a part of me, buried down deep and one I'd never admit to, wishes I could too.

But I can't. I'm just not built that way. No one expects me to be any different. Just like Harper, everyone loves me like I am. And that's good enough.

Isn't it?

My phone buzzes in my hand. I look down at a text from Harper.

She's at my house. Go on over. She has no plans.

My heart begins to thump a rock-and-roll-style beat. I slip my phone back into my pocket.

With a final glance at the sky, I climb back into my truck and hope I don't do more damage than I might've already done.

CHAPTER FIFTEEN

Avery

"Crap."

I grab a towel and toss it over the skillet handle. Moving the sizzling pan off the heat, I look at the eggs I carefully broke a few minutes ago. They're a giant mess.

As I'm watching, the grease around them pops, and a bullet of red-hot liquid smashes into my forearm.

"Ouch!"

I shove my arm under the sink faucet, wincing as I flip on the coldest water it can manage. My head hangs as I wait for the burn to dissipate.

My arm burns, but that's not my biggest problem. What's worse is the heaviness in my body. It's like I ran a mile and someone forgot to tell me. But even if that kind of thing were possible and I were the kind of girl who could run a mile and not die, I'd know that wasn't the cause of this drag.

It's because I kissed a blue-eyed devil.

"Why did I do that?" I lament as the burn begins to ease. "I'm stupid, stupid, stupid."

My head dips deeper. The hiss of the water soothes me somehow and lifts me gently out of my funk. Those words echo through my mind, and I'm reminded of what Harper said about mental dialogue.

"No," I say out loud. "I'm not stupid. That's not fair. I'm not even careless," I add. "I made a choice to kiss Penn Etling, even if it wasn't the most spectacular decision I've ever made."

But his lips were pretty spectacular.

My shoulders stiffen as my brain and body go back to war. It's hard to deny the way my stomach clenches when I think of his hands on the small of my back and the warmth of his breath against my skin. Even if I can't deny it, I can argue it when I realize I'm standing at the kitchen sink hours later, still thinking about it while he's probably making another girl feel the same thing.

His kiss was spectacular, being he has plenty of practice, Avery.

But it's more than the kiss that has me a mess. It's more than the feel of his body against mine. It's the genuine interest in my answers to his questions and the patience he has while he waits for them. It's the feeling in my stomach when he looks at me. It's the way he invited me to sit with him and Matt at Mucker's and the inclusion I felt with him and Matt and Claire.

It's all that. And I'm afraid it's gone.

I pull my arm out of the water. It burns instantly.

"Shit."

Back in it goes as I inspect it for visible damage. Just as I start to get a good look, something raps the kitchen door. I peek around the corner to see a shadow of a person through the white curtain.

"I'm coming." I push the lever to off and try to find a towel to dry my arm. "Who is it?"

"It's me."

Stopping in the middle of the kitchen, arm dripping with water, I look at the door at Penn's shadow. My head swirls with confusion. *Why is he here? Is he looking for Harper?*

"Harper isn't here," I call out.

"I know. I came to see you."

Oh, so that's what that text I got a bit ago from Harper was all about. Damn her.

His response is so matter of fact, like he routinely swings by the house to see me, that it drives me a little crazy. A part of me doesn't want to see him. The only way I got away from the library without talking to him again was by immersing myself in a conversation with Meredith.

Why would he want to see me now, anyway?

"Ugh," I say, shaking the water droplets from my arm. "What do you want?"

"Can we talk without a closed door in between us?"

"I don't see why that's necessary."

The shadow moves. From the looks of it, he's laughing. It makes me grin.

"Just let me in, Ave," he says.

"I . . . Why?" It's almost a whine, a plea not to do this.

Clearly, the reasoning I used to justify kissing Penn didn't work. One could even say it was an excuse. *Maybe* it was. But now it's happened, done and apparently not over yet, and I have to deal with it, and I don't want to.

Why can't I be forced to deal with other things instead? Like a box of chocolates or a trip to Greece?

I make my way slowly toward the door in the hope that he'll be gone by the time I get there.

"Fine," he says. "We can have this conversation through a door if you'd like, but I really thought that you—"

I jerk the door open. His eyes go wide for a split second before a smile slips across the lips I just touched with my own.

"I'm kind of busy," I say.

He tries to keep a serious look on his face. It's ridiculous to watch, and also kind of charming, but I attempt just as hard to look neutral.

"Doing what?" he asks.

"I was making dinner. And burning myself." I look down at my arm. "That really freaking hurts."

A red blotch lies halfway between my palm and my elbow. Heat pours out of it like the grease is still somehow there, even though I know it's not.

Penn reaches for my arm, but I yank it away.

"Let's not," I say. When his eyes crinkle with mirth, I look away. "So, door is open. What do you want?"

"I brought you something."

He bends down and picks up a tackle box. It's red and plastic and looks like the one every country boy has in the movies.

"Thanks." It's more of a question than a statement as I watch him hold out the box. I take it. It's heavier than I anticipate. "You brought me fishing supplies. How . . . nice."

He rolls his eyes. "No. I didn't just bring you fishing supplies. Open it."

There's nowhere to set it unless I use the kitchen table. And if I do that, I'll have to let him in.

I glance up at him only to realize that he knows this. It's the smirk that gives him away.

"Fine," I say. "Come on in."

"I thought you'd never ask."

"I wasn't going to," I say as I turn around.

I set the box on the table. Penn closes the door and then walks to the other side of the table so he's facing me. Instead of opening it, I take a step away.

"Why did you bring me this?" I ask.

His brows pull together. "What kind of question is that?"

"What do you mean, 'What kind of question is that?' It's a question I want you to answer."

He bites his bottom lip, probably to keep from smiling.

"What?" I ask. "Why are you doing that?"

"Doing what?"

"Smiling."

"I'm not," he says as his face splits into a wide grin. "I mean, I wasn't. Now I am."

I blow out a breath, unnerved by this whole thing. There's a chair pulled out beside me, so I sit. He follows suit.

We watch each other from the safety of our sides of the table. I search his eyes for some sign of what this is all about.

"Not that I don't love staring at you, but will you just open the damn box?" he asks.

"What's in it?"

"You'll know if you open it," he says, exasperated. "Good lord, Avery. Why are you so difficult?"

My jaw drops. "Me? I'm not difficult. You didn't even have to work that hard to kiss me."

There. I said it. It's out in the air. The elephant in the room is out of its cage. Or savanna. Or wherever elephants are kept.

His eyes twinkle. "Ah, so you think this is some kind of parlay from that? Is that your hang-up?"

"I don't have a hang-up," I say, tucking a strand of hair behind my ear. "I just don't understand what the point of it is."

He leans back, resting his hands in front of him. He frowns as he takes me in.

"Don't people do this?" he asks. "I mean, Neely baked Meredith a bunch of cookies when they moved to town. And Claire just bought a dozen doughnuts from the café for some woman that moved into the house next to her." He spins his hat around so it's sitting backward on his head. "Maybe I got this all wrong."

I'm speechless. I open my mouth, but nothing comes out. I don't even really know what to say. That stupid backward cap makes him even more attractive, and that's not what I need right now.

"I'm sorry if I fucked this up," he says, starting to get up.

"No," I say quickly. "Um, no. You didn't mess anything up, Penn. I just . . . I'm not used to this kind of thing."

He settles back in his seat with more than a dose of hesitation. "What do people in California do when you get a neighbor?"

"Ignore them."

A laugh spills into the room, but it's more from disbelief than entertainment.

I play with the latch on the box, snapping the black piece that holds it shut over and over. There has to be something that goes along with this. Something I'm not thinking of. If someone does something nice for you in Los Angeles, it's because they need a favor.

"So, there are no strings attached to this?" I ask.

"What kind of people are you used to?" He raises his brows. "I mean, hell, Avery. I'm not the nicest guy in the universe, but I wouldn't bring you something and expect something in return if that's what you're getting at. And quite frankly, I'm a little offended you'd think that."

My heart sinks as I take in his face.

"I'm sorry," I say. "I didn't mean it like that. I'm just used to people that don't make a move unless there's a reason behind it—and the reason isn't ever to just be nice."

"That fucking sucks."

"Yeah. It does." We exchange a soft smile, one that fills me with a warmth that I never want to leave. I flip the latch and pull apart the two halves of the tackle box.

And I laugh.

"This is not what I was expecting," I say.

He leans forward, peering into the box like a child at a birthday party. He looks up at me through his dark, thick lashes. "Do you like it?"

"Yeah," I say with a giggle. "I do."

I take out a white pencil. The tip is a plethora of colors, and I can imagine that when you sharpen it, the shavings look like rainbows.

"This is nice." I hold it up. "Very colorful."

"Okay. To be honest here, Mia gave me that. But the colors reminded me of paint, and I thought that since you're an artist, you might like it."

My heart tugs in my chest. "I do. Thank you." I reach in and take out the next item. "A multipurpose tool. Smart."

"Knowing you're a city girl, I figured you didn't have one. Every country girl needs a good multitool. Never know when you're gonna need to fillet a fish or screw something in—like your speaker. Did you ever get that hung?"

I set the tool down. "Let's not ruin the moment. Moving on . . ."

The next item is a bright-red flyswatter. I hold it up.

"So, that's for flies by design, but you'll really need it for mosquitoes in the summer. But it can be used in the bedroom if . . ." He stops when I smack the table in front of him. The grin on his face is priceless.

"Fly- or mosquito-swatter. Got it. I'm sure that will be handy." I set it down and spy a bright-orange candy wrapper with peanut-butter-filled chocolate cups. "Oh, I love these."

"I knew you would."

I laugh. "Did you really?"

"Doesn't everyone?"

"Not people with peanut allergies," I point out.

"Do you have allergies?"

"Just to bullshit," I say, picking up the last item from the box. It's an expired ticket to a circus. I laugh. "What's this?"

He turns his head so he's looking at me out of the corner of his eye. "That is a ticket to the Dogwood Lane Tour."

"Funny. It says it's a ticket to the Long Family Circus, expired in 2018."

“Well, it has multiple purposes.” He turns to face me. “If you want someone to show you around, a tour of the paths less traveled, you can cash that ticket in at any time.”

“No strings attached?”

He rolls his eyes and falls back in his chair. “Why do you think everything comes with a string?”

“Because they do.”

“Like . . . what string would I attach to an expired ticket to a circus? Make me dinner afterward? Although, by the smell in here, I’m not sure I’d want you cooking for me.”

I pick up the flyswatter and smack it at him. He ducks, laughing so freely that I can’t help but join him.

His laugh is addictive. It’s interesting that he doesn’t know how normal it is to have strings attached to everything. He’s almost . . . naive. There’s not a hateful bone in this man’s delectable body. And I like it. I like the easiness of this in the face of the kiss.

It feels good. I didn’t expect it to be like this, and I’m not quite sure what to do now.

Once we’re settled and the room is quiet again, I take a deep breath. I don’t want to go too deep with this and tell him who my mother is or that I grew up with the family known as America’s New Camelot. I don’t want that. I like the way he looks at me now. Like I’m just Avery Perry, hairdresser and painter.

Still, he’s made an attempt at friendship, and I should do the same.

I take a deep breath and prepare to open up to him a little. It only seems fair. Maybe it’ll help him understand where I’m coming from.

“One of the reasons I moved here,” I say carefully, “is because everyone I know wants something from me. Not just me, but from everyone. No one just does anything nice for the sake of being nice. It’s to get a leg up, to move up the ladder.”

He narrows his eyes. “And you were able to move people up the ladder.”

"In some ways, yes," I say with a gulp. "But I just . . . I don't trust people. I think people are fake more often than not. Whether they try to be or not is a different question and one I've battled with therapists over my whole life. Either way, I'm tired of all that. I just want to relax and be surrounded by people who I know aren't putting on airs."

"That must have really sucked."

That sentence, five simple words, sums up my existence in California to a T. It sucked. It always sucked. It sucked from the day I caught my mom doing cocaine in the bathroom and she bought me a fancy watch in return for never telling my dad. I knew, from that moment on, that nothing was as it seemed. If my own relatives kept secrets with bribery and lies, how much worse would it be outside the family unit? Nowhere felt safe from the manipulation.

"Yeah," I say softly.

I rip open the candy and offer Penn one half. He takes it. We eat the chocolate in silence, kind of feeling each other out through the quiet.

The longer we sit, the more comfortable it gets to share the same space with him again.

We nibble on the candy, exchanging little smiles here and there. It's peaceful and relaxing, and I find myself letting go of the stress of the afternoon.

"Want to go for a walk?" I ask.

His face lights up. "Sure."

CHAPTER SIXTEEN

Penn

Well, this isn't how I expected this evening to go.

Avery's hands are in her pockets, her hair floating behind her in the breeze as we walk toward the field behind Harper's house.

But I'm not complaining.

She's calm and collected and so unbelievably pretty. I hope she's like this partially because of me. Or even because of the chocolate, since I gave that to her. Either way, I'll happily claim responsibility for putting that look on her face.

I feel lighter now that there's no weirdness between us. The weight that was on my shoulders is mostly gone, and I have no intention of ever letting that happen again.

"Do I have to use the ticket for this?" She glances at me cheekily from the corner of her eye.

"Nope. This is a freebie. But it won't be as interesting as the Dogwood Lane Tour. Just warning you."

She grins, dropping her gaze to the grass. We move along quietly as the sun makes its final descent over the horizon. Birds call good night as we pass through a grove of trees.

"Thank you," she says. "Your present was really thoughtful."

"It's not a big deal. Just stuff I had in my truck, mostly." Even though that's true, there's still a surge of pride in my chest. I felt like a moron putting that bundle of randomness together, but I didn't know how to actually say, "For once in my life, I'm worried I fucked up by kissing you." "But I'm glad you liked it."

She stops walking and stares off across the field. The grass is so green this time of year, and flowers fill the ditches and ravines. I wonder if she likes it because it's natural artwork in a way. But something about that feels too personal to ask.

"You like to fish, huh?" she asks.

"Was the tackle box your first hint?"

"That, and you have a fish tattooed on your arm." She points to a piece of my sleeve. "Is there a reason you have that permanently inked in your flesh? Or do you just like fish so much that you wanted to live with one forever and ever?"

I hold out my arm. Colorful ink is etched on my skin from my shoulder to my wrist. Each tattoo holds a story, whether it's a sentimental memento or just a relic from a drunken night. I like them all. I don't regret any of them.

"I got the fish when my grandfather died," I say. "He was a great fisherman and probably the reason I love it so much. I was a little rambunctious as a child. I know that's hard to believe," I crack as she laughs. "He taught me how to sit still and focus on one thing while we were fishing."

"He sounds nice."

"He was a cool guy."

It's my turn to gaze across the grass as I wonder what my life would've turned out like had he not passed away when he did. He was my rock, my shield when things were bad, my guidepost for how I wanted to live my life. I loved going to his house. There was a feeling I'd get as soon as I walked in the door. It might've just been a slight buzz from the cigar smoke, if that's possible, but it was the only place I could really let my guard down. I didn't have to watch my back or brace for the possibility of a fight breaking out.

I wonder if he'd be proud of me. If he'd look at how I've turned out and think I didn't do too badly.

I hope so.

Avery shifts her weight, running her fingers through her hair. The motion flips my attention back to her.

"Was the fish your first tattoo?" she asks.

"Nah." I hold my arm out again and rotate it back and forth. "The skull was my first one. Got it when I was sixteen, in Daniel Layman's garage."

She makes a face. "Um, was that safe?"

"Probably not. But you have to start somewhere, right? And my mom wouldn't sign off for me yet, said it was a step closer to becoming my father." I watch as she bends down and picks up a broken acorn. "What's your mom like?"

"My mom was a bit of a . . . What did you call me the other day? A fun-sucker?" She laughs, throwing the acorn across the field. "My mom was the ultimate fun-sucker."

I join in her laughter. Our voices mix together in the easiest way. I like the sound of it. It does something in my chest that I'd rather not explore.

"The star was my first legal tattoo," I say before I can freak myself out with deep thinking. "Then the rose. The red dye is fading now." I run a finger over the ink. "I got this one for my mom."

"That's really sweet," she says, grinning softly.

"Yeah, well, it's probably sweeter than she actually was." I kick a rock as we walk again. I think about my mom and how hard it must've been for her to be married to Dad. "Maybe that's not fair."

"What's not fair?"

I stop walking. "My mom had a lot of shit to deal with. My dad wasn't around much, and when he was, it was complete chaos. People in and out of the house. Drugs. He'd get pissed and just whack you across the face." I cringe, the sting of his hand fresh against my cheek. "It was a hell of a life."

"Penn," she says with a gulp, "I'm so sorry."

She looks at me with wide eyes that are full of concern. I stare at her, absorbing the fact that I just shared that . . . and that she cares. Both are so out of the ordinary that it takes a full few seconds for me to accept reality.

"I never would've thought you had that experience," she says softly. "You're so . . . kind. It's hard to imagine someone like you coming out so . . . good . . . after going through all that."

"I can't say it didn't have an effect on me. I'm sure it did. I'm sure a lot of my fuckups are because of how I grew up."

She places a hand on my arm. Her eyes shine in a way that makes it feel like we're the only two people in the world. "Anyone would be affected by that. Hell, I've had years of therapy because of my parents, and they weren't physically abusive."

"Everyone has shit to deal with, right?"

"I guess so."

We start to walk again. Crickets chirp beside us as the air begins to cool. There's a steadiness, a peace, even, that descends around the two of us as we venture farther from the house.

"Tell me something," she says. "Whatever you want. Tell me about another tattoo."

"Well," I say, searching my arm for something to show her, "this one I got on vacation when I was eighteen. I don't know why I thought a sea turtle was a grand idea, but there you have it." I run my hand over my skin, skipping over the pair of dice on my forearm, and land on the cross. "This one is to remind me that God is always watching."

"I like that."

"Me too."

She tucks her chin and stays a step ahead of me as we wander through the grass. It feels good to do this with another person, to talk about things with someone who just might give a damn. And with someone who doesn't expect a joke to be cracked.

"Do you have any tattoos?" I ask.

"Um . . . yeah." She looks at me in an almost panic before ripping her eyes away just as quickly. "I got one to rebel against my mother, actually. Like you."

She searches my eyes—for what, I'm not quite sure. I let her see what she wants to see because I have nothing to hide. I wait for her to say something, to tell me what she was looking for, but she doesn't.

We stop in the middle of the field. The final rays of the sun shine down on us almost like a spotlight. I want to reach out and touch her, to feel her skin against me. But I'm afraid that if I do, she'll look at me like she did today when we kissed.

That's never happened to me before. Usually, if a girl initiates a kiss, she's all in. Or at least in for a good make-out session, and she certainly doesn't pull away like she's just done some tragic thing. It was like a punch in the stomach, and not for the reasons I imagined it would be. I figured my ego would be a little sore. Fuck my ego. I was worried something was wrong with her and it was my fault.

What's that say about me?

"Penn . . ." She tilts her chin to look me in the eye. "About earlier . . ."

"You don't have to say anything about it," I tell her. "It's fine." She still looks worried, so I try to lighten the mood. I don't know what else to do. "I know I'm hard to resist."

She rolls her eyes, but the grin splitting her cheeks softens the blow. She motions for me to follow and heads back toward the house.

My pulse beats harder with each step. The closer we get to the house, the sooner this night will be over. It's an odd feeling to wish for more time with a girl whom I'm not sleeping with. But I like it. I like her. I like talking to her and telling her things about me and hearing things about her.

It's messed up, and I'm not sure how to rationalize it all, especially when I add in how much I liked kissing her today.

"Avery?" I say.

She stops and looks at me over her shoulder. "Yeah?"

I want to wrap her up in my arms as the temperature drops again. The sun slips behind the tree line. It's dark and quiet with only the lightning bugs dotted across the landscape.

I'm out of my element here, but I'm *here*. With her. After everything that happened today, we're together, and it's okay. There's an urge in my stomach telling me to be honest with her in the hope that we can do *this*, whatever it is, again.

As I look at her staring back at me, I'm not sure what to say. It's because I'm not sure what I want. I wanted to fuck her brains out when I first met her. I'd still do that happily. But if that's not what she has in mind, then I'd rather see her smile than not see her at all.

It's hard to believe I'm thinking this way.

I take a slow, deep breath.

"I want you to know," I say, "that I really liked kissing you today. But I will never kiss you again or make it uncomfortable for you if that's what you want, and I didn't mean to do that today, if that's what happened. I actually feel bad about it, and I didn't know I could feel bad about things like this, and I kind of don't know what to do so I'm just standing here rambling like a moron."

She opens her mouth and closes it again. Her weight goes from side to side before she seems to find the words she's looking for.

Maybe I should just get in my truck and leave. Clearly, I'm an idiot. Who stands in front of a girl like her and jabbers away about their feelings?

Fools, that's who.

"I'm going to be honest," she says finally.

"Please do."

Her eyes soften. "I wanted to kiss you today. As much as I wanted to, I also didn't."

I try to process that information—that she wanted to kiss me and she didn't want to kiss me. I have no fucking idea what that means. *How does that work?* "Okay . . ."

She takes a deep breath. "You are a good-looking guy."

Can't argue that.

"And you're funny, and apparently, you can be sweet. Who knew?" She laughs softly. "Of course I wanted to kiss you. Every girl wants to kiss you, don't they?"

I shrug, making her chuckle.

"You didn't make me uncomfortable," she says. "Don't feel bad. You did nothing wrong."

"Is this an invitation to kiss you again?" I joke.

She narrows her eyes.

"Sorry. Too soon. Got it."

She shakes her head. "Honestly, I felt like I was leading you on. You're the guy that knows what you want and you get it and you're unapologetic—rightfully so. But I know what I want, and I want to get it too."

I don't respond. I just watch her rattle off her monologue, because I'm stuck at the part where I know what I want and I get it. *Do I?* Because right now she's what I want, and I'm sure not getting it.

"What is it you want?" I ask.

She looks off into the distance. "Once, when I was a teenager, I was on a plane flying somewhere to see my dad. There was a couple sitting across the aisle from me." She smiles to herself. "I remember it like it was yesterday. They talked to each other so passionately, completely engaged with what the other was saying. They held hands and shared their pretzels and were just so happy." She looks at me. "They'd been married for thirty years."

"Wow," I say.

"I've never forgotten that. It was a moment in time that I've carried with me forever because that day I decided that's what I wanted. It was only recently that I realized I couldn't get that in California—not in the life I lived there."

I jam my hands into my pockets. Thirty years is a long time to be married to one person. It's longer than I've been alive. I've never met anyone willing to put up with me for three weeks, let alone thirty years.

"I want that level of connection," she says, looking at me. "I want something deep and passionate. A man who thinks I'm interesting and values what I have to say. Who wants to have sex with me all night and then laugh with me all day. I want to build a life with someone, and if I keep kissing guys that have no interest in that, it'll put me farther behind." She forces a swallow. "I've spent a lot of my life alone. There have been many days I wondered how long it would take anyone to notice if I died. I'm on a mission to not re-create that life. I hope that makes sense."

I try to imagine the scene she's describing. There's a hollowness that takes root in my chest. How lonely must that have been? Even I, the guy who rejects having a girl spend the night, am never lonely, because I have Matt and Dane and Claire and Mia. I have a list of people who call me if I don't show up to the café for breakfast. Hell, even Mick at the bait shop will call if I don't swing by there at least once a week, and it has nothing to do with the ten bucks I spend on worms that I really don't need.

"I'm really sorry you've had to think about something like that," I say. "But I'm glad you're here."

She nods. "Me too. I just have to figure out how to be around you and not want to kiss you all the time." She grins. "Can you just not be as cute? Or be mean sometimes? That would help."

"That's fucked up." I laugh as I think about being mean to her. I couldn't be. Even if I were pissed, I couldn't be mean to her.

"Tell me about it."

I look at her standing there, as pretty as the day is long. My chest hurts for her as I watch her work through something inside her head that I'm not aware of.

As much as I like Avery, it doesn't change anything. I still can't see myself settling down with someone or having to be responsible to catch someone every time they slip. I can barely catch myself. But I respect what she's saying. A lot. But fuck it if having her be so strong and opinionated—even to my detriment—doesn't make her even sexier.

A pang ripples through my chest. I wince at the pain.

I look up at her. "I'll tell you what."

"What's that?" she asks, looking up at me with hope in her eyes.

"If you need a friend, I'll be your friend. I promise not to speak every word with some kind of sexual overtone, and I won't ask you out every day either. Just sometimes." I wink. "But seriously, I'd like to be your friend, even though that sounds so kindergarten."

I'll just jack off every night in the shower.

Her face lights up. "Really?"

"Sure. I mean, you're looking to marry someone, and I just want to get laid, so—ouch!" I dart backward as she swats at my shoulder. "That hurts."

"Oh, it does not." She chuckles, her cheeks pink. She looks at the ground. "Are you sure, Penn? I know I probably seem like an oddball—"

"You totally do. No one has ever just wanted to be friends with me in my entire life."

"Guess I'm the first," she says with a light shrug.

"Guess so. *Friend.*" I start to turn away but am caught off guard by the curve of her neck. *Damn.* "Okay, quick amendment to our friendship."

She laughs. "Already?"

"Yeah. There's no sense in starting a friendship off with a lie, right?" I run my hand down the side of my cheek.

"This is true."

"I'll overlook your unwillingness to kiss me if you can overlook some innuendos and maybe a *little* flirting. What?" I say with a laugh as she shakes her head. "I'm me. You're you, and you're fucking hot. And I've kissed you once now, so I know what that tastes like. Deal?"

She nods in an exaggerated cue that a deal has been made. But, funnily enough, I don't quite believe she likes it.

I know I don't. But what choice is there?

"Fine. I'll accept some *minor* flirting," she says. "Now, if you don't mind, I'm going inside. The mosquitoes are starting to bite, and I forgot my flyswatter."

"Perfect," I say, heading toward my truck. "I hope your dreams are as sweet as your ass."

She laughs. "You said minor flirting."

"That was minor," I say as I reach my truck. "You don't even want to know what I wanted to say."

She laughs, but I know she likes it.

I watch her walk back inside the house before I turn to my truck. After I've climbed in and turned on the engine, I sit for a minute.

I just told her I could be her friend.

What the hell? How am I going to pull that off?

"Friends, huh?" I say as I put the truck in reverse. "This should be interesting."

CHAPTER SEVENTEEN

Avery

I almost miss my turn.

The sun is so bright that the glare on my windshield hid the entrance to the old library. Luckily, the minivan in front of me is going about two miles an hour, and it gives me enough time to hook a quick right.

There are a number of vehicles parked outside but plenty of available spaces left. I take the one next to Penn's truck. The black-on-black beast towers over my red compact car. I can't see inside the cab due to the window tint, but I'm fairly certain he's not close by, because the cells in my body are calm.

Friends. It's the word that rolled around my brain all night. It's a great term, one that exudes ideas of camaraderie and fun outings. Just probably not the experiences I was thinking about as I lay in my bed after my bath and thought about Penn.

Being friends with him is the answer. It's the only option, really. I just hope I can keep myself nice and even-keeled around him and be friendly.

I grab my bag full of sketch pads and pencils from the back seat. Digging through it, I make sure I have everything I need to get started on the mural today. A flurry of excitement washes over me as I process getting to spend the entire day being creative.

Tap! Tap!

My head whips to the side. Penn is standing at the passenger-side window. Dressed in a faded black T-shirt with an oil company logo flaking off the front and jeans that show off his trim waist, he looks better than anyone should at nine in the morning.

Fucker.

Popping open my door, I get my bag on my shoulder. Then I climb out.

"Nice of you to join us," he says with a grin.

"Meredith said to be here 'in the morning.' That's not an exact time by any stretch of the imagination."

"I'm just giving you shit. How's your arm?"

The red spot has mostly gone away, but the area is still tender. "It's okay. Sore, a little. Who knew eggs could be so dangerous?"

"Me, actually."

I wait, expecting a joke about him fertilizing eggs or the fear of it. The longer he goes without a comment, the more suspect he becomes.

"What?" he asks.

"I'm waiting for an egg joke."

He shrugs. "I don't have one."

"Bull."

"I really don't." He laughs. "I'm trying to override my brain and only think clean thoughts." His head goes from side to side like he's reconsidering. "Most of the time. My thoughts were pretty filthy when I saw you in that shirt." He winks, walking backward toward the door.

"So, how'd you know eggs are dangerous?"

"When I was learning how to cook, I had a lot of grease blisters." He takes in my reaction. "What? You didn't think I knew how to cook?"

"Um, actually, no."

"Your quick judgments of me wound me deeply." He snickers. "Joking. I had to learn to cook if I didn't want to starve. I'm pretty shitty at it, but I do like it sometimes."

"That's . . . awesome," I say, trying to stop the image of Penn cooking with no shirt on. "What else do you like to do . . . Don't answer that."

He gives me another smile, this one a smidgen back from being devious, before turning around and dipping into the building.

I pause by the bucket holding the door open. The warmth of the morning encompasses me like an old friend, and I find myself excited for the day. It's an odd feeling. My mornings used to begin with a headache, followed by coffee, followed by a pep talk to get me through whatever I had to do. I thought that was life. I figured it was just the way things were because it's all I'd ever known. Fighting for a job, pretending the world was peaches with clients, getting berated when you don't know something because some pampered celebrity thinks everyone exists to benefit them.

I was wrong.

This morning greeted me with possibility. There was so much adventure on the horizon that I sprang out of bed. It's amazing what getting to do what you love all day can do for your spirit, as opposed to feeling like you get your spirit sucked out of you as the days go by.

I step inside the building and stop. It's like a pretty-people convention in front of me, and I'm not prepared.

Penn is standing next to a pile of lumber, a pencil shoved over his ear. The addition of a carpenter's belt makes his shoulders look even wider. The entire display is enough to make me drool. But there's more.

Matt is standing next to him. He looks up and waves. His light-brown hair and sweet smile are enough to melt a girl. But then, standing next to Meredith, who's wearing a pale-yellow dress with what I think are pearls, are two more hotties. With strong bodies and tanned skin, the two men wearing button-up shirts look like they walked in from a department-store magazine.

"Avery, good morning," Meredith says. "How are you today?"

"I'm good. Ready to get started."

"Great. I'd like you to meet my stepsons, Trevor and Jake Kelly."

The one on the right sticks out his hand. "I'm Trevor. It's nice to meet you."

"I'm Avery," I say, giving his hand a shake.

"And I'm Jake," the other says. His green eyes sparkle. "It's a pleasure to meet you."

"Likewise," I say.

Penn's stare burns into the side of my face, but I ignore him. With Meredith and these two in front of me, I can handle only one tornado at a time.

"Meredith told me you were new in town. My fiancée, Haley, is hoping to meet you," Trevor says. "She's lived here forever and would love to show you around."

"Or I could do it," Jake offers. "Haley's a busy—"

Crash! We all jump and look to our right, where Penn and Matt stand. Matt looks at the floor while Penn looks at me. He grins, but it's not the happy-go-lucky kind of goofy Penn grin. It's forced.

"Whoops," he says. "Sorry."

His antics amuse me to no end. He had to have heard Jake's comment. Why he cared I don't know, since he declared us friends last night, but he apparently didn't like something about it.

"Thanks, Jake," I say, turning around. "I'll keep that in mind."

"I was thinking about the mural," Meredith says. "I know we talked briefly about it, but I'd really like to incorporate Dogwood Lane into the art. Really pick up on that hometown angle, you know? Make the kids proud of where they're from. I think that's so important."

"I love it," I reply. "I had a similar vision, so this really works. I sat down with Harper last night and jotted some things down. We're on the same page, I think."

"What are you thinking?" she asks.

"Well, in general terms, I'm thinking about finding out what this town means to the locals and really bringing that to life. Making it grand—an in-your-face snapshot of the town through the years."

Meredith claps her hands and almost squeals. "Yes. That's brilliant. Run with it. Have fun with it. Tell me if you need my help or advice, but I want you to just have at it, Avery."

My insides squish as her trust in my abilities is heaped on me. I think I might burst. "Wow. Thank you. I'm excited."

"If you want to get the supplies you need and just bill me for it, that's fine," she says. "Or you can make a list, and I'll be sure to get them."

Jake cuts in. "Let's rephrase that with a bit of practicality. She'll get the list to me, and I'll get it here as soon as possible."

"That's what I said," Meredith says.

"No, it's not," Jake, Trevor, and I all say at the same time. It gets a round of laughs from all four of us.

As discreetly as possible, I glance toward Penn. He's using a pencil like the one he gave me last night to make marks on a board. It makes me happy, and I'm not sure why. It's a pencil, for heaven's sake.

He's so focused on what he's doing that he doesn't see me checking him out. I take the opportunity to study him. He's so careful as he marks the wood, so controlled as he stops and points at something on the plans. Matt listens to what he says and nods.

"Jake," Meredith says, drawing my attention away from Penn, "I need you to get the window company down here soon. I have big ideas for the shutters."

"I know it's a foreign thought," Jake says, "but everything can't be on Meredith Time."

"That doesn't work for me," she says.

"Of course not." Jake gives me a grin and a little wave. "Trevor and I have to be going. I'll see you at the house later, Meredith. It was nice meeting you, Avery."

"You too," I call after them.

"And head by the flower shop and say hi to Haley. She'd love that," Trevor says over his shoulder.

Once they're gone and Penn and Matt are back to cutting lumber, Meredith and I walk toward the wall that will hold the mural.

"I'm glad you got to meet them," Meredith says. "They're so smart, both of them. Trevor lives here now with Haley. Jake isn't around as much, but you'll see him from time to time, and you can always reach out if you need anything." She stops walking and faces me. "I know Jake was a little flirty. I haven't mentioned that you and Penn are an item."

"What?" I blurt out as another boom rips through the room.

We look over to Penn, whose eyebrows are shooting skyward, and to Matt, who can't contain a chuckle.

"Penn and I aren't a thing," I say, keeping a side-eye on him. "I have no idea why you thought that."

"Really?" She looks at me and then to him. "That's surprising. There's a lot of chemistry between the two of you."

Penn's features smooth out as he goes back to measuring his board. "I can't help it. Women are always drawn to me."

"Given your attention-seeking ways, they don't have much of a choice, do they?" I poke.

He ignores me.

"Well, now that that's all out and awkward," Meredith says, "I need to go. I have brunch with the head of permitting for the city to try to get an animal license for this address. I had no idea this would be such an issue."

Matt clears his throat as he approaches us. "I was actually thinking about that. Maybe if you can block off those meeting rooms in the back and almost make them their own structure, it would help. There would be a clear separation between animal and child, at least unless you intentionally mix them."

Her eyes light up. "That is a great idea. From a construction standpoint, do you know how to do that? Is it hard?"

"Nah. It's just framing," he says. "Nothing more than we're doing out here."

"Perfect. Actually," she says, biting her bottom lip, "could you go with me, Matt?"

"Where?"

"To City Hall. I might need you to talk construction." Meredith makes a face. "I'd feel better if someone knowledgeable was at my side, fighting along with me."

"I bet Matt would love to spend the morning with you," Penn teases. "This physical stuff is hard since he's so freshly recuperated."

I've known Matt for only a few days, but I think if he could kick Penn in the face, he would.

"Great. Let's get over there now so we can chat a little in the car," Meredith says. "I like to walk into a meeting knowing exactly what we're going to say."

"Sure thing," Matt says, giving Penn a look like he's going to kill him later. He drops his belt on a piece of wood and follows Meredith out the door.

The room settles, the sounds of their voices drifting away, and it's just Penn and me. We watch each other, neither of us wanting to be the first one to break the silence. Finally, Penn shrugs and goes back to work.

I take my sketch pad out of my bag. The design I started to work out last night is on the first page. When I wouldn't give in to Harper's pokes and prods about my evening, only telling her I'd been sketching, she threw out a suggestion. A thunderbird, Dogwood Lane High's mascot, sits in one of the dogwood trees. It's a cute touch.

Slumping against the wall, I lower myself until I'm sitting. The floor is cool beneath me as I take in the spot where the mural will go. But after a few minutes, my attention is dragged to Penn.

A bead of sweat glistens on his forehead as he focuses on his work. I wonder if Meredith would mind if I just painted a mural of him, preferably shirtless, instead.

Forcing the thought out of my mind, I go back to the sketch pad. But as my hand starts to doodle again, it pencils a set of abs instead of the lake I was planning.

"That might be one way to get more views on this thing," I mumble and laugh before I can stop it.

The sound catches Penn's attention. He leans forward, his palms resting on a stack of lumber as he looks at me.

"What's so funny over there?" he asks.

"Just wondering how bad Matt is going to hurt you for sticking him with Meredith," I say, erasing the quick version of Penn's stomach as fast as I can. "She's nice. I don't know why you two try to avoid her."

"She's nice. She's just full of so much . . . enthusiasm. Who gets that excited about renovating a building?"

I shove off the floor and get to my feet. "What if someone was going to build a huge pond so kids that were in trouble or had extra energy could go and learn to . . . fish? Cast a line? I don't know the lingo."

He laughs. "That would be super awesome of someone."

"No one says 'awesome' anymore."

"I do," he says flatly.

"Fine," I say with a sigh. "Anyway, this is Meredith's fishpond thing. It makes her feel good to make people happy and to think she's making a difference in the world."

"Well, making other people happy makes me feel good, too, if ya catch my drift."

All I can do is shake my head.

He moseys across the room and stands next to me. Peering down at my sketchbook, he nods. "This is great. Did you do all this?"

"Yes."

He reaches for the book. "Can I see it?"

"Oh, um, sure," I say, handing it over.

He walks around the room, inspecting my sketches with the care of a surgeon. I bite my nail as I watch him pore over each little thing. A few times, he looks up at me with what looks like awe, and it gives me chills. Pride swells in my chest as I take in how impressed he is.

No one has ever really taken my art seriously. Sure, my father would use my art connections to benefit a charity auction he was involved with from time to time, but painting and drawing were considered my silly little hobbies. They were nothing compared with my sister's talent of finding married men to sleep with.

Not having that in my face every day is more of a relief than I even dreamed it would be. I never truly understood how cold my life was until I got to Dogwood Lane and experienced its warmth. This kind of community should be something everyone gets the chance to have in their lives.

"How much time did this take you?" he asks.

"I don't know," I say, feeling my cheeks heat. "I worked on it for a few hours last night. I wasn't sure what direction Meredith wanted to go. I was just kind of messing around."

"Holy shit, Ave." He gives me a huge, wide grin. "What else can you do?"

I couldn't smile wider if I tried. I grin from ear to ear, my cheeks aching as I all-out beam at his compliment. "A girl can't give away all her secrets."

"Hopefully a boy can dig around and discover some more." He wiggles his eyebrows until I giggle. He seems to catch himself, and his features smoothen out. "In all honesty, these are beyond impressive."

"Let's not get crazy."

He hands the book back to me. Our fingertips touch, rocketing a blast of energy through my body. His eyes go wide, but he recovers quickly—probably quicker than me.

He blows out a breath. "Better get back to work."

Work. Yup.

As he turns and walks away, I swear I hear him mumbling something about friends.

I resume my spot on the floor and try to focus on sketching the lake. The pencil goes back and forth across the paper, and my brain bounces back and forth between Penn and the drawing.

People who are ridiculously attracted to one another can be friends . . . right?

I look up to see him wiping his face with the edge of his shirt. A slice of his abs shows just above the top of his pants.

My gaze flips back to the sketch pad like I've been burned.

Friends, I remind myself. *We are friends.*

I look up to see him grinning.

With no benefits.

Sigh.

CHAPTER EIGHTEEN

Avery

A shot of pain courses up my arm.

"Ouch!" I say, cupping my shoulder with my other hand.

"You okay?"

Penn is standing across the room, his brow furrowed in concern. The light coming through the windows is now muted, and I wonder how long I've been sitting here, sketching.

I read somewhere once that "flow" is a psychological state that means you're in the zone, fully immersed with both involvement and enjoyment in an activity. It's not an easy frame of mind to get into, and a lot of people never do. I don't unless I'm drawing or sketching or painting. Even doing hair doesn't get me there, so being able to bust out my sketch pad daily is a dream come true.

"How long have I been sitting here?" I ask. The last things I remember are Matt bringing Penn and me sandwiches, and then Matt leaving and saying goodbye. I have no idea how long ago that was.

Penn looks at his phone. "About five hours."

"Crap." I get to my feet, my back and bottom yelping from sitting on the concrete floor. "Why didn't you get me up?"

"Sounds like a personal problem," he cracks. "Kidding. I did try to get you up. I even did a striptease over there, and you weren't interested."

Now I know he's lying.

I work my shoulder around, trying to stop the pinch that's burning inside it. Penn tidies up the area he was working in. Tool cords get wrapped up and sawdust swept into a neat little pile and then tossed into a makeshift trash can.

For all the hell he catches from Matt, he seems to be a hard worker. He barely took a break as far as I can tell, and by the looks of the wood laid out in squares on the floor, he seems to have gotten a lot done—even more so when you figure that he sent Matt off with Meredith and then sent him for lunch. I think he's taking it easy on his friend, even though I'm sure he'd never admit it.

The sketch in my hand is more final. Dogwood trees will stand on either end of the wall, their branches draping over the top. The lake will be featured front and center, along with other local favorites. I even worked in the bright-yellow sign that welcomes you into town. Still, there are a few more spots that need to be filled, and I'm not familiar enough with the area to know what to add.

I look up at Penn. "Hey."

He holds a tape measure with the end sticking up in the air. "Were you admiring my eight inches?"

I snort but secretly find his ridiculousness adorable. "Um, no. I had no idea you were holding eight inches."

"Oh, you thought I meant this was eight inches . . ." He clicks a button, and the tape rolls back into the device. "Clearly you haven't had much exposure to the difference in what an inch or two can do. What's up?"

I laugh. *Minor flirting, my ass.*

"What do you think of when you think of Dogwood Lane? Since you know it better than me. I have a couple of spaces to fill on the sketch, and I'm not sure what to put."

He wipes his brow with the back of his hand. "The lake, for sure, but you've got that. The old cannon in the park. Everyone in town has had their picture taken riding that thing at some point or other." He grins. "The train trestle on the far end of town. It goes across the creek that feeds the lake."

I scribble down his ideas. He goes back to cleaning up.

An idea comes to me slowly, more in feelings than in images. I watch Penn move around the room and notice how careful he is about everything he does. It's not what I expected. At all. Come to think of it, he's not what I really expected him to be, and I don't know what to make of that.

I flush.

"Hey," I say again.

"Are you bored or something?"

"No. Why?"

"Because you keep saying 'Hey.'"

I slip my pad back in my bag and hoist it on my shoulder. "Forget it."

"No. Tell me."

"No," I say, shaking my head.

"Ave . . ."

"Stop calling me 'Ave,' by the way." I don't really mind the nickname, but I'm sort of embarrassed that he thinks I was pestering him.

He rolls his eyes, not taking me seriously at all. "Tell me now."

"I don't like being told what to do."

He looks at the ceiling. "Fine. Please tell me what you were going to tell me."

The way he says it is downright adorable. It's a tongue-in-cheek, "I'm trying so hard to play your game" kind of way that makes me grin.

"I was going to see if you had plans tonight, but—"

"I don't." He says it immediately without even letting me finish. "I'm free."

My stomach twists. I sort of just spewed this whole thing without really thinking about it, and now that he's free, I realize what I might've gotten myself into. Not that spending time with Penn is a bad thing at all. It's quite the opposite.

"Well," I say, trying to settle my heartbeat, "I was wondering if this was an okay time for me to cash in my ticket?"

A look of pure bewilderment is slowly replaced with complete shock. "You mean to tell me that is gonna work?"

"It probably wouldn't have except for the fact that I happen to need some help from someone who knows their way around."

"Fuck, yeah. Let's go."

"Now?" I ask.

"You just asked me if right now is a bad time, and now you're acting surprised that I'm—"

"No, you're right," I say, brushing an errant lock of hair out of my face. "I'm sorry. Yes. Now."

He heads for the door and motions for me to follow.

Once we're outside, he moves the bucket holding the door open and locks the building. I head to my car and deposit my bag. When I turn around, he's standing behind me.

"It's taking you long enough," he says.

"It's been two minutes." I laugh. "I'm ready now."

"Let's go."

Before I realize what's happening, we're shoulder to shoulder, going down the sidewalk.

The breeze rolls gently around us as we walk beneath a giant pine tree. The air is scented with the woodsy, citrusy smell of the trees. It settles some of the adrenaline pumping through my veins.

"You didn't bring your sketch pad," Penn notes as we pass a bench.

"I know. Sometimes I think having it on hand when you're experiencing something takes away from your creativity. It's kind of the same thing as losing a moment because you're trying to take the perfect picture for social media."

"I don't do social media."

"Nothing? Not even one site?"

"Nope. If I don't know you in real life, I don't need to know you online. Besides," he says, "I've looked at that stuff long enough to know it isn't good for you."

"How do you figure?"

"I don't know. Have you ever logged off one of your app things and felt better about yourself? More motivated? Have you ever thought, even once, 'Man, I'm really kicking ass over here'?"

I consider this. My timeline is full of my Los Angeles friends and their curated content of parties and events. Their lives look picture perfect, except I know the truth.

"True. But it makes it easier to check in with my parents and my sister," I say. "There are good uses for it, you know."

He just shrugs.

I take in his profile. His jawline is rugged and sharp. I'd venture to guess his nose has been broken at least once, but somehow it gives his face character. There's a mole next to his nose that's so small that I haven't noticed it before. I wonder what else there is to know about him.

"Have you always lived here?" I ask.

"I went to preschool right over there." He points to a little gray building with a faded rainbow sign. "I cut Claire's hair one day. Oh, and then this other time"—he grins—"it was pouring rain. There was a dog in the play area outside, and I let it in. Want to talk about getting in trouble."

I laugh. "You've been ornery from the beginning, then."

"So it would seem."

We walk together quietly. A car passes every now and then, and Penn waves at each one. I wonder if he actually knows them all or if it's some form of southern hospitality I don't yet understand.

He seems content to just walk and enjoy the quiet. It's not at all like my old friends and their constant use of their phones. Heck, even the men I dated spent more time on their devices than talking to me. Penn isn't even talking to me. He's just being with me.

"Let's cross here so I can show you the church." He starts across the middle of the street. There are no cars coming, but there's no crosswalk either.

"Isn't this illegal?" I ask, speed-walking to keep up with him.

"Probably."

"Um . . ."

When we make it safely to the other side, he looks down at me. "Live a little, Avery."

I instantly miss "Ave."

We take an alley behind a big brick building before coming upon an old church. The stained glass windows are breathtaking as they reflect the late-afternoon sun.

"See that?" Penn asks. "That spot up there in the steeple? Where it kind of looks broken but it's not?"

"Yeah."

"There are musket balls stuck up there from the Civil War."

My jaw drops. "Really?"

"Yeah. Tennessee is the only state that had a battle fought in every single county during the war. Only Virginia saw more battles than we did."

He says this like it's common knowledge and takes off again. This time, I remain a few paces behind him.

My mind is reeling. *What else does he know?*

"Matt and I were convinced a ghost lived up there," he says, pointing to the top of a building that looks deserted. "We used to sneak in there with little ghost-hunting kits we made up. I think Dane and his friends would try to scare us sometimes and make us think we'd made contact, now that I think about it. It was a good time."

I imagine a little Penn with his flashlight and rubber boots and can't help but smile. "Those must be great memories. I can see why you and Matt are so close now. You've been friends forever."

"Yeah." His arm brushes mine as we step over a broken piece of sidewalk. The spot where our skin touched is hot. "Did you do stupid stuff like that as a kid?"

"My childhood was nothing like this." I laugh. "It was basically an instructional on how to grow up and not get in my parents' way."

His forehead creases. "What's your mom do?"

I look at his face and watch him watch me. There's something pure and untainted about it, and I don't want to spoil that yet.

"It doesn't matter," I say.

He takes his hat off and runs his hand through his hair. "Well, my mom tried to do the right thing. My dad just made it impossible."

"What is he like?"

"These days, I don't know."

He puts his hat back on again. There's a sourness to his face that makes me regret asking about his father. I remember bits and pieces that he mentioned ten years ago, but I have no idea what happened after that. I'm not sure how much I remember is truth and how much has been skewed by time, anyway.

"He and my mom didn't really get along. Dad tried to drive a wedge between me and her. When I was a little kid, I didn't understand that. I just thought his presents were the best thing ever."

His tone is full of sorrow. It hurts my heart to watch him struggle with thinking about his dad.

"Things were basically okay until I was sixteen. On my sixteenth birthday, he tried to recruit me into a biker gang."

"A what?" I bark.

I'm sure I misheard him. I had to have. A biker gang? What? But one look at his face tells me all I need to know.

"Yeah. A biker gang." Penn heaves a deep breath that's laced with years' worth of stress. "He got me up in the middle of the night and said he needed my help." His eyes glass over as his pace slows. "I was all about my dad, you know, so getting to help him was a huge thing. Until I realized what he needed help with, and I balked."

His eyes stay fixed on something in front of us. It doesn't hide his pain. The war passing across his face is as plain as the day is long. I had no idea he was carrying around something so . . . tragic. The way he seems to struggle with hearing the words out loud makes me think he doesn't share this information often.

My spirits sink.

My hand goes to his arm without thought. He looks down at it, and some of the glassiness goes away, but not all. "I don't know what to say, other than no kid should be put in that position. Hell, no person should, and I'm sorry you were."

"Yeah, well, shit happens, I guess. I just couldn't . . . do those things." He gulps. "And I took a lot of ass whippings for my failure to step up."

We walk a little farther, and he points out Haley's flower shop but doesn't say anything. I wish I could lay my head on his shoulder or at least wrap my arm around his waist, but I can't. And not being able to hurts.

I squeeze his biceps in my hand, hoping he feels a little support. "I'm sorry I brought it up," I say.

"It's okay. How would you know? Besides, he's in prison now for a bunch of stupid shit, and Mom is dead. I can do whatever I want without fear of repercussions."

He stops so abruptly I almost trip. The trees above us whisper in the wind as he holds his arm out.

"See this?" He points to a jellyfish on his arm like it's the most important thing in the world. Whether it really is or its importance lies in changing the subject, I don't know, but I'll go along with it.

I peer at the design on his skin. The tentacles are blasts of color that are breathtaking. My heart leaps in my throat when I see it's wound around dice.

"I see it," I say.

"I got the jellyfish after Dad went to prison. They survive using instinct and adapt as the currents take them into new places." He stares at the ink. "Every time I look at this, I remember to follow my instincts and that no matter where I end up, I can survive." He takes a deep breath and smiles faintly. "Gotta roll with it."

His words bring tears to my eyes. I flutter my lashes in the hope that it dissipates the droplets before they fall down my cheeks.

"You're one of a kind," I say through the lump in my throat.

He gives me a tight smile. "I don't like to talk about this. I think I've just talked about it more with you than I ever have with anyone."

"I'm honored."

"Yeah, well, don't be. I'm just using you for cheap therapy." He winks before raising his eyes and looking around. The fogginess in his beautiful blues is gone as he inhales a lungful of air. "I don't think there's much else to show you."

You've shown me more than I ever imagined.

I'm unable to make sense of all the sides there are of Penn Etling. Who would've thought the guy whom I was sure could speak only in innuendos could be so thoughtful? Smart? Inspiring?

I must be losing my mind.

Turning to ask him where we're headed now, I catch him staring at me. My cheeks flush. "What?" I ask.

"Am I doing a good job of being your friend?"

"Yes."

"Okay. Because I'm not sure what that really looks like. I'm just doing my best."

"You're friends with Claire and Alexis, right?"

I hold my breath because I'm not sure what to expect his reaction to be. I'm not even sure what his friendship with either of them really is . . . and I might not want to know. Although given Claire said I was the *only* person she's ever seen shoot Penn down, perhaps that's my answer. *And I really don't want to know.*

Penn grins and drops his chin. "Yeah. Totally the same thing."

He laughs quietly before raising his head again. His eyes swim with an emotion I can't quite name, but it makes me smile.

"Now let's get back," he says. "I have some fish to catch."

CHAPTER NINETEEN

Penn

I hand Gerald, Mucker's delivery guy, twenty-five bucks. "Keep the change."

"Thanks, man," he says.

"No problem."

I shut the door and head down the hallway toward the kitchen.

The walls of my rental need to be painted. They've needed to be painted since I moved in six years ago. I keep thinking I'll bite the bullet eventually and just do it, but I also keep thinking that maybe I won't live here forever.

I've had a dream for years now, ever since I was a teenager, of building my own place out by the lake. Building it with my own hands. It would have a big fireplace in the living room and a kitchen large enough for my friends to come over and watch a game or exchange presents on Christmas Eve like we used to do at Grandpa's.

It would take a lot of money and even more energy, and I halfway think it would be a waste since it's just me. I don't need all that. And when I think about other options, like finding someone who would be happy living like that, too, I backtrack really fast and reconsider painting.

"Here ya go," I say, sliding the pizza box onto the table. "Half sausage and pepperoni for me, half sausage and mushroom because you're gross for you."

Matt looks up from his phone. "Dane just sent me a text. He's coming home early."

"Why?" I open the box and take out a slice. "I think if I ever went to Florida, I might not come back."

"Right?" He puts his phone on the table. "I guess Mia stepped on a shell and sliced her foot, so the ocean and even walking hurts. And I guess Meredith called him."

"Why? We're there. Why did she bother him?"

I chomp the pizza harder than necessary.

"I guess her schmoozing with the permit people didn't go well. She stayed after I left and I didn't see her again, so I didn't know how it panned out. Dane said she said they won't budge on joining her two little brainchildren, convinced that animals and kids together are a liability."

I point at him. "Makes sense."

"Now she's determined to open some kind of animal sanctuary or some shit, and Dane thinks it's a big opportunity."

My pizza hits the box lid with a thud. "I'm never getting a vacation, am I?"

Matt laughs. "Falling off a ladder will get ya six weeks."

"Except I'm not a baby and could never live with myself for pussying out like that."

"You'd have a hard time living with a bleeding spleen too. Just saying."

We exchange a grin. It lasts a half a second before he can't take it anymore.

"You aren't going to eat that pizza, are you?" he asks.

I pick up the piece I tossed on the box. "You mean, this one?" Sauce squirts onto the table as I take a giant bite. "Yup."

"You're going to die of some strange bacteria. You can't just eat things that have been lying on random surfaces."

"What's the difference between the top of the lid and the bottom? It's the same thing, bud."

"It's not. I can't explain it, but it's not."

"I think they took a part of your brain out when they fixed your uterus."

"My spleen, damn it. Spleen."

I get up and find a couple of glasses. I fill them with ice and grab sodas. "It pains me to say this, but Meredith hasn't been quite as pushy this time."

Matt takes a cup and a soda from me. "I think she just has her hand in more cookie jars this time. She can't micromanage us if she's not there."

"Don't say that," I whine as I sit back down across from him. "You just jinxed us. The universe is now handing its beer off to Meredith's poodles, saying, 'Watch this.'"

Matt laughs. "Sorry. You're probably right."

"No doubt I'm right, and I'm blaming you." I reach inside the box and flick a mushroom from my side to his.

"Dude, don't touch my food," Matt says.

"Don't taint mine with your fungus."

He settles back in his chair. "Speaking of taint . . ."

"Totally not where I thought this was heading." I pop open my soda and pour it into the cup. "But whatever. Go ahead. What's wrong with your taint?"

"Shut the hell up, Etling," he says, shaking his head. "I was trying to segue over to discussing Avery."

"And you were doing that with 'taint'? What kind of animal are you?"

"I was angling toward you tainting her, but you cut me off before I got it out."

I take a long drink of soda. When I set the cup back down, I wipe my mouth off with my hand. "Do you just sit around and wait for the proper segues? Or do you ever just say, fuck it, and say what you want?"

"I try to be polite about things."

"That's your first problem." I take another bite.

As I move around, my chair, a yard-sale find when I moved in years ago, creaks under my weight. One of these days, I'm going to sit down and it's going to drop me on my ass.

"What's going on with you two?" he asks. "I can't figure y'all out. She's not fawning over you, and you're not chasing her tail like a dog in heat, but you clearly want each other. I'm perplexed."

Me too. Me fucking too.

I shove the rest of the slice of pizza into my mouth to give me a couple of extra seconds to contemplate my answer. I get what Avery and I are doing for the most part—nothing. She wants to be the female version of Matt, I think. How do I put that into words for someone else?

Do I say we're friends? Matt will laugh me out of the kitchen. He knows me too well. He'll say the only girls I've ever been just friends with are Haley and Neely and Claire—and almost not even Claire.

There's no way I can say I don't want to fuck her because I'm not sure I can get past the first two words without calling bullshit on myself. I. Want. Her. I want her so much that I've not even been with anyone else since I met her. And it's not because I'm trying to turn over a new leaf. Fuck that. It's because she's the only one I'm thinking about, and when Alexis or someone hits me up, I instantly compare them to Avery and opt out. It's unnerving.

Is there a way to say I want to wrap her around my cock and kiss the ever-loving fuck out of her at the same time? But I can't because if I do, I run the risk of seeing *that* look in her eyes again. The one that seems . . . scared. Or maybe even worse, lonely.

"It's complicated," I say finally.

Matt's eyes go wide. "Motherfucking hell, Etling."

"What?" I tug at my hat in some kind of nervous twitch. "What's that supposed to mean?"

He doesn't answer. Instead, he sits back in the broken chair's companion and crosses his arms over his chest. A grin so smug I'd knock it off his face if he were anyone else sits happily on his lips.

"Fuck you," I say.

"Simmer down, lover boy."

My jaw sets. "I'm not gonna punch you, but I'm not above kicking you off that chair."

He just laughs. He laughs and laughs and laughs, and all the while, I get more confused.

"Why do you find this so funny?" I ask.

"Oh, the same way you think me falling off a ladder is funny."

"You know, I really don't think it is. I just screw with you."

His arms drop to the table with a thud. He leans forward and looks me in the eye. "And I really don't think this is funny either. I think it's awesome."

"No one uses 'awesome' anymore." I don't believe this, but for some reason saying what Avery told me makes me happy.

"Says who?"

"People," I say.

"Well, people are dumb."

Looking at the ceiling and rubbing my eyes, I regret inviting him over for pizza.

"I'm not good at this shit, okay?" I say. "I'm in a jam here and am trying to work it out like I think you would. Or fucking Dane would. Hell, even like Trevor if I'm in a pinch. But I don't know how to do this with her."

"And why not?"

"Because . . ." Because I don't know. Maybe because I'd ruin it. Or it's possible that she'd eventually figure out I'm a screwup and leave.

Even more possible is that she'd want to be serious-serious, and I'm not about that life. "I don't know why. I just know."

"You sound like a child."

"Go fuck yourself."

Matt grins. "Look, the fact that you even realize you don't know how to do *this*, whatever *this* is, with her and want to figure it out, is telling."

"It tells you to leave me alone? Perfect."

His smile fades. "Penn, listen to me. This is *normal.* It's called feelings, and you can't die from them. They won't make your dick stop working, and they won't ruin your life, no matter what you think."

"You're a comedian."

He doesn't look fazed. "Want me to break this down for you in the simplest terms?"

"Honestly, no. But you're going to, anyway. So do it now so you don't come up with a reason to come over tomorrow and talk me into buying you pizza again so you can get the nerve to say your spiel. Just get it over with."

He should be slightly offended by that, but he's not. He might even be proud, and I'm left to ponder where I went wrong in my delivery.

Shit.

"Why are we friends, again?" I ask.

"I ask myself that every day." He gets comfortable, which is a bad sign. "Now, what's happening here is that you're willing to not fuck Avery or pursue her for the ultimate objective of fucking her in exchange for spending time with her."

I scrunch my face. "You make it sound so gross."

He laughs. "It's not gross. It's not something I ever thought I'd see out of you, but here we are. And I'm kind of happy about it."

"Well, good for you."

I pick up my empty soda can and take it to the trash. It's more for a reprieve from Matt's dissection than to clean up the kitchen. As I'm watching the metal can hit the liner, I think about what he said, and I can't dispute it. He's right. I'm not fucking her just so I can be around her.

What does that even mean?

My heart pounds in my chest, and I want to grab my balls and make sure they're still there.

"Penn?"

"What?"

"Breathe."

"I'm breathing," I say.

Matt stands. He picks up his can and walks it over to the trash. "A relationship isn't the worst thing—"

"Whoa. Hold up. How did we get here?"

"Where?"

"To discussing relationships."

Matt grins. "I know you think you'd fail at a relationship, but how do you know? You've never tried."

"Because I'm self-aware. I know how I'm wired, and I'm not wired for exclusive relationships," I insist. "It's all fun and games until someone realizes who you are. Everything is roses until you don't do what they want. The blowback from that is avoidable, and I want to avoid it. Period."

"But that's saying that those things will happen."

"Matt," I say, shaking my head, "they will happen. You can create a facade for the world, like the walls we build at work, and make it palpable. But who you are down deep, the 'you' that someone would get to know if you're in a relationship, is a different person sometimes."

"And sometimes it's better. You can really relate to them. Share things with them. Root for them."

"And sometimes it's worse."

Avery's face pops into my brain. The smile painted on her lips as she showed me her artwork is something I hope she never loses. And the main way to keep that from happening is to keep her away from me.

I need to get laid.

CHAPTER TWENTY

Avery

So . . ." Harper adds pieces of garlic bread to the edges of our plates. "How is it going at the library?"

I carry the plates to the table in the small eating nook. Harper follows me with our drinks.

My new life in Dogwood Lane has been crazy. Balancing both Hometown Hair and the mural means days are full, but days are full doing what I love. I've been here two weeks now—working with Meredith for almost a full week, and I've never been so fulfilled creatively.

And then there's Penn.

I smile to myself as I take a seat next to the wall.

Penn and I have developed the strangest, yet most normal friendship I might have ever had. It surprises me every day when I see him, whether it's at the library or the café or if he comes into the salon just to say hi, how comfortable I am with him.

He genuinely seems to want to be a part of my life. He brought me fudge from Rockery because I mentioned in passing that I'd never tried it. He makes small talk when I get to the library, and he asks questions about the mural like he cares about it. Maybe about me, even.

"The library is going great," I say. "I'm getting the design on the wall so I can start actually painting. Meredith is so excited, and it's hard not to be just as excited when she's gushing about what we're doing. And Penn and Matt," I add, "are transforming the interior of that space with new walls and ceilings. I've never watched someone do that. It's pretty amazing, but they make it look so easy."

Harper sits across from me. "I'm happy for you."

"You know what?" I say, chomping down on a piece of garlic bread. "I'm happy. I can say that and mean it for the first time in my life. This is really a dream come true. A financially unstable dream, of course, but a dream, anyway."

"I warned you," she says with a laugh.

There's something off about her laugh, though. It's restrained, a little pulled back. When I sit back and take her in, I see the worry lines around her eyes.

"If you need me more at the salon, I can be there," I tell her. "You're my first priority."

"I'm not your first priority, and that's fine. I shouldn't be."

She focuses intently on her spaghetti, refusing to meet my eyes. Her voice sounds normal, but her behavior gives her away. The hair on the back of my neck stands up.

"Harper, what's wrong?"

Her fork twists a load of pasta up and into the air before she shoves the whole thing into her mouth. "Your mom called me today."

The words are garbled. I think I misheard. But the somberness on Harper's face tells me I didn't mishear anything.

My mom called her today.

Shit.

"This should be fun," I mumble. Clearing my throat, I look back at her. "What did she want?"

"She wants to tell you herself."

"Don't do this to me. Can we not just get it over with? Please."

The longer it takes her to spill the beans, the more the knot in my stomach feels like a ball of mangled spaghetti. Harper doesn't get worked up about LA stuff; she doesn't care. So whatever this is has to be beyond a "I broke a nail at the Women's Gala" kind of thing.

"Harper?"

She takes a deep breath. "She's divorcing your dad."

I sit still. Do an internal check-in because something about this should shock me or devastate me or trigger some sort of emotion.

Waiting for a feeling to knock me sideways, I close my eyes. I wait longer. How is it possible that apathy and indifference are what I feel? My mother is divorcing my dad. Yet . . . I've got nothing.

"You okay?" Harper asks.

"I'm fine." I open my eyes. "Why is she doing that?"

One brow lifts. "She's in love with the twenty-seven-year-old son of the owner of Ialine Productions."

"The same son of Michael Ialine that she tried to get me to date a couple of months ago? He's younger than me." I push my plate away. "Wow. I don't even know what to say."

My stomach burps, the acid quickly building as all the pieces come together. The fact that my parents' marriage is ending is no surprise. Quite frankly, I'm surprised it lasted this long. But to see Mom end it to get a leg up in her career—because that's what this is, no doubt—is utterly disgusting.

Ugh.

"I wonder if she even knows his middle name," I say.

"That's random as hell."

"Not really. My mom is detonating her marriage over a boy toy that she knows nothing about."

"Maybe she does. You don't know that."

I slow blink. "She doesn't. Trust me. She's seeing her name in lights right now, and that's the only name she's worried about. I'm not even shocked. This was another decision based on what's best for her."

Harper bites her lip. "Do you want a drink?"

"Actually, yes."

She scoots her chair back and heads to the kitchen. While she preps a rum and cola, I think about the bomb that's been dropped in my lap.

Should I call them? Should I care? Is Dad okay?

Dad left Mom once. That's what landed me in Dogwood Lane the first time.

Harper places a drink in front of me before taking her seat again.

"You know my sister will love this," I say. "The sympathy she'll get when this hits the magazines will fuel Oakley's fire for days."

"I wish I could say that's not true, but you're right."

She takes a drink as I twirl my cup in my hand. Being away from that life even for just a couple of weeks is enough to make it seem even crazier.

"Sometimes I think the 'anonymous source quoted with insights' is her. I know it sounds bizarre, but I believe it's possible."

Harper slides her plate back in front of her and lifts a piece of garlic bread. "Okay. Let's change subjects."

It's no wonder I love this woman. She gets me. She knows I'm not ready to talk this to death. Besides, what is there to say?

"To what?" I ask.

She shrugs. "Anything is fine with me." She crunches through the bread and watches me, crumbs dropping onto the table. She grins. "By 'anything,' I really mean Penn."

Just hearing his name makes me relax. Instantly, I imagine his laugh and feel the energy that ripples off his body.

Over the last few days, it's been harder and harder to toe the line with him. I haven't forgotten my reasons for keeping him at arm's length. He's still adamantly in the "don't want more than a fuck-buddy" camp. It's just that when I see him be kind day after day, watch him work with an attention to detail that most people don't give a crap about, and witness how he treats his friends and those he works with, it's hard to remember all the reasons for staying away. Harper was right—he's a great guy.

"Penn is . . . Penn," I tell Harper. "I don't know what you want to talk about."

"We can start with the smile you got as soon as I said his name."

"I . . ." I start to argue with her, but I can feel my cheeks ache. "You were right about him."

"In what way?"

"He's nice."

"That's it? 'He's nice'?"

I laugh. "What do you want me to say? I mean, I didn't expect him to be all the things he is. There's a lot more to Penn than I imagined. It's like . . ." I think about how to say it. "He's like a mural that the longer you look at it, the more interesting bits you find."

I think back to the stories about his dad. Why the fish on his arm is so important to him. All the things he knows about Dogwood Lane and the love in his eyes as he speaks about the town in which he was born.

The way he ribs Matt and the respect he has for Dane, even if he calls him a dumbass at least once a day.

His smile pops into my head as he tells me about cutting Claire's hair in preschool and ghost-hunting with Matt as a little boy. And the dice tattoo. The damn dice tattoo. It occurs to me that I know more about him than I did my best friends in LA.

A chill races over my skin as a realization hits me out of left field.

My stomach sinks.

A lack of respect is what's taking down my parents' marriage. It's the root of why I left California. I tout that I want something real all the time in all aspects of my life. Penn heard me, and he's volunteered sensitive information about himself to forge a friendship with me.

I haven't even respected him enough to tell him we slept together—a piece of considerably more important information that I would be pissed if he held back.

"What's wrong?" Harper asks.

I shift in my seat and stare blankly at the wall. "I just had an awful realization about myself."

"What kind of a realization?"

My attention lands on my aunt. The concern on her face melts a little of the anger I feel—anger at myself. I sink back in my chair and sigh.

"You know, it always hurt my feelings when my mom would forget the things that were important to me. My ballet recitals or parent-teacher conferences. She even missed me walking across the stage for graduation. She got there twenty minutes late."

Harper frowns.

"But it hurt so bad to always be on the fourth back burner that I finally stopped telling her things. If she didn't know, she couldn't be expected to show up. It was a self-preservation type of thing."

"It makes sense. Probably not super healthy, but it makes sense."

"But it's turned me into someone that wants that connection with people, Harper, but I don't always give it. Maybe I can't give it. Like, I want you to care about the things in my life. Not 'you' but the theoretical 'you,'" I say when she looks confused. "I want someone to want to show up for me. But I don't always give them a chance to."

"Sounds like you have a problem on your hands."

Ouch.

This stings a little, but she's right. And this isn't my mom's problem. It's mine.

I think of the sadness on Penn's face as he shared the stories about his dad. The man who thinks he's allergic to relationships is better at them than the woman desperate for one.

"You know," she says, testing the waters. "I suck at relationships. Fact. But I'm really good at friendships. And the first block you have to lay in a friendship is trust. A part of that is trusting them with bits and pieces of your heart and believing they'll show up when you need them."

She pats my hand before she gets to her feet. As if she knows I need a few minutes alone, she gathers our plates.

"I'm going to clean the kitchen up. If you need me, I'll be in there, okay?"

I nod. My eyes are watery, so I don't look at her. I just keep thinking about Penn and how I owe him so much more than I've given him. If nothing else, I owe him the truth. About me and about us.

Sliding my phone out of my pocket, I find his number. It rings four times before he answers.

"Yeah?"

"Hey, Penn. It's Avery."

"Hey. What's up?"

I slosh my drink around, watching the liquid slam into each wall of the glass. "Are you busy right now?"

"Depends who is asking and why."

"Well, I'm asking, and it's because—"

"Then nope. Not busy," he says with a chuckle. "Doesn't matter why."

A shy smile touches my lips. "Great. Can I meet you somewhere?"

"Well, here's the deal: I'm elbow deep in paint."

"Are you at the library?" I gasp. "Are you messing with my mural?"

"Calm down," he says with a laugh. "I'm not at the library, and I'd never touch that mural. It's art."

A ball of warmth settles in my stomach. "Sorry. Okay. Can I come to where you are, then?"

"I'm at my house, but you're welcome to come over. I'd meet you somewhere else, but it would take me forever to get this paint off me. It's in my hair. I think it's in my nostrils, even."

I laugh. "Okay. I'll be there in a little bit."

"Bring your painting clothes."

"I don't have painting clothes," I say.

"Then what do you wear to paint? I've ruined these jeans for sure."

I rise to my feet. The anxiety about telling him the truth about us subsides as the excitement at seeing him takes over. "Usually something I don't want to ruin, but I don't usually paint like a child so it's not a real problem."

"Well, I do. So just prepare yourself for that."

"Will do. See ya soon, Penn."

"See ya, Ave."

The line goes dead.

I stare at his name on the screen. The reason for the call and for going to see him blasts back and hits me straight in the heart.

What am I about to get myself into?

CHAPTER TWENTY-ONE

Avery

"Come in," Penn shouts.

I push open a well-worn door that designers would pay big money to replicate. It's the color of tobacco with streaks of caramel and has enough dings and dents that I would ask if it was purchased at an antique store if I didn't know better. Penn may be many things, but an antique collector, I'd venture to say, is not one of them.

The house is airy. Ceilings go on for what feels like forever in the main entryway. The wallpaper is probably from the seventies with a cream background and orange-and-brown flowerlike designs. A chandelier hangs, and the light dances from the crystals dripping off it.

"I'm in here," Penn calls out.

His voice comes from ahead and to my left. An oversize doorway with ornate trim in solid wood leads me to him.

He's standing in the far corner, a paint roller on an extended handle in his hand. He's covered. White paint is everywhere, including his nose.

"Getting any on the wall?" I tease.

He grins. "What brings you by on this fine evening?"

I mosey around the room, taking in his space. "Oh, just bored."

"Really?"

"Yeah."

A couch is shoved into the center of the room. It's a blue-patterned corduroy, and I flop down on it.

"You should really cover this," I tell him.

"Let's just say I didn't expect to get this messy." He sets the roller down in a tray of paint. He grabs a towel off the back of a covered rocking chair and wipes his face with it. "This is why I leave the painting to professionals."

"Were you just so inspired by me that you had to redo your house? That's adorable, Penn," I joke.

"It was really a way to lure you over here." He winks as he walks across the room and sits on a limestone fireplace ledge. "So, what's happening?"

I point at his face. "You missed a spot."

"Just one?" He chuckles, wiping the white blob off the tip of his nose. "Did I get it?"

"I think you got all you're gonna get."

His hand falls slowly to his side, a soberness trickling across his face.

"Good thing I'm practiced in accepting that, huh?" he asks.

My throat squeezes shut as his eyes find mine. They stay locked together for a split second—long enough for me to know for sure that he was talking about me.

Finally, he looks away. "Nah, I've been thinking about painting for a long time. Just decided to bite the bullet and get it over with. I was tired of knowing it had to be done."

Boy, do I understand that.

"I never feel that way about painting or creating," I say. "I do feel that way, though, about human interaction."

He laughs. "Depending on the human, I do too."

His chuckle peters away, and a silence descends on us. I know he's wondering why I'm here.

An energy jolts through my veins as I try to get the courage to tell him. I want to word vomit and run. Just spew, "Hey, we slept together a bunch of years ago and I've known it from the minute I saw you but didn't tell you and now I feel like an asshole so we're cool, right?"

I force a swallow and eke out a nervous grin. "Penn . . . ," I say but am stopped when his phone rings through the room.

He gets up and finds it next to the paint can. I watch him look at the screen. He silences it.

"It was Alexis," he says.

"Oh."

His shoulders move in a circle as if he's working out a knot. He crosses the room and sits on the limestone again.

"I haven't talked to her since that night at Mucker's."

"Penn—"

"No," he says, waving me off. "I know you probably don't care, and that's fine. I just wanted to say that for whatever reason and I did and now we can move on." He works the towel between his hands as he looks at the floor. "I probably just made this super weird, didn't I?"

"Actually," I say, forcing a swallow, "I was going to make it weird. So, I'm glad you did it first."

His head snaps to mine. A look of concern splashes over his eyes as the towel stills. "What do you mean?"

I don't know.

Suddenly, I'm not sure what I'm doing.

My mind races, wondering why I thought this was a good idea and pointing out that even if I level with him, all it is going to get me is knowing I did the right thing. *Why stir the pot when the pot was fine to start with?*

I look into his eyes.

My heart beats so loud that I can't hear him speak. I see his mouth move and watch his jaw tighten in suspicion. It's not a look of anger, but one of worry. Like he's worried about me. Not about what I'm going to say or how it will affect him, but how it will affect me.

I want to cry.

"What's going on, Ave?" he asks softly.

I take a deep, shaky breath. "I've been thinking a lot about you."

"Nice."

I smile. "You've really been an open book with me. I don't think you do that a lot, do you?"

"Nah. People know what's happened in my life because they've been around for it. But I don't talk about it. It's none of their business."

"But you told me."

He flinches at the observation. It's as if it's never occurred to him that telling me intimate details about his life was an anomaly. He works it over in his mind before tossing the towel on the floor.

"I guess it just came out," he says.

"Well, it occurred to me tonight that I haven't really told you anything about me."

"No. You haven't."

"I know."

"Why not?"

I move around until I'm as comfortable as I can be. I have so many things to say and I don't know where to really start but starting with "we had sex" seems rougher than my family. So I go there.

"My mother is Jasmine Perry," I say point-blank.

"Okay."

I wait for the name to sink in. For the slow blink. For the gush about how wonderful her movies are and if she's as amazing in real life as she is on-screen and if I really know James Hollyfield, the biggest actor in Hollywood who my mom is (correctly) rumored to have had an affair with.

When a few seconds pass and Penn doesn't even blink, I figure I'll break it down for him.

"Jasmine Perry from *The Breaker Party. Cull and McGill,*" I say, naming off a couple of her biggest movies. "*Top Shelf.*"

He nods slowly, as if the pieces of who she is and who I am are hard to fit together.

"I know. It's hard to believe," I say. "She looks like she's twenty-five and is in better shape than me and—"

"She's a picture on a screen, Avery. She doesn't hold a fucking candle to you."

It's not the words so much but how he says it that stills something deep inside me. The genuine kiss of the words, the honesty in his tone assuages my anxiety over this whole conversation a bit—not to mention how amazing it makes me feel for him to say something that sweet. No one has ever said anything like that when it comes to comparing my mom and me.

"Penn . . . I don't know what to say."

"'Thank you' works fine." He grins. "So that's why you were talking about not embarrassing her and people using you. Your mom is famous."

"Basically."

He folds his hands together and rests his elbows on his knees. "Is there a reason you're telling me this?"

"I told you. I haven't said much of anything about me and you have, and I wanted to even the playing field a little."

"I'm not in this *friendship* for information."

My throat tightens. "Then what are you in it for?"

He stands as if he can't sit any longer. He moves aimlessly around the room. "I don't know. You're just really easy to talk to and not bad to look at." He grins at the floor. "Really, though, being with you makes me feel like I'm seen. Like you don't care that I *allegedly* blew a snot rocket into Mrs. Johnson's gradebook my freshman year. And you don't look at me and see the goofy guy that everyone knows I am." He looks up at me with a hesitation that stops my breath. "You see the guy I think my grandpa told me I could be."

My chest heaves as his voice starts to crack. "Penn, don't you make me cry, you dickhead."

He laughs, wiping his nose with the back of his hand. A white streak of paint is left in its wake. "Now I feel like Matt, all pussified with feelings and shit. If you ever tell him I acted like this, I'll deny it."

"I would never," I say with a laugh. "But you're right. I do see a man that could be anything he wanted to be. You work harder than anyone. You don't miss a detail, whether it's when you're building a wall or looking at sketches or listening to Matt tell a story. You're kind and can be sweet and—"

"Let's stop there. I'm starting to feel weird." He makes a face.

I laugh. "Fine. But you get the picture."

"One I'm going to try to forget," he jokes. "So, your mom's a movie star. What about your dad?"

"He directs movies. He hasn't had a hit, though, in ten or fifteen years, which is why my mom called to tell me she's divorcing him for a guy with better connections."

"That's harsh."

"What? The way I said it or the way she's acting?"

"Both, but I don't fault you for it." He runs a hand down his chin. "You and I are alike in a strange way."

"How do you figure?"

"Both have fuckups for parents. Both turned out okay, more or less—more for you, less for me, but you get the idea."

"Stop that," I say, shaking my head. "You turned out great. Especially considering the circumstances. You have to stop all that negative internal monologue."

He grins. "Did you hear that on a television show?"

"No." I laugh. "I heard it from Harper, actually."

He joins in the laughter, settling across from me again. There's a sweet look of contentedness on his face as he studies me that warms my heart.

"So the objective here is for you to tell me things about you, right?"

"Basically. I mean, if you care."

He nods like I'm crazy. "For sure, I care." His face lights up. "I have an idea."

"That scares me."

"As it should." He drags the rocker from the other side of the room and places it facing the sofa. "Here's what we're going to do because I don't trust you at this point not to get all sappy because fun fact: I don't do . . . *that* . . . well."

I giggle. I fucking giggle.

"Okay," I say. "What are we doing?"

"Rapid-fire questions that will satisfy your need to tell me things and my desire to know certain things in a painless and feeling-free kind of way. Deal?"

"Deal."

"Good." He gets settled in front of me. "Dog or cat?"

"Really, Penn?"

He sighs dramatically and looks at the ceiling. "Dog or cat, Ave?"

"Dog, I guess," I say. "But that makes it sound like I have a thing against cats, and I don't. I love cats, except for the hairless ones because they look evil and unnatural."

"The definition of rapid-fire is that we do this fast. That means you can't expound on every question or we'll be here all day."

"But you said you want to know things," I point out.

"I said I want to know *certain things*, not all the things." He sticks his tongue in his cheek. "Got it?"

"Sorry." I laugh. "I'll try to do better."

"Great." He grins. "Pepperoni or mushrooms?"

"Pepperoni. Never mushrooms."

"I'm letting you pass because you got the correct answer, but remember: rapid-fire."

"I didn't know there were correct answers," I say.

He just grins. "Blush or Bashful."

"I don't know what that means."

"Correct answer. Morning or evening?"

"Evening," I say, laughing.

"Truck or SUV?"

"Who is driving?"

"Me."

"Then truck," I say matter-of-factly.

I don't add how hot he looks in his truck with the big tires and black-on-black motif. He did say this was rapid-fire, after all.

The look in his eyes changes. It morphs into a darker, more serious vibe.

"House in town or cabin in the woods?" he asks.

I tap my chin. "Cabin in the woods, but I hate phrasing it like that because it sounds scary. I mean, did you see that movie—"

"Rapid-fire."

"Sorry," I say, trying not to laugh.

He narrows his eyes. "Would you ever fillet a fish?"

"Ew. No."

"Wrong answer," he says, falling back in his chair. "You were batting a thousand, and then you go and fuck up the most important question of them all."

I burst into laughter, smacking him on the knee. "Those were subjective questions."

"With right answers." He crosses his arms over his chest. "You really wouldn't fillet a fish?"

"No. Absolutely not. I have no interest in killing anything."

"I'd kill it. You'd prepare it."

"I don't care," I say, my voice a full octave higher than usual. "I don't even really eat fish."

Like I've just called him the worst name in the book, he jumps to his feet. "You don't like fish?"

"No," I say, standing too. "Is that somehow offensive to you?"

We stand toe to toe. There's a smile sitting just behind his lips that he's holding back. I know I shouldn't stare at them, but I can't help it. I want to see it break.

He moves one step and then two. His body shifts so that we're even closer. The air fills with a mixture of his cologne and wet paint, and the two things, possibly my two favorite scents in the world, wallop me.

My breathing gets ragged, my chest rising and falling at an increased pace. I look up at his eyes to see that they're hooded.

I shiver, the proximity of his body in addition to the heat in his eyes causing a riot to break out beneath my skin.

"Is this offensive?" he asks, moving closer yet again. His Adam's apple bobs as he stands just inches from me. "I know I said I wouldn't kiss you, and I'm trying like a motherfucker to back away right now . . ."

My brain shuts down. It's like my body knows it's going to set off an alarm, so it just cuts off the blood supply.

Our bodies are nearly touching. The fabric of our shirts almost colliding as we drag in labored breaths. He reaches for me and then stops, his hand dropping to his side.

Whether it's right or wrong, I want to kiss him. I need to feel his touch. And I think he wants, and possibly needs, that from me too.

"Do you think we can manage this and not mess everything up?" I whisper.

"I don't know," he says with a husk in his tone that is like a match to my libido.

"We agreed this was a bad idea."

"No, *you* said it was a bad idea," he points out. "I agreed to agree with you."

I grin. "Well, it *was* a bad idea. It might be a bad idea now. But . . ."

"I have one stipulation," he says softly.

My stomach clenches at the tenderness in his voice. My legs are heavy. Every piece of my body from head to toe readies in anticipation of Penn.

He reaches down and places a hand on my hip, his fingers wrapping to the small of my back. I gasp at the contact of his palm cradling a part of me I usually hide from people.

"What's that?" I ask.

"If I kiss you, you cannot look at me like you did last time." He dips his head so he's looking at me dead in the eye. "If you can't promise me that, I will walk away."

I know what he means. I know exactly how I looked at him the last time, and the fact that it apparently still bothers him makes my body sag into his touch.

"I promise," I say.

He takes his sweet time guiding me in front of him. His other hand cups my other hip and lights my body on total fire. Every cell is singed with heat and sensation overload.

I'll never be the same after this.

"Let's roll with it, then," he whispers.

That line, those five little words are enough to make me remember what else I wanted to talk to him about.

"Penn," I say as his lips find mine.

All. Thoughts. Cease.

He jerks me forward so there's nothing between us but the clothes on our bodies. His fingers skim the skin beneath the hem of my shirt, leaving a trail of electricity behind. My nipples bead against the pressure of his chest tight against them.

The hardness of his body is a glorious juxtaposition of the gentleness of his lips, and I think I might die in this moment, in this house, and in his arms.

His palms drag against the sides of my body, skin on skin. His hands are rough from holding lumber all day but handle me with such care that my legs go weak.

I run my fingers through his hair, pulling him closer to me. He tastes sweet, like soda, and smells like everything I've ever wanted.

I'm here for this. Checklist be damned. To hell with my internal voice and the bruises from people who didn't deserve my time.

This is where I want to be.

"Penn," I whisper as our kiss breaks.

He kisses across the side of my face, along my jaw, and behind my ear. I angle my body to try to get some contact with my clit because I think I might explode.

His hair slips through my fingers as I close my eyes and feel him kissing along my shoulder. Cool air wraps around my body as my shirt is caught in his arm and pulled toward my shoulder.

I'm ready to volunteer to remove it altogether when he pulls away.

His eyes are wild, his breath as uneven as mine. He steps back and looks at me like he's just seeing me for the first time.

My heart races, adrenaline filling my body as I take in the bewildered look on his face.

Something is wrong. Something is very, very wrong, and I have no idea what it is.

I tug my shirt back down. "What's going on?"

He runs his hands over his head, a look of confusion painted across his gorgeous face.

A sinking feeling settles in my stomach. I fight the bile that's threatening to come up my throat.

My mind is on overdrive, re-creating the last few seconds and trying to figure out where things went wrong. But there's nothing I can come up with, and he's not answering me.

"Penn?"

"Um, you have some paint on your face," he says. He tugs at his hair before dropping his hands to his sides. "I have to meet Matt in a couple of minutes. I forgot. Can I call you later?"

"Yeah," I say, making the word into a three-syllable answer. "Sure."

He nods and heads toward the door.

I follow in a state of pure confusion. There are so many questions popping into my head as my brain turns back on—so many that I don't know where to start.

Rejection begins to take over as he swings the door open like he's dismissing me. It's as if he got what he wanted, or discovered he really didn't want it to start with, and is just clicking the off button.

Fuck that.

He swings the door open. "I'll call you."

I nod, untrusting of my voice or the feeling of pressure on the bridge of my nose. I won't cry. Not in front of him.

He stands still as I walk out. I don't bother to look up at him or tell him not to call. He won't. I'm not sure I want him to right now, anyway.

Climbing into the car, I catch the door to the house closing in my peripheral vision. His overt lie about Matt ripples through my brain, and a dose of humiliation washes over me.

I realize I'm not going to make it to Harper's.

Tears stream down my face as I look at the closed door with confusion.

"Guess I couldn't look at you that way, but you can me, huh?"

With tears trickling onto my shirt, I back out onto the street and head home.

CHAPTER TWENTY-TWO

Penn

What. The. Actual. Fuck?

The engine roars as I hammer it up Matt's road. I didn't call ahead to warn him I'm coming—or to warn him I'm coming with this kind of attitude. He won't be pleased, but neither am I at the moment.

There has to be some logical explanation for the pair of dice on Avery's side. I'm not good at logic or math, but Matt is. I just need to calm down and wait for him to give me the odds and prove that Avery Perry is not Abby.

Why would she lie to me? Then or now?

How stupid do I look right now?

I slam the steering wheel with the palm of my hand.

"This is why you don't actually like people," I tell myself. "They never are who they say they are."

I think of all the things I've told her, how I half-assed broke down about my dad, and wonder what she was thinking. Wow, this guy still has daddy issues ten years later.

Fuck.

I slide my truck against the curb. The rubber squeals at the contact, but I don't care. I hop out and make my way up Matt's sidewalk like a wounded badger, ready to fight. He must have heard my truck because the door opens before I even get there.

"This is gonna be fun," he grumbles. "What happened? And why are you covered in paint?"

I storm in. The door shuts behind me.

"Do you need a beer?" he asks.

"I don't know what I motherfucking need."

"Beer it is. Follow me."

We make it to the kitchen. As he rummages around his fridge, the disbelief starts to turn more into anger. And embarrassment.

Matt hands me a bottle, top already off. "Drink before you talk. Let's get a head start on the situation here."

I eye him over the rim of the bottle as I do as I'm told. The liquid is cold and shocking, but I don't taste it. I don't feel it pool in my stomach like I usually do. I don't feel anything other than the overwhelming sensation that everything is wrong.

We stand in Matt's kitchen, the one he decorated with old farm utensils. It's an odd motif, and I've told him this a hundred times.

"Do you ever think about taking that old hook and throwing it at the wall?" I ask. "Could be a good stress reliever."

"First, I think it would break. It's from the 1800s. Second, I don't like hanging drywall that much."

"That's why I'm here," I say.

"For drywalling tips?"

"No. For your logic. You're good at that shit."

Matt chuckles under his breath. "What did you do now?"

"Nothing," I say with as much emphasis on the word as I can place. "Believe it or not, I didn't do *anything*. Not anything wrong, anyway. I did everything right. For the first motherfucking time in my life, I did it all right, Matt."

He drops into a chair. Unlike my chairs at home, it doesn't squeak. I'm too amped up to sit, so I just pace across the kitchen instead.

"Okay," Matt says. "I'm ready. What are we dealing with here?"

"What do you think?"

"Penn, no offense, but you could be talking about virtually anything right now. I'm scared to even guess."

I whirl around and look at him. Surely he knows what I'm talking about. I don't get mad like this. I've never stormed inside his house and rambled like a lunatic. My heart never feels like it's going to burst out of my chest, either, and in the case there's a freak exception, it's never, ever about a woman.

Ever.

"Oh," Matt says. "Avery."

"I did everything right," I promise. "I tried not to say anything stupid. I didn't chase after her. I was polite, Matt. *Polite.* Me. I was polite." My empty bottle goes into the trash. "I was thoughtful, I thought."

He doesn't say anything. It's like he wants me to word vomit everything before he reacts, like maybe I'm going to let some offense slip and make his job easy.

There's no offense. He'll see.

"We talked about things," I say. "You know, we discussed things that go beyond the weather. I thought we . . ." My insides bunch up and I don't know what I think. Or thought. Or should think.

This is all a mess.

Any humor in Matt's eyes evaporates as he sees the pain I can't hide in mine. He leans up and places his bottle in the middle of the table. I don't know if he's offering it to me or he's just getting it out of the way, but I take it. He doesn't say a germophobic word about it.

"May I ask what happened?" he asks.

"Do you know how I told you when I first met her that I thought I knew her?" I ask.

"Yes."

"But neither of us knew an Avery Perry, so we just assumed I was mixing her up with someone else."

"Right. And I told you not to mention that—"

"—so she wouldn't think I was a dick! This is your fault, Matt!"

He hangs his head. I think the son of a bitch is laughing, but I can't be sure.

I hold my forehead in my hands. My temples throb, probably from trying to process so much information in a short period of time.

"This is not my fault," he says. "Whatever in the hell happened to set you off like a hillbilly firecracker is not my fault."

"If I would've told her I knew her, then this would be a different story."

"So you do know her?" he asks.

I yank out a chair across from him. But I don't sit. Instead, I drape my arms over the back of it and look at my friend.

My world is imploding. A night that meant so much to me so long ago is now relevant—no, entwined—with a girl I just met that I probably really like if I let myself think about it. And I was starting to let myself think about it, I think.

"Do you remember the day my dad got arrested?" I ask.

A shadow falls on Matt's face as he nods. "Yes."

I close my eyes as I remember the rage in my dad's eyes. The way he held my mom like she was a rag doll. How she screamed at me to leave him alone, but I knew that if I did, not only would the cycle of abuse continue but also one of us would end up dead. And it wouldn't be him.

He gripped my throat. Spit in my face. Explained, in detail, what a disappointment I was to the Etling name. As I listened to his venom and felt the pain of his hits, both verbal and physical, I knew I had to do something. And when he finally let me go with a promise to continue our *discussion* later, after he had one with my mother, he locked me out of the house.

In my truck a few minutes later from a couple of streets away, I called the police and told them where they'd find a domestic dispute and enough cocaine to lock my dad up for the rest of his life.

"I thought he was going to kill me that night," I say. "There was something different about him. It was evil. Just inhuman, honestly." I take a huge swallow of air. "I'm the one that called on him."

The words taste bitter on my tongue. Still, a weight is lifted from my shoulders as I expel the truth to someone for the very first time.

My chest shakes as I drag in uneven breaths.

I called the police on my own father.

I look up at Matt warily. His eyes grow wide as he absorbs this information.

"Penn, man, I had no idea. That must've been hard as hell."

That's one way to put it.

"Not my favorite memory in the world," I say. "But after I did it, I drove out to the lake. I didn't know what to do."

"Why didn't you come over?"

"It's hard to go to someone's house that has a decent family when yours is as fucked up as mine was. It makes you feel like there's something wrong with you."

"There's nothing wrong with you, Penn. You are not your parents."

I shake my head. "I know that. But I couldn't put on a face for you and Dane."

He wants to offer me his sympathy. There's a reminder coming that everything worked out and my mom died having had a little peace and that I turned out okay. But he keeps it all held back. I'm glad for it.

"I was sitting out there," I say. "It was Fourth of July weekend. I watched the fireworks and pretended my grandpa was there because he'd understand. I realized he was trying to prepare me for this for years, and I just . . . I felt so fucking alone. I didn't think anyone would understand." My lips turn upward. "And then this girl came out of nowhere."

Matt's face transforms into shock when he sees where I'm going with this.

"I still don't know how she found me. No one ever comes down that path, but she did. She had hair the color of coal and the thickest black eyeliner. Her lips were stained like she'd been biting them all day." I chuckle at the thought of Avery looking like that now. "She was also in the same mood as me."

"It was Avery?"

"It was *Abby*," I say, lifting a brow. "We hung out that night. Talked about our shitty lives and how much our DNA might affect us, whether we had a shot at being normal people or not. And we had sex and she left and all I remember specifically about her was that her name was Abby and she had a pair of dice tattooed on her rib cage. A 'fuck you' to her parents, she said." I tip back the rest of Matt's beer. "Before she left, she wished me luck and told me, 'Roll with it.' I never saw her again."

Talking about this night with Avery in mind feels too hard to believe. But it's true. I know it in my gut. It explains so much. Why I was drawn to her in the first place. Why I kept thinking I knew her. Why I felt a connection or some crazy shit with her from day one.

Matt stands up, his hands stuck in his pockets. "And I'm guessing you somehow figured out that Avery was Abby."

"That's where you come in."

"I'm not following you."

I force a swallow. "What are the odds that Avery would have the exact same tattoo in the exact same spot as Abby?"

"Same numbers?"

"Five and five, and in the exact same position."

"I mean, I don't know the exact probability, but it's not good." He grimaces. "But I think you know that."

I toss Matt's bottle in the trash too.

Even with his validation that I'm not crazy to think she is the same girl as the night on the lake, I can't make sense of it. Why wouldn't she say anything to me? She has to remember who I am. How many guys are named Penn, after all?

Because I didn't lie to her.

That night carried me through the darkest part of my life. If she hadn't shown up, I don't know what I would've done. I was almost frantic when she arrived, from replaying the call I had just made and understanding the ramifications that would be coming my way.

Would I have done something stupid? Cracked? Acted out? Maybe. I don't know. But Abby—Avery—showing up gave me something to think about instead.

But now everything feels different, like there's a cloud that I can't shake.

"I asked her when I first met her if I knew her, and she acted really weird," I say. "It's because I did."

Matt comes around the table and puts a hand on my shoulder. "You're going to be okay."

"Why did she lie to me? Or not tell me? Do you know how stupid I look right now?"

"You always look stupid." He shoves my shoulder before letting it go. "You just need to talk to her."

"And say what?" I fight back the urge to get angry again. "She's always saying how people just want shit from her. I didn't ask her for anything, and she couldn't even tell me who she really is." I snort. "She wants something real. I was a hell of a lot more real than her."

Matt sighs. "I can't argue that logic. Hey, look at that. You're being logical. I'm standing here watching the transformation of Penn Etling. What a day."

I give him a menacing look, to which he laughs.

"Maybe she figured you'd just think of her like one of your harem."

"I don't have a harem," I say through gritted teeth.

"Maybe she thought it was pointless to rehash that night because you two weren't going to have anything real together, anyway. You don't do that kind of thing, and you've made sure everyone knows it. Or maybe that night meant something to her, too, and she didn't want you to make a mockery out of it."

I shake my head because he doesn't get it. She wasn't afraid to make a connection with me because we already had. We fucking connected. I know that because it's gone now, and I feel the loss in the middle of my fucking chest.

"This is exactly why you're better off not to care," I tell him. "Do people do this all the time? Do they care about people and spend their energy constantly trying to make things right?"

He laughs. "Yes and no. This kind of thing is unique, though. Most people remember who they sleep with."

I fire him a warning glare. He ignores it.

"You do this all the time, anyway," he says. "Who snuck pizza into the hospital for me when I was on a liquids-only diet after I fell and was starving? You. And who went to Lorene's and fixed her step without being asked? You. And who unclogged the gutters at the café last fall because the guy they hired to do it didn't show? You." He shrugs. "You already spend your energy making sure people are okay. This time, it just happens to be a woman you aren't actively fucking."

"It's not that easy."

"Of course it's not. It never is. Things always look easier on paper. But you just have to make a choice about how you want to handle it and go be a man and do it."

I slow blink. "Does that mean you aren't just going to tell me what to do?"

"That's exactly what it means."

I balk. "But you always make my adult decisions for me."

"And I've been waiting for the day to arrive to put that back on you. Lucky for me, today is that day."

Maybe it's lucky for him, but it's shitty for me because I don't know what to do.

My spirits fall as I realize there is no easy answer, and if there were, Matt wouldn't give it to me, anyway. This is the shit I don't want in my life. I avoid it at all costs. Yet here I am, giving a fuck, and I can't turn it off.

"Can I get a rain check?" I ask.

"Ha."

He studies me as if he isn't sure I can handle this task. I can't. I try to get that point across as strongly as I can, but when he smiles, I know I've failed.

"I'll tell you what," he says. "I'll give you a road map. Will that help?"

"Will it end with a solution?"

"Yes."

"Then it will help. Gimme."

He takes another bottle of beer out of the fridge and opens it. "Option one: go fuck Alexis. Perfect way to nuke this entire situation. Avery will never talk to you again."

I wince. Not an option.

"Option two: admit you can live without her but want to be on decent terms. Go home. Finish painting or whatever you're doing that has you covered in white paint. In a day or two, someone will hit you up and you'll go do Penn things with them and your life will be back to normal. You'll see her at work, and you'll be the old you."

I don't want to be the old me. Not really. The old me didn't have Avery.

"Option three: decide you can't live without Avery in your life. Go to Harper's and hear her out. Consider that maybe this was complicated for her, too, and that you want to give her the benefit of the doubt just like I did the night you wrecked my truck."

"I didn't wreck it. A deer did."

"Anyway," he says, "if you take option three, you'll have to suck up any embarrassment or fragile-male-ego syndrome you might have. Approach this option with the understanding that maybe she's not feeling too great about this either."

For the first time since I left my house, enough adrenaline has emptied out of my veins for me to think back clearly.

There were tears in her eyes. Was she crying? Did I make her cry?

Fuck.

My stomach feels heavy and rotten as I picture her pretty face twisted up. I run my hands down my face as I wonder if she'll even talk to me now.

"Now the choice is yours, but I have to go to Dane's. They're home and Neely is down with the stomach flu, so he needs help getting the car unpacked."

We head to the door. Matt follows me to the driveway. I start to climb into my truck when I stop.

"Hey, Matt," I say as he approaches his vehicle.

"Yeah?"

"Not to be all girlie, but thank you."

"It's called having class, not being a girl, you idiot," he says. "And you're welcome."

"You could've just said you're welcome."

"Bye."

I turn on the engine and grip the steering wheel. My gaze lands on the dice tattoo on my arm. My stomach flip-flops. I've looked at this ink a million times since I got it, and it always brings me a certain feeling. That's different today, and I hate it.

I can't do this forever. I have to figure it out.

Sitting in the driveway, waving at Matt as he backs out beside me, I think about everything he said. There's really only one option.

Jerking the truck into reverse, I pull out onto the road.

CHAPTER TWENTY-THREE

Avery

"I tried."

My reflection is blurred by the steam from my shower. I wipe it off again, but it just steams right back up, kind of like my eyes have done for the last hour. I blink them clear, and they fill right back up.

Crying makes me mad. I hate it. I'm so good at not doing it. It goes with the territory of having your feelings continually hurt—you learn to not cry. The fact that I'm crying now, or on the verge of it, is really freaking annoying.

I give my teeth a quick brush before heading into the hall. Harper is watching television in the living room, some show about a hot veterinarian who rescues animals in destitute conditions. I wonder vaguely if there's an equally hot people doctor who rescues humans who are stuck in the same routines over and over.

Maybe I tried too hard, I think as I head into my bedroom. *Maybe my attempt at being real with Penn scared the crap out of him.*

Getting dressed, I mull the incident over again.

He was fine until we kissed. No, he was better than fine. He was the Penn I've gotten to know.

What on earth made him pull a one-eighty and basically kick me out?

I sit on the edge of my bed and dry my hair with a towel. The friction feels good, therapeutic, even, and I keep going long after it's dried.

"And I was worried I wasn't being fair with him," I say. "What a joke."

I'm tossing my towel into a laundry bin when I hear a soft knock on my door. I feel bad for not wanting to talk about this to Harper because I know she's worried, but I don't really know what to say. *Penn rejected me.* I don't want to say that out loud.

"What is it, Harper?" I ask. "I really just want to be alone."

The door pushes open, anyway.

"Harper, please. I'm fine. I just . . ."

Penn is standing in the doorway. Paint is still smeared all over him, and his hair is still a mess from my fingers a little while ago.

I sink down on my bed. My chest feels tight as I give up on trying to figure out my emotions. They just *are*.

"What do you want?" I ask.

"I want to talk to you."

"I'll be honest," I say. "When you said you'd call, I doubted that. I'm having a hard time believing that you're here."

He must feel like it's safe to come in. The door closes behind him, placing us both in the same compact room together.

It's not big enough—not for our bodies, and not for all the things happening between us. I get up and open a window as if that will somehow add more space.

He stands by the door, hat in his hands, eyes so wary that I want to punch him and kiss him at the same time.

What a feeling this is.

"I'm not good at this," he says.

"You're not good at what? Explaining why you just freaked out on me?" I grab a brush off the dresser and pull it through my damp hair. "It occurred to me on my way out the door that you blindsided me the way I did you the other day. Were you just evening the score?"

"Avery, no."

"Then what was it?"

His Adam's apple bobs. "Will you sit down?"

"Nope."

I'm not giving him the dominant position over me, especially not in my own bedroom.

He sighs. "I'm sorry for . . . I don't know if you actually cried, because I kind of mentally checked out or something. But if you did, I'm sorry for making you do that."

My brush slows a little.

His shoulders slump as he sits on the bed. He jams the hat on his head. "Can I ask you something?"

My stomach rumbles with anticipation mixed with anxiety as I try to decipher which way this is about to go. Thoughts spin in my head like a Tilt-A-Whirl—so fast that I don't know how I want this to pan out.

I'm surprised he's here. Embarrassed from earlier. Angry that I care.

Yet seeing him like this softens all that because seeing him without his cocky grin bothers me. A lot.

"I guess," I say.

"Have you been to Dogwood Lane before?"

My brush slows more.

There's a piece of red-hot lava that lodges itself in my stomach. His words are too carefully curated, his tone too unnaturally even to be anything but a lead-in to something else.

He knows. My hand stalls over the top of my head as I force myself to breathe. Even if I'm right and he's somehow figured it out on his own, I want to tell him first. I owe him that.

"Penn," I say, setting the brush down. "I . . . I have something I want to tell you."

"Why don't you go ahead and do that?"

Swallowing is hard with the lava in my throat, and breathing is difficult with the weight of a secret like this on my chest. I have no idea how he put things together or when he did or what it means, but I know I should've told him sooner.

But it's too late for that.

Our eyes lock like they always do, and I wonder, if we didn't know each other and found ourselves in a busy city, would we still find each other like this? Because it feels like it. It feels so natural to be around him, like something inside me searches for something inside him.

I don't know what to say or how to say it. Words refuse to come to my tongue. My fingers grip the hem of my shirt. I walk in front of him.

My chest rises and falls with such depth that I wonder if it's possible to die from too much oxygen.

He looks up at me. His features are tight from what I think we both know is coming. I want to cry again but manage to hold back my tears as I slowly lift the edge of my shirt on my right side.

I wait for his reaction. His eyes are glued to the two dice on my ribs, the two dice that are the same two as on his forearm. His weren't there when we were together before, and I can't help but wonder why they're there now.

He reaches forward and grips the backs of my legs and pulls me into him. His cheek buries into my stomach as he holds me the tightest I've ever been held.

I cradle his head in my arms and pull him against me.

My emotions are scattered across the room, blending together into a muddled masterpiece. I don't know what I feel or what I'm supposed to feel or what I even want to feel. *Did I just lose him? Was he mine to lose? Do I want him? Can I risk that?*

We stay like that for a long minute before he pulls back. His eyes are raw, the shields down as he peers up at me with a vulnerability that rips my heart out.

"I should've told you," I whisper.

He nods.

"I was going to. Today. But then we were kissing before I could get it out . . ." I exhale sharply. "That's how you knew. You saw my tattoo."

He stands, giving me time to back up. His expression is pained. "Yeah. I wasn't expecting to see that. I don't really know what I said or how I made you feel, and again, I'm sorry about that."

"I'm sorry for not telling you."

"When did you know it?" he asks.

I smile sadly. "As soon as I looked at you."

This pleases him. I can tell. He runs a hand over his mouth as he paces a small circle in my room. I give him the space to work things out in his head. I've had time to think about this, to work it out in my head. I'm sure he needs time to process it too.

Finally, after what feels like an eternity, he stops.

"Why did you leave?" he asks. "Why did you give me a fake name?"

I take a deep breath, my room suddenly too small.

"I left because my mother summoned me. She called crying the next morning, saying she couldn't get through my father's affair without me being home. And I have to say, I really thought she might be serious, and I was thrilled she wanted me around." I throw my shoulders back. "But she didn't. She just wanted me to tell her attorney that I'd met my father's mistress to help her case."

"What a bitch. Pardon my language."

"It's the reason I didn't tell you my name. I could've said I was Avery, I guess, but I didn't know if you knew that Harper was my mom's sister, and I just wanted to not be me for a night. For one night, I just wanted to be anonymous. Angry. Pissed off at the world. I wanted someone to like me without knowing I was Jasmine Perry's daughter."

His body stills. "I'd have liked you regardless of whose daughter you were."

I smile at him. "But you know what I mean, right? You felt like people judged you because of your family. That's what I was afraid of. I just wanted complete anonymity to feel whatever I wanted to."

He picks at a tiny hole in the thigh of his jeans. "I can understand that." His gaze flips up to mine. "That's the night I put my dad in jail."

I blink once. Twice. My heart crushes against my ribs as I watch an unnamed emotion pass through his eyes.

"Why didn't you tell me that?" I whisper.

"Because I didn't want you to know that's the kind of family I was from. So like I said, I can understand that."

He goes back to fiddling with the hole in his jeans.

I stand in front of him. Reaching out, I take his face in my hands and lift his chin. I look him right in the eye so he doesn't miss a word I say.

"I would've liked you no matter what family you were from too," I tell him.

He takes a breath and lets that settle over him. Finally, he grins. "Thanks."

I release him and back away.

As if a piece of my life has been snapped into place, I feel a serenity like never before. And as I watch Penn watch me, I realize there's a peace between us, too, in a way I couldn't have imagined.

"Abby made such an impression on me," he says cheekily, "that I got a tattoo for her."

"The dice?"

He nods. "She was the only person that I felt like didn't judge me, make excuses for me, or blow me off."

I grin. "I think I kind of did blow you off that night, if you catch my drift."

He laughs, his dimple setting deep in his cheek.

I take his hand and pull him to my bed. We sit together quietly, our hands locked together with an intensity that I'm not sure either of us means to happen but neither of us pulls away from. Having him here like this is the most intimate moment I've ever had with a man, because we're sharing something that matters. We're choosing to participate in this, even though it isn't easy. Even though it kind of hurts a bit. Even though it could change everything.

"I was embarrassed that you didn't recognize me at first," I say softly. "And then, once I didn't say anything, it was kind of hard to just bring it up. I was stuck and I didn't know what to do, but I was going to tell you today."

He shakes his head. "I was just shocked. I've thought about that emo girl named Abby over the years, wondering what happened to her. I'd almost convinced myself that I made her up as a coping mechanism or something." He blushes. "I saw that on a television show once."

I laugh. "I was real. Abby was real." I think back to what I must've looked like that night with my black hair and bloodred lips. "That was not my best stage of life."

He shrugs. "I thought she was pretty bangin'."

"Did you?" I prod.

"Almost as hot as she is now." He squeezes my hand before letting it go. "I should hate you," he says.

"Why?"

"Because before you came to town, I had my balls. Now, I'm talking about my feelings, giving a fuck about how you feel, and I haven't gotten laid. At all. I don't even know me anymore."

I bump him with my shoulder. "Yeah, but you're the new and improved Penn Etling now."

"I was pretty damn perfect before."

"You're welcome to go back to it," I tell him. Even as the words slip by my lips, I inwardly cringe.

He might take me up on it. I might die if he does.

He bites his lip and looks at the ceiling like he's considering it. The longer he goes, the more worried about it I become.

"Nah," he says. "It was getting pretty tiresome to be me with my phone ringing all the time and the girls just all over my cock. I needed a break from it."

"Oh, geez."

He shrugs. We sit quietly for a while, the only sound coming from Harper's television show.

As I study his handsome face, I realize that this is the realest I've ever been with another person. The vulnerability I feel exceeds anything else at the moment. There's no shield, no plan to prevent myself from getting hurt by Penn. There's only trust that he wouldn't do anything to wound me.

It's a revelation that sparks something inside me. I've given my time and energy to men who didn't try half as much as Penn. And even though I want more, and I do, maybe something could work out between us.

Just as I'm trying to formulate how to start a conversation to see how he feels, he stands up.

"Come on," he says abruptly.

"Come on, what?"

He snorts. "Can you please think about what you say before you say it?"

Come on what. I hit him.

"Where are we going?" I say politely.

He grins. "We're taking a road trip."

"And where are we taking a road trip to?"

"Why do you ask so many questions?" he asks. "Just put some shoes on, or don't, and let's go."

I put my hands on my hips. "And why should I trust you?"

"It's a little late for that. We're on the 'talking about feelings' level. There should be some trust there. But if you ever bring this up in public, I'll deny it like a motherfucker."

I can't hide my laughter. "Deal. Now, back to where we are going: Can I wear what I have on?" I ask.

"Do you think I care what you wear?" He holds out his hands. "I mean, if I had my choice, you'd wear nothing, but I'm going out on a limb and guessing you won't go for that."

The smile he gives me dissolves me on the spot.

He's back.

"Fine. Let's go," I say.

He wraps his arm around my shoulders and leans his head against mine. I think he might kiss the top of my head, but I'm not sure.

What I am sure of is that this was way easier getting into than it will be getting out of.

CHAPTER TWENTY-FOUR

Avery

"Oh, wow." The words escape my lips before I even realize I'm saying them.

The sight before me, even without Penn in it, is spectacular. The deep-blue waters of Dogwood Lake ripple in the fading sunlight.

Everything feels amplified out here. The greens are more vivid, the birds happier, and the air a little sweeter than anywhere I've ever been. It's just like I remembered but . . . *more.*

"What do you think?" Penn asks. He holds his hands out to his sides like he's showing off the little area nestled out into the middle of the forest. "Ring a bell?"

"Of course it does."

I turn in a circle. The tree canopy overhead is thick and lush. The large oak tree we lay under that night is still there, minus the ants. I laugh.

"What?" he asks.

I point at the tree. "Do you remember the ants?"

"Fuck yes," he admits. "I came out here with a can of ant killer the next day. That's against my usual code of conduct, but I had welts everywhere for two weeks."

"Those were fun to explain to my mom."

He laughs. "I bet. What did you say? That a stud you met in the woods fucked you on a . . . what was it? A jacket?"

"That's not what I said, and yes, it was a jacket."

I walk to the water's edge and gaze across the lake. It's so peaceful with just the occasional fish or bird breaking the surface. On the other side is a giant hill that's covered in trees and looks like it reaches the sky.

"How did you find me down here that night?" he asks.

"Honestly? By accident." I climb back up the little slope from the water and stand next to Penn. "I'd left Harper's to get some fresh air. I got to crying so hard I couldn't see, so I pulled over up on the road. And I heard your voice and took a chance."

"I could've been a serial killer."

"Yeah, but you weren't."

"Yeah, but I could've been."

We exchange a grin.

He puts his arm over my shoulder and pulls me into his side. I fall into him, my head leaning against his chest. It feels like the most natural thing I've ever done.

My arm snakes around his waist. I can feel the muscles in his lower back flex as he moves. It's sexier than any smile or any touch or any act I've ever seen because it's unintentional. Just a strong man letting a woman rest against him. And maybe, a strong woman letting a man rest against her.

"I feel like most people probably label things that feel like this," he says roughly.

The hesitation in his tone is obvious and one I can't deny. It's something I can't say I don't share as well.

This is all new. Really, really new. And even though it feels like I've known him for a lifetime, I haven't.

I have to trust myself enough to know what's right for me, and I have to trust him enough to know he wouldn't hurt me.

And I don't think he will. *But do I ask him?*

"I'm not totally sure where you're going with that," I say cautiously.

"Where do you want me to be going with that?"

I consider this. "I don't know. I don't want to jump to conclusions."

"I . . ." He gulps as his fingers play with the hem of my shirt. "I think we're really good friends. And that's a good thing. So, maybe, you know, we could try something else." He looks at me, his eyes shining. "I'd like to see what happens."

My heart starts to beat frantically. Of course this is what I want. I know it as soon as he says the words. But the logical part of my brain warns me to take it easy because a tiger's stripes don't change overnight.

"I've seen enough . . . *friendships* to know that what you call them doesn't matter," he says. "I know a lot of people that label a woman a girlfriend or wife, but they don't act any different than before. It's like sticking a piece of paper on a grain of rice and calling it a meal."

I laugh. "Nice analogy."

"It might not work, but you know what I mean."

He strokes the top of my arm with his fingertips so lightly that I wonder if he realizes he's doing it. I lean into his touch. The rough pads of his fingers send shocks through my body with every brush against my skin.

He spins me around slowly so I'm facing him. My breath halts in my chest.

The look in his eyes is intense, but tender—raw, like he's waited on this exact moment for so long that he's having a hard time holding himself back.

My body tightens as a shiver rips through my body.

He holds my gaze with a slight crook of his brow. It's like he's warning me about what's to come and is giving me an out.

Not a chance, buddy.

He seems to read my mind, because a wicked grin slips across his face. He widens his hips so I'm standing between his legs and looks down at me with hooded eyes.

"Now, before this goes any further," he says, "I'm going to be fucked up about this after. I don't know how, exactly, but I'm absolutely sure things won't be the same way they are right now. If you have any reservations, tell me. We'll get in the truck and go home."

His usual confidence is marred by a streak of nervousness. I don't want him to be nervous. I want him to be Penn in every way.

There's only one thing I know to do.

"I actually have one thing," I say.

His brows pull together. "Really?"

"Yes." I keep my face completely straight. "What if you don't deliver eight inches? I mean, you've basically promised me that, and I'm not sure how I'll feel if I'm disappointed."

He bursts out laughing. "You little shit." He cups my face in his large hands. "You always make me smile."

"Well," I whisper, angling my body toward his, "if you'd stop talking, I could make you really, really smile."

"Damn you," he groans.

His mouth dips to mine. Our lips touch, and I swear fireworks tear through my veins.

His hands drop to my throat, then to my shoulders and down my arms. They course roughly down my back until he's gripping my ass and hauling me into his chest.

The years since we were here last, on top of all the kisses and almost-kisses of the last few days, add up to this moment. His lips devour me—my mouth, my tongue, my jawline. It's like he can't get enough.

I can't get enough.

I moan as he kisses the side of my neck, his fingers finding the edge of my shirt. He lifts it up and over my head, tossing it somewhere near the oak tree. I feel the clasp of my bra release. He steps back far enough to remove it.

The air kisses my nipples right before he does. He licks one, then the other before swirling it with his tongue. He palms the other, taking the pebble in between his fingers and sending shocks of desire through my body. I press him against me by the back of his head.

He nibbles and kisses a path back to my lips and presses a final kiss to my cheek. "You are so fucking beautiful. Do you know that?"

I stand in front of him, shirtless, my imperfections bare for him to see. All he has to say is that I'm beautiful?

I've never been called beautiful by anyone. My knees go weak as he watches me like I'm a piece of artwork he's always wanted to see.

"I'm the luckiest fucker alive," he says quietly.

Emboldened by his reaction, I remove my shorts. Facing away from him so he can see the black thong parting my ass cheeks, I hook my fingers at the waist.

"Damn, Ave."

His tone is rocky. How much he wants me is evident in the words, and I wonder how hard he is right now.

I gulp.

Dragging the thin piece of fabric over my hips, I don't give the first thought to the bow of my legs or the cellulite on my ass. It would be impossible to consider anything negative when Penn Etling is looking at you like you're the best thing he's ever seen.

My heart pounding in my chest, I step out of my panties. I hold them up by one finger as I turn around.

His eyes are wide as he watches me with rapt attention. His shirt is gone now. The sight of his body is enough to make me forget what I was doing.

Defined abs that aren't cut too hard rock his center. Sex lines, where his obliques meet his lower abs, point to a bulge in his pants. His shoulders are thick and solid, and I want to run my fingers along them and feel his strength.

In one quick move I don't see coming, he grabs ahold of me.

His lips find mine again, his mouth hot and hungry. As his tongue works me over, I unbutton his pants and shove them down. He breaks the kiss just long enough to get them off and out of the way.

"How," he says, kissing me. "Do." He kisses my throat. "You." His tongue traces a line to beneath my ear, where he plants another kiss. "Want this," he whispers before nibbling my earlobe.

I squeal as his teeth get the lobe a little too hard. His laugh against my throat reverberates through my body. The chords assimilate in my groin, making me even wetter.

He picks me up. I wrap my legs around his waist as he kisses me again. This time, there's no rush as he lazily moves his mouth over mine.

My fingers run through his hair, my breasts pressed against his chest as he carries me toward the path. He kicks at something before he drops to his knees.

The kiss is broken as he lays me on my back on my clothes. I peer up at him as he kneels between my legs.

"Stay put," he says.

I nod.

Without breaking eye contact, he gets to his feet and slips his boxer briefs off.

I gasp.

Holy fucking shit.

I wouldn't have staked my life on the fact that I could give you an exact measurement of eight inches. But he's close enough.

He grins as he searches through his pants pockets, then pulls a condom from his wallet.

"You are the slowest man at this ever," I complain.

"I'm not sorry. I have the best view of any man ever."

"You could've been more prepared."

He snorts. "Yeah, like you were a given or something. You're lucky I have a condom at all."

I watch him roll the protection down his shaft as he walks to me. He drops to his knees again and grips my hips with both hands. The spots where his fingers press into my skin burn.

He gives me a smile so soft it's almost shy. It pings something deep inside my heart.

Bending down, he places a kiss on my chest. I close my eyes as I absorb the moment. It catches me off guard because tenderness isn't what I expected.

But damn it if it doesn't feel perfect.

My hips are lifted. The head of his dick spreads me open. His eyes snatch mine out of the air.

I hold my breath as he slides the tip around, getting it wet and making me ready to lose my damn mind.

"Penn—ah!"

He thrusts himself deep inside me. There's no fanfare, no warming me up to the intrusion. Just a shock of pleasure ripping through my core.

My back slides against my clothes as he thrusts in again.

"You meant now, right?" he asks, a hint of a laugh to his voice.

"Mm-hmm . . ." I moan, squeezing my eyelids together.

His hands dig into my hips, keeping the motion steady and hard. My back arches as I give myself to him.

This is not the teenager I slept with before. This is a man, all man, taking what I'm offering and giving me something back.

That's what I feel more than the delicious push toward a climax—the fall of Penn's shield. The hint of vulnerability in his eyes, the care to each move he makes, and the gentle undercurrent of every touch is the sexiest part of this encounter.

He presses in, deep and hard, until the sound of our bodies sliding past each other echoes across the water.

The pressure inside me, from my groin through my core, gets stronger and stronger. Each drive brings me closer to the brink.

"I'm so close," I warn him as my back bites into the ground.

A small moan joins the cacophony of sounds, and I feel my body starting to give. Warmth spreads through my veins, my vagina liquefying as it prepares to come apart around him.

He moves one hand to the center of my chest. The weight of his fingers over my breasts is enough to send a shock roaring through me. I topple over the edge.

"Penn," I almost shout as my senses are shredded.

He picks up pace before shoving inside me one last time. I can feel the swell of his cock as he falls apart.

My heart pounds in my ears, but not loud enough so I miss the guttural groan of him losing himself.

Panting, I watch him come undone. His face lifted to the sky, his eyes shut in a bout of pleasure—it's the sexiest thing I've ever witnessed.

He drops his chin. I bite my lip and prepare for a variety of responses.

None of them are what I get.

He slips out of me without a word. Instead of getting up or cracking a joke, he wraps me in his arms and pulls me against him.

My breath stalls in my chest as he rests his chin on the top of my head for a long moment. Before he pulls back, he leaves a kiss in its place.

There is a wariness in his eyes, an uncertainty of what to say. I don't know what to say either. Even so, I'll be damned if this gets weird. It was too perfect.

"I have to say, you didn't lie," I say, trying to lighten the mood and draw attention away from too many feelings.

"What about?"

He offers a hand and helps me to my feet. I brush off my legs and back as I try not to smile.

"Eight inches was fair," I note.

He laughs as he gathers our clothes. Mine get a quick shake. Grass and twigs fall off them.

"I told you," he says. "I'm great with tools."

I take my clothes from him and slip my shirt over my head. Looking him up and down and then back up again, I grin. "I'd have to agree."

He shakes his head as he buttons his pants. "Let's get you home so we can clean you up."

"Harper is going to love this," I say. "Maybe I can tell her I fought a lion in the woods. That's believable, right?"

He stands still. "I was, um, meaning my house. But I can totally take you to Harper's."

I hold my shorts in my hands. Looking up, I take him in. He's watching me with what I can only think is hope.

I grin. "Your house will be great."

He smiles but doesn't say a word.

He doesn't have to.

CHAPTER TWENTY-FIVE

PENN

I could get used to this.

The ceiling fan sends ripples of cool air over my naked body. The sheet that's supposed to be covering me is askew, a remnant of a long, altogether enjoyable night.

And morning.

Because Avery doesn't play around.

She's curled up next to me, her head on my chest. One of her arms is stretched over my stomach, and a leg is entwined with one of mine. I tug the sheet up around her, making her as cozy as possible. If she doesn't wake up, she won't leave.

Now I sound like a lunatic.

I brush her hair away from her face. Her lashes are long and displayed along the tops of her cheeks. She looks peaceful and happy. When I think I had something to do with that, a peace settles over me too.

I'm fucked. I know it. I don't know what to fucking do about it, but I'm out of my depth here. How I got here, in my bed, with Avery Perry, a.k.a. Anthill Abby, makes my head spin. Add to that the fact that I'm not actively freaking out, and I might as well be admitted to a mental institution because people aren't supposed to do *this*—wake up one morning and feel like a different person. I learned that on a television show once too.

She stirs, her arm lifting off my body as she stretches. The little sounds she makes as she wakes up are adorable.

Her head tilts as she looks up at me with sleepy eyes. "Hey," she says.

"Hey."

She holds my gaze for a moment before rolling onto her back. I think about dragging her back against me, but there are laws about holding people captive and I'm not sure I'd let her go.

That probably should terrify me. Strangely, it doesn't. Not yet, anyway.

A yawn slips from her mouth as she gets her bearings.

"Every part of me hurts," she says. "Parts of me hurt that I didn't know could hurt."

"Those city boys don't know how to put it down, huh?"

She smacks my chest.

I sink back into my pillows and watch her sit up. Her breasts are heavy and have the most natural, sexiest hang to them.

"One, two, three, or four?" I ask her.

"I have no idea what you're talking about."

"I'm doing research."

She takes an elastic off her wrist and ties her hair in a knot on the top of her head. "Okay. Is the answer, 'The start to a Coolio song for five hundred'?"

"I have no idea what you're talking about," I say, giving her answer back to her.

She sighs. "What am I actually choosing?"

"One would be Anthill Anonymous. Two would be Rocky Root. Three would be Crazy Cowgirl, and I'm going with Miscellaneous

Missions for number four, only because I'm not sure what to focus on. There was a lot going on at four this morning."

"I can't with you," she says, looking at me like I'm nuts.

"What? I want to know what you liked best. How else will I improve?" I wait for her to answer, but she doesn't. "Fine. It was totally Anthill Anonymous, wasn't it? I mean, it was super cool to fuck someone I didn't know—only I really didn't know you because you lied about who you were."

"Penn," she says, laughing, "the first time we were together was one of the worst times I've ever had. With anyone. Ever."

My jaw drops. My ego might be wounded but she practically begged for it last night, so that helps.

"You're joking," I say.

She shakes her head from side to side. "You were a mess. Fumbling around—"

"It was dark."

She pats my chest. "It's okay. I gave you another chance."

"You gave me three more."

"Want another?"

I growl as I move to cover her body with mine. But before I can, my phone goes off on my nightstand.

"Get it," she says.

"It can wait."

"No, get it. I need to pee, anyway."

She jumps out of bed, her ass jiggling as she hits the floor. My eyes are glued to the round globes until she's out of sight.

"Damn." I grab my phone and check the screen. *Fuck.* "Hello," I say, followed by a sharp exhale.

"Good morning, princess," Dane says. "What's happening today?"

"How was your trip?" I ask, hoping to avoid a discussion about me for as long as possible. I'm not sure what Matt has told him, and I'm not in a place to argue or defend my position at the moment.

Hell, I'm not sure what my position even is.

"Eh, fifty-fifty," Dane says. "How did things go while I was gone? Did you piss anyone off that I need to know about before I run into them?"

"Nope." I settle back against the pillows again. "I was actually on excellent behavior. I made a lot of people happy."

He laughs. "Oh, I bet."

"Not like that."

"Whatever. Hey, we're all heading to the café for breakfast. Meet us up there in twenty."

Avery walks back in the room. She's still completely naked. Her body is round and full and tight and my cock gets hard just from a glimpse.

I yank the sheets off my body and grab myself with my free hand.

"I'm kind of busy this morning," I tell him as Avery crawls across the bed. "Probably gonna have to pass on breakfast."

"Bullshit. You're coming."

"I fucking hope so," I groan.

I hiss as Avery straddles my legs, her breasts sitting on my legs. She bends forward, swatting my hand away and sucking the tip of my cock into her mouth.

"Dane, I gotta go."

"I don't care who you're fucking, you better be there—"

I end the call and send my phone sailing across the room.

&

"I told you he'd come." Mia runs to me before I even get in the door of the café. "Hey, Penn."

"Hey, you. How was Florida?"

"Hot. So hot." She motions for me to bend down, so I do. Her hand cups around her mouth as she whispers in my ear. "It was hot as Hell, but Dad doesn't like me saying it. Neely says it's a place and a proper noun, so it's not technically a bad word if used correctly. But you get the idea."

I stand back up and catch a glare from Dane. I laugh.

"Mia, I'd like you to meet my friend Avery," I say. "Avery, this is Mia Madden."

"Well, hi," Avery says. "It's nice to meet you. I love your braid."

"Neely did it. She's sick, but she still got up and French-braided my hair."

"She must be nice," Avery says.

"She is." Mia skips over to the big round table in the corner and climbs into a chair between Matt and Dane. "Hey, Dad. Penn's here."

Dane looks at me, then at Avery, and then back to me. Avery glances at me and I can see the bout of nerves in her eyes, so I put my arm around her waist.

I'm a little anxious too. I don't know what my friends are going to say or think or what assumptions they'll make. Even more, I don't know how to respond to those.

I'm still me. Because I have Avery on my arm doesn't mean I've inherently changed. Sure, things might be more complicated than I imagined they could be, but I haven't worked out how that's going to pan out. And I sure as fuck don't want to be ribbed about it.

"Dane, this is Avery," I say. "Avery, this is Matt's brother, Dane."

"It's nice to meet you," she says.

"You too. I've heard a lot about you," Dane tells her. "My favorite story was you turning Penn down."

My jaw sets. "Really, Matt?"

"What?" Matt says, sitting back in his chair. "Did you really expect me to keep something that epic to myself?"

"You mean when Avery turned Penn down?" Claire comes up to the table with two cups and a pitcher of coffee. "That was one for the record books." She looks at Avery. "How are you this morning?" She raises her brows with an "I got ya" kind of look.

"I'm good. You?" Avery asks. She toys with my hand on her hip.

"Pretty decent." Claire flips her a smile as she pours the two cups of coffee. "You want your usual, Penn?"

I nod. "What would you like, Ave?"

"Ave, huh?" Dane presses his lips together. "This must be serious if we're at nickname status already."

"Shut it." I turn my attention back to Avery. "I get bacon extra crispy, two eggs over medium, and hash browns—unless it's Friday, and then I add a cinnamon roll."

Avery laughs, moving away from my hold. It's a smooth move, but definitely intentional. "I'll just have a cheese omelet, if that's possible?"

"Done." Claire nods and scurries back to the kitchen.

I pull out a chair beside Matt and the one next to it on the other side. Avery takes the one not by Matt, and I couldn't be happier about that.

"Have you checked out the library yet?" I ask Dane as I move the two cups of coffee Claire poured in front of Avery and me.

He shakes his head. "Not yet. Meredith did call first thing this morning and seems happy with what you guys have been doing. She thinks you have about a week left. Does that seem right?"

"Yeah, probably."

Dane looks at Avery. "I hear you're an artist."

She winces. "Not really."

"Yes, you are," I tell her. "Don't sell yourself short."

Dane grins, settling back in his chair. "You know, I didn't believe it until I saw it for myself. But Hell has frozen over."

"Don't say 'Hell,' Dad. We just discussed this."

"Mia . . . hush," he says.

She stops coloring and looks up at him with absolute seriousness. "You just lectured me about saying Florida was hot as Hell, and I meant it as a proper noun. Is it okay or not?"

Avery giggles. "You're a smart little girl."

Her hand drops to my thigh under the table. The innocent touch sends fire through my veins. If this keeps up, we're going to have a problem.

"I am. I—Haley!" Mia scrambles out of her seat again and launches herself toward Haley. "I missed you."

Haley stands next to Trevor. In all the years I've known her, I never had her pegged to be with a guy like Trevor. He's nice enough, I guess, and he knows construction. That's a plus. But there was a time where I thought I was going to have to kick his ass. Wouldn't have taken that long by the fancy shirts he wears, and I wouldn't have minded it much either. But since Haley is happy and Trevor seems to keep himself in check, I let him live.

Haley's eyes land on Avery. She gets Mia back in her seat as she comes around the table.

"These boys don't have any manners, and I apologize for them—except for Penn. He can apologize for himself," Haley teases.

"Good morning, Haley," I say as sarcastically as I can.

"Good morning." She extends a hand to Avery. "I'm Haley, but you probably know that by now. I'm been fixing to come down to the library or over to Harper's and say hello, but I haven't been able to get away from the shop long enough to have a conversation."

Avery shakes her hand. "I'm Avery, as you know. It's nice to finally meet you."

"Trevor said he met you the other day. Said you're really talented."

"Thanks." Avery looks at the table. "I've been wanting to stop in and see your store. It's so pretty from the outside."

"Oh, do. Come by. Or we can meet up here one morning and have our own girls' brunch without the boys. We can ask Claire when they'll have their caramel-topped doughnuts. They're the best."

"Sounds good. Count me in," Avery says with a laugh.

I sit back in my chair, coffee in hand and knee resting against Avery's, and watch her interact with my friends. It's effortless. Besides the introduction part, no one watching would even think she's just meeting them.

Dane catches my eye. There's something pensive, maybe even proud, about the way he's watching me. It reminds me of how their dad looks at him or Matt when they're building something and aren't paying attention.

I shrug. Dane smiles. And for whatever reason, I needed that.

Every time I start to feel comfortable, my nerves kick in. This is all really different, something I've never done before, and my propensity to mess it all up is pretty high.

I have to get out of my head.

"What's everyone doing today?" I ask.

Mia makes an exaggerated, wide-eyed face at me. "I'm getting ready for Dogwood Day this weekend. It's only my third—fourth favorite day of the year," she says. "After Christmas, my birthday, and the Summer Show, Dogwood Day is the best."

Matt leans against the table. "It is the best. Who doesn't like cotton candy and bouncy houses and games that cost ten dollars to win a fifty-cent prize?"

"Right?" Mia misses the point. "Will you get your face painted with me, Penn?"

"What do I want my face painted for?"

"Because it would be awesome. I will get a butterfly and you can get . . ."

"A princess," Dane teases.

I fire him a glare.

"No," Mia hisses. "What about a giraffe?"

"I do have a long—ouch," I say as Avery elbows me in the side. "Memory. A long memory."

Mia shrugs and goes back to coloring with these expensive markers that Dane buys online like the sucker he is. I mean, I'd probably buy them for her, too, but still.

Claire comes back and sets our food in front of us. "Do you two lovebirds want anything else?"

My stomach drops as my head whips to Avery. She places her hands in her lap and steadies her gaze on Claire.

"We're fine. Thanks," she says slowly.

"Lovebirds?" Mia looks at me like she does when she knows I have a candy bar in my truck. "Are you two in love like my dad and Neely?"

"No," I say much too quickly. "We're . . ."

I look at Avery. She's watching me with wide eyes. I don't know what to say, especially to a ten-year-old.

"We're friends," I say finally. "Avery and I are really good friends."

Dane leans forward and grabs Mia's glass. His gaze pins me to my seat. "Mia, finish your milk before it spills."

My friends start talking, jabbering about Dogwood Day and where Neely's purple bag disappeared to. I tune them all out.

I watch Avery chat with Claire, her head falling back in laughter, and wonder why this is so tricky.

Maybe getting off six times in the last fourteen hours is making me weak.

Or maybe it is because Avery fits so easily into my life without complicating it too much.

There's one last possibility, one I don't want to really consider. Is this feeling I'm experiencing the same one Dane feels about Neely, and I'm too scared to admit it?

Nah, I think. *It can't be that. You haven't gone more than a week without sex for a long time. That's what this is. Sexual satisfaction. Exhaustion. That's all.*

I bet my aura is a pale orange this morning.

Avery looks at me, and I wonder what color her aura would be today. Just as I'm about to ask her opinion, she grins.

"How are you, *good friend*?" she asks.

"Um, fine. You?"

She takes a piece of bacon off my plate. "Just pondering what it would take to be classified as a great friend."

I shift in my seat. Leaning in, I whisper in her ear. "You'll never get there if you keep stealing bacon off my plate."

She turns her head. Her lips brush against my cheek as she finds my ear. "Maybe I don't want to be your great friend." She snatches another piece of bacon. "Maybe good friend is my limit."

I scan the table. No one is paying any attention to us because they're too immersed in Dane's story about a sand dollar.

Dropping my hand under the table, I squeeze the inside of Avery's thigh. There are too many things happening that I can't control, too many ideas bouncing around my head that I can't make sense of. So I focus on the one I know.

I tap her leg close enough to the spot where her leg meets her groin to get her attention. A small gasp lets me know I have it.

"You want to get out of here and see if we can go from six to seven?" I ask.

She grins, dropping the bacon. "Check, please."

All I can do is laugh.

CHAPTER TWENTY-SIX

Avery

A white banner with navy-blue lettering welcomes us to Dogwood Day. People wander about, stopping at little booths, and gathering in groups while they eat corn dogs.

It's the perfect afternoon for a festival, although I'm not sure that's the right word for this event. It's small and quaint and probably doesn't even fit the official definition for a festival.

Still, it's lovely. The breeze moves the air in a lazy way, lulling me into a state of bliss.

Penn walks beside me. His jeans have a little fraying at the hems and a couple of stains here and there. I wonder if he bought them that way or if he wore them to a state of perfection. The blue T-shirt that's stretched across his body is the softest cotton I've ever felt, and I could just nuzzle my face into it and call it a day.

Except he would end up taking it off and then I'd take mine off and things would progress from there. Not that I would mind.

I look up at him and catch him watching me.

"What?" I ask.

"You look pretty today."

"Thank you."

He flashes me a shy smile and looks away.

Even though he's seen me naked and contorted into various positions, and even though he's made it clear just how much he admires my body, having him say I'm pretty is a whole new thing. There was a vulnerability in the way he said it. It was as if he wasn't only talking about my looks or body or cleavage—he was talking about *me.*

That feels nice.

We've spent the week together. Getting to know someone has never been so fun. I know he burns toast every single time, brushes his teeth multiple times a day, and loves the smell of lemon. And he loves to kiss and cuddle and is willing to play *Jeopardy* every time it's on.

But there's always a hesitation—something that holds him back just enough to keep from really putting his guard all the way down. It's there when we're alone but even more apparent in the presence of others. It makes me nervous.

"Penn, how are you?" A man wearing a brown pullover and smarmy smile heads our way. "I haven't seen you in a long time."

"Blame Dane. He's been keeping me busy."

The man looks at me. "Maybe Dane's not all that's been keeping you busy, huh?"

Penn gives him a tight smile, takes my hand, and walks away. "See ya later."

"Good seeing you."

Once we're out of earshot, I can't help but ask, "Who was that?"

"His name is Patrick," Penn says. "Word has it that the night a guy named Bobby Jones went missing, Patrick was the last guy to see him." He looks over his shoulder. "Never got a good feeling off that guy."

"He feels icky."

"'Icky.' Good word."

He grins, hesitates, and then takes my hand in his.

Laughter from a group of little girls running down the center of the blocked-off street fills the air along with scents of cinnamon and cotton candy. A giant lemon is perched on top of a food truck that sits next to a tent set up for donations to a local food bank.

"This is the sweetest little thing I've ever seen," I say, taking in the game of bingo to our right and ignoring the wobbliness on Penn's face. "People still play that?"

"Every Thursday night at the senior center. Actually, there was a brawl with these two seventy-year-old men a couple of months ago over whether the ball was *B* or *G*. I'm talking this fight, if that's what you want to call it, had the police called and everything."

"Oh, gee," I say with a laugh.

"No. It was *B*."

I shove him with my shoulder as he chuckles. "Hey," he says, pointing across the road. "See that little building?"

I follow his gaze to a narrow slice of a building between two larger ones. It's a deep green that probably is held together by decades' worth of paint. There are letters just above the mildewed overhang, but I can't make them out.

"What about it?" I ask.

"That place used to be Bernie's. You could walk in and get a soda on the left at this sandwich-shop kind of thing. The rest of the top floor was a pharmacy." He tugs my hand and guides me around a group of kids throwing bang snaps at the ground. "In the back, there was a set of stairs that took you to the basement. They sold furniture or appliances or something down there."

"It looks like it's been closed forever."

"Well, since I was seven or so, probably. When the big chain pharmacy came to Rockery, that place closed. They couldn't compete. But everyone here remembers Bernie's. Maybe you could include it in your mural somehow."

My heart fills. He's always thinking, always remembering things like my mural or shutting the door to the old library so Meredith's dog doesn't run out—even though he verbalizes his dislike for said dog constantly.

We venture down a little farther, taking in the stands selling homemade purses and trinkets for a dollar. A crowd cheers as a man overseeing a game hands a plastic baggie filled with water and a goldfish to a little girl.

I breathe a sigh that comes from my soul. This place feels like home, a place where you could start a family and be a classroom mom and bake cobblers for banquets.

I glance over at Penn. *Maybe someday.*

"Those remind me of Floater," Penn says. "Most traumatic thing of my single-digit years."

"Fun fact: I've never had a pet."

He flinches, like I just told him I'm from Mars. "Never? You've never had a pet? Not a fish or a dog or a cat? Nothing?"

I shake my head. "Nothing. Not even a hamster."

"I think you'd be a dog person, as much as you like to cuddle. Hamsters are boring. Cats are cool but more standoffish. They'll let you pet them when they want to be petted, and you can go fuck yourself the rest of the time."

I laugh. "Really? They're that bad?"

"They're really that bad." He checks out for a minute, gazing into the abyss. "I've been thinking about building a cabin."

He says it in a way that makes me unsure whether I was supposed to hear it or if I'm even supposed to comment.

"Well," I say, "the paint at your place isn't that bad. It's fixable."

He looks down at me and grins. "Yeah, but maybe it would be better to just forget it and start fresh. What do you think?"

"I—"

"Hey, Penn." A loud voice comes from behind us and we whirl around. A man is making a beeline our direction. "How are ya, buddy?"

Penn slips his hand from mine. "Hey, how are you, John?"

"Hanging in there. You know how it goes."

I step back out of instinct. The angle of Penn's body and the loss of his hand makes me feel like I'm intruding.

"Who is this?" John looks me up and down.

"This is Avery," Penn says. "Avery, this is John. I did some work at his place last summer."

We exchange hellos before they turn their attention back to some construction talk. I glance around, wondering if there's something I can go look at as a way to excuse myself, but there's just children's games and political booths.

"So, is this your girlfriend?" John asks.

"No," Penn says. "We're just friends."

I watch Penn struggle with his words. His eyes dart to mine as if he's not sure how to handle this question. I'm sure as hell not handling it.

It's not that I expect him to call me his girlfriend, but it's the almost offense he takes to the question that bothers me. As if calling me that stings.

"Avery is new to town," Penn says in a flimsy attempt at changing the subject. "This is her first Dogwood Day."

"It's great." I force a swallow. "It was really nice meeting you. Hey, Penn," I say, turning toward him. "I'm going to go check out a booth over there."

With as natural of a smile as possible, I back away and scoot over to the first booth.

We aren't labeling this, I remind myself. *We are still just friends. Even if I might be ready to settle on being exclusive, he's not.*

Could he be embarrassed of me?

I wish I had a friend to talk this out with.

My hand shakes slightly as I pick up a pin shaped like a die. *Roll with it.* That's what I used to say.

Maybe this is a sign.

"How much is this?" I ask, holding up the black-and-white decoration.

"Two dollars."

I fish out a couple of ones from my pocket and set them on the table. "Here you go," I say.

The guy wearing a hat with a ponytail sewn on the back nods. "Thank you."

I spin around and almost run into Penn.

He's a wall of muscle and energy that blocks my way. It would be easy to slip my arms around his waist and to plant a kiss in the middle of his chest like I did all night last night. But there's a strange vibe rolling off him that keeps me from it.

"I, um, just bought a pin. See?" I hold it in the air.

He checks it out but doesn't move. "Cute."

"Cute?"

"Awesome?"

"I hope you'd think so," I say, stepping around him. "Since you have two printed forever on your arm."

He follows me as I head back into the throng of people.

"Well, my two had a little meaning behind them," he says.

I slow, my heart picking up speed. "Oh, yeah?"

"Yeah."

He touches my elbow. I turn in a half circle until I'm looking up into his eyes. He looks uncertain, as if his normal swagger and confidence are missing and he's not sure why. Uncertainty is still the name of the game as the confidence that usually oozes from his pores is missing.

A microphone shrieks behind us as someone does a sound check. Music begins to play, and the voices around us begin to talk louder to be heard.

Penn steps closer.

"I got those to remember a girl named Abby. The girl that listened to my story one night by the lake and didn't judge me. Didn't tell me what to do or feel. Didn't tell me I was right or wrong. That was the first time that had ever happened to me."

I sag, the weight of his words sinking into me.

Over the last decade, I knew that night was special . . . to me. I never dreamed it was so important to him.

"Abby felt like someone finally liked her despite her bad dye job and weird lipstick," I say past the lump in my throat. "That boy listened to her rants and commiserated with her situation, and she really believed she could've told him there was an article about her on the newsstands and he wouldn't have cared. That was the first time that ever happened to me."

He sticks his arm around my shoulders and pulls my head against him as we start back down the road.

"You had enough of Dogwood Day?" he asks.

I look up at him. "We said we'd have dinner at Dane's."

"We did, but I think I need to be alone with you more."

The look in his eye suggests sex, but I'm still not sure if he doesn't want me to be a part of his world. Everyone knows him, and although the people we've met have mostly been friendly, he hasn't been at ease. He did say to me that he wasn't sure how to do this and we are a pretty new thing, so I need to give him the benefit of the doubt.

It's just that I want him to want me as much publicly as he does privately. That's my problem and not his. Maybe I'm just reading too much into this. It's possible he's trying not to lead me on, and if that's the case, it's the right thing for him to do.

I needed time to tell him we'd slept together. Maybe he needs time to come to terms with this too.

"Okay," I say. "Let's go."

He lays his cheek on the top of my head and guides me back to the car. We get looks from bystanders and the occasional wave as we pass different booths. But he never stops to say hello. And I wonder why.

He opens the truck door and holds it as I climb in. Before he shuts it, he peers up at me.

"I had fun with you today," he says. "Thanks for coming with me."

He doesn't wait for an answer. The door closes.

As I watch him walk around the front, I think about his reactions to things. He's coming around slowly. Changes don't happen overnight.

I hope.

CHAPTER TWENTY-SEVEN

Penn

"There he is." Matt steps away from the plans Trevor dropped off yesterday. "Hard time getting out of bed this morning?"

I survey the room. Besides Matt and his wonderful attitude, it's empty.

Avery left my house a few hours ago to go by Harper's for clean clothes, and then the two of them were going to have breakfast together. I, on the other hand, needed sleep.

I'm exhausted. Tired in every way. Physically worn out, which I didn't think was possible from sex, and mentally beat from overthinking this whole thing every time I get a quiet moment.

Dogwood Day fucked me up. It was the first time she and I were together in front of everyone in the entire damn town. A part of me was proud as a fucking peacock that she was there with me, yet another part of me was paralyzed. What will those people say when they see me in a few months and Avery is with someone else?

That thought makes me want to punch something hard, but that doesn't make it any less true. She'll finally see me for what I am and leave. It's bound to happen.

I'm just not sure how I'll fare when it does.

I dream about her at night. We're at a cabin, and she's sitting by a window with a paintbrush in her hand. I'm standing in the doorway, watching her. I'm so damn happy. And then I wake up and feel the loss of that immediately.

"Well, you'd have a hard time getting out of bed, too, if you've been through what I've been through," I grumble.

"By the looks of it, you've been through Hell."

"A Hell of my own creation."

"Use a comb next time you come to work," Matt says, throwing up his hands. "Or at least put on a hat."

I grab my belt from the corner and fasten it around my waist. My gaze catches on the dice on my arm like it's done a million times since I got the tattoo. Only these days, I get all fucked up about it and have to pause and stare. It's something I would've made fun of other guys for doing. But I'm starting to get it now.

It's like she gets me without me having to explain myself. Even more, she *wants* to get me. At least for now.

"Where is everyone at?" I ask.

"Avery went with Meredith to pick out paint. Since we're just about done in this room, they can get some paint on the walls. I asked them to wait for you because I knew you'd appreciate spending the morning with Meredith, but they left."

I flip him the bird.

"Jake is here somewhere. I think he's just killing time before he meets his dad for golf," Matt says.

"Of course they golf," I say, trying to remember where I left off yesterday. "They probably have Sunday dinners and give each other ties for Father's Day."

"Probably."

I've told myself my whole life that I don't care about that shit. I mean, how much smarter or better off does it make you if you and your pops have a standing golf time on Saturday mornings? And who golfs, anyway? It takes years off your life.

"I think I left my hammer in the back room," I tell Matt. "Be right back."

It takes a few minutes to find where I stashed my tool. As I turn to leave, my gaze falls on the table by the wall that Avery sat on when she kissed me. That feels like it was forever ago, like she's been in my life for ages.

I think back over the last couple of weeks. She's been patient with me. She's given me room to figure this out as best I can. She makes me feel good about myself, and I love hearing her laugh. Even more, I like knowing she's an arm's reach away in the middle of the night when I can't sleep.

Maybe I'm overthinking everything. She's certainly not like any other woman I've ever known.

I feel lighter as I start down the hallway again. Avery's voice filters down the corridor.

"There you are," I whisper, my face breaking into a smile. My steps get quicker as I march toward her voice.

"I've been here for a few hours already," I hear her say. "Meredith is the best person to paint-shop with."

"I'm the best person to shop with period," Meredith says, as I round the corner. She takes off her sunglasses and hooks them on the V of her shirt. "You and I need to go to Nashville one weekend. We'll take Haley and make it a girls' trip. It'll be a blast."

Avery laughs. "Count me in."

I can't help but notice how happy she looks as I set my sights on her. Her cheeks are rosy. There's a bounce in her step that I decide I'm taking credit for instead of giving it to Dogwood Café's omelets.

Meredith looks around the room. "Jake is going to bring the paint in. Where do you want it?"

"Let's see . . . Can he put it in that corner back there?" Avery points across the room. "I'll set up a little staging area."

"Have him come through the side door," I say. "He'll have to carry them a lot shorter distance."

Meredith nods. "Let me go tell him before he gets them out of the car." Her heels click against the tile as she scurries back out.

I wrap my arm around Avery's back and pull her into me. I kiss the top of her head and pause to breathe her in.

"Stop staking a claim to her and get to work," Matt jokes. "She's yours. We all know."

"I'm not staking a claim," I say, making a face at Matt. "And I can get more work done in an hour than you can in five."

Avery pulls away.

"Both of those statements are lies," Matt says.

"Let's have a build-off. We each build a frame for one wall and see who finishes first." I toss out the challenge and reach for Avery again.

She walks toward Matt instead of letting me grab her. I make a face to lure her back in, but she's not looking at me.

"I'd kill you. Wouldn't even be hard," Matt says before looking at Avery. "If I beat him, will that make you rethink your relationship with Penn? I wouldn't want to cause problems in paradise."

She puts a hand on her hip and lifts her chin to me. "I don't know. Would you call this a relationship, Penn?"

I shrug, my stomach knotting tight. I have half a notion to tackle Matt for doing this.

"I don't know. We decided to not put a label on it, didn't we?"

Avery's gaze cools as she turns it back to Matt. "We're friends."

"Interesting." Matt raises his brows. "Guess I didn't understand the definition of 'friends,' but there are lots of things I don't know. As long as you two have it figured out . . ."

Meredith calls for Avery, who gives me a tight look, one that leaves me a bit rattled, and heads toward the boss lady.

Once she's gone, Matt sighs.

"What?" I ask.

"Do you know what you're doing?"

"Always."

"No, really. I'm asking you a serious question."

"Yes, Matt. I know what I'm doing." I glance at the plans in front of him. "Why? What has your panties in a bind?"

He puts his hand in the middle of the plans so I have to look up at him.

"What?" I ask. "Stop being a dick."

"I'm trying to help you here."

"Help me with what?"

He shakes his head. "Didn't you just see any of that? Your little game of being *friends* with Avery is getting old."

"It's not a game," I counter.

"Then whatever it is. The words you use. The denial. Penn, she wants you to . . . you know, be proud she's with you. Stake a claim to her. Say she's your girlfriend."

My stomach twists around. I think he's serious, but I don't know if he's right this time. Avery gets what's happening here. We're getting to know each other. Having fun. Whatever it is, it's working, and Avery understands.

Doesn't she?

He shakes his head like he's not done sorting through something. After a few seconds, he seems to give up. "Come hold this. It's hard to keep it straight and hammer it at the same time."

We get to work on the final frame, trading off hammering and holding. The joint effort makes it go quickly, and the repetitive motions let me think.

I'm trying so hard to walk some kind of line. To treat her the best I know how without making her think I have it figured out. Because I don't.

If the world were perfect, I'd scoop her up in a heartbeat. But it's not—it's far from it. And the last thing I want in my life is to fuck up someone else.

She deserves the guy she thinks I am—or the one she hopes I am. Because I'm not that guy. I couldn't be if I wanted to, and when people realize I'm not who they think I am, things turn to shit.

I don't want to see that revelation in her eyes. Ever.

"I think that's it," Matt says.

We both look up as Avery, Meredith, and Jake come in through the side door. They're chatting back and forth like old friends.

Matt claps my shoulder. "They're just talking."

"I know." I clear my throat as I watch them. "Am I supposed to be jealous?"

"Jealous of what? Your *friend*?" He moves on to another frame. "This is the kind of thing I was talking about, Penn."

Meredith takes a call and scoots outside. I just stand there and watch Avery chitchat with Jake and not even look at me.

Is Matt right? Does Avery want to be mine? Do I think she's mine? It certainly feels like it right now.

Too many emotions misfire inside me to think straight. My blood runs hot and cold at the same time. Matt's words echo in my head as I think back to the chilly look she shot me before she walked over there.

The bubble building inside me is borderline frantic. Seeing her with Jake after the weirdness a minute ago is freaking me out.

Fuck.

Can I be more for her? Do I have it in me? Or should I let her go be with a guy like Jake who understands how to do things like this?

That thought takes the heat in my blood to a terrifying level.

Her laugh is light as they move closer. "Oh, I know. Trust me," she says. "This has been a little culture shock for sure."

"The first time I came down here from Nashville, I pretty much hated it. It was just because I didn't understand it. Now I find myself spending more and more time down here," Jake says. "You just don't realize how busy the city life is until you spend a weekend here."

"That's so true," she says. "I'll be sitting around at night these days and realize I'd still have another hour in traffic in LA."

My stomach churns harder the longer their conversation wears on. It's like a glimpse into the future if I don't do something.

"I could totally see myself settling down here," Jake says.

"Me too. I mean, I hope I do," Avery gushes. "It's so easy to imagine getting married in one of these Tennessee barns, having babies here, going to potlucks."

Babies? What?

A cold sweat breaks out across my skin. I propel myself forward to her.

"Hey," I say. "How's the mural coming?"

She watches me carefully. "Good. I'm getting the second dogwood tree mocked up today. Should start coming together now."

"Your girl is very talented," Jake says.

"Oh, I'm not his girlfriend," Avery says sharply.

Jake's surprise is genuine.

My reply is immediate. "Avery . . ."

"I thought you two were together," Jake says. "Sorry if I got that wrong."

Avery's eyes find mine. She doesn't smile or smirk or even frown. She's just neutral, and I think that hurts worse than anything.

It's like a sore that won't heal, a rusty nail that sticks so deeply inside you that you know you'll fight that infection for a very long time. This is a pain that's going to stick around.

I feel sick.

"We're friends. Right, Penn?" she asks. "No stakes claimed. Public relationships aren't our thing."

There's a thread of hope in her eyes, but hope for what? What does she want from me? Marriage? Babies?

A trickle of sweat rolls down my back.

It's too soon. All this is too soon. I can't. When I try to love someone, everything falls apart.

"Yeah. We're friends," I repeat. The words hold less conviction than they did a while ago.

At that, Jake turns his back on me and leans in to speak to Avery. I'm seeing red, but what the fuck am I meant to do? Do I smash him and cost Dane a job? Do I even have a leg to stand on?

"Well, if you're available," Jake says, "I'd like to go to dinner tomorrow night?"

My body flexes. Jealousy sears my veins. "You can fuck off."

"Penn!" Avery gasps. "What are you doing?"

I level my gaze to my adversary. "Talking to Jake."

"I'm sorry. You just said . . ." Jake looks between us.

"Jake, can you excuse us?" Avery takes my elbow and ushers me to a room off the main area.

The light is too bright, the air too warm. Avery spins me around and stands in front of me like she's some kind of giant.

"What are you doing?" she demands.

"What do you want me to do? Stand there and listen to that fucker ask you out?"

She narrows her eyes. "First of all, *that fucker* is nice. Second of all, that sounds fair to me, considering every person we see when we're together you're quick to assure that I'm not your girlfriend."

"We aren't labeling things. That's what we decided, right?"

"Yes. Sure. That's right. And by definition, that means you don't get the right to march into a conversation that doesn't concern you and act like a jerk."

I don't know what to say. She's wrong. She does concern me. It certainly feels that way, anyway. But I don't understand why, just because I don't want to put a bunch of rules and regulations on us that I'll never be able to follow, I can't stand my ground.

"Look," she says, "I'm not mad at you for this. But when we went into this . . . agreement, or whatever it is, I didn't think I'd be portrayed as your naive little fuck-buddy."

"What are you talking about? Why do you think that?"

"Because it's true. You kiss my head and have your hand on my ass and then tell everyone that'll listen that we're nothing special. Like I'm an Alexis or whomever, and I'm not. And to be honest, I'm sick of pretending like I am."

My head spins. *I don't understand. Does just being her friend mean I'm not supposed to touch her? I have to commit to her to get to be seen with her in public?*

How does this work?

"Well, you get out of my bed and come here and talk to Jake about having kids," I shoot back.

Her jaw drops. "Yeah. I did. And that's such a weird behavior, isn't it? For a woman to see herself as a mother someday. To talk about her hopes and dreams and goals." She shakes her head in disgust. "I don't know what's wrong with you."

"What's wrong with *me*? Are you serious?" I try to wrap my head around what she's saying. "You spout off about wanting something real. I'm the realest person you know, Ave. I've never been anything but one hundred percent real with you."

She stills. "But have you been real with yourself?"

I groan as frustration seeps out of me. "And what does that mean?"

"Have you even looked in the mirror once since this thing started and asked yourself the tough questions? You just . . . you tell yourself you can't be this and you can't do that, but those things are exactly what you want."

"How do you know what I want?" I fire back.

"Because I see it in your eyes, you idiot. Everyone knows. And if you think you're being real with me, you need to get real with yourself first."

"Did you see that on TV or something?"

"No. It's a fact of life."

She looks at me with a coolness that sends an icy dagger right into my chest. I wish I could say something witty or nonchalant and walk away, but I can't. All I can do is stand here and bleed and hope I can get it stopped before I die.

But the longer she looks at me like that, the more I think there's only one end to this story. She wants all the bells and whistles of life, and I applaud her for that. It works for a lot of people.

It doesn't work for me. *She knows this. What's she doing?*

Some people are built to understand how car defrosters work. There are even others who can switch back and forth between metric and imperial measuring systems in their heads.

Defrosters work for me. I'm decent at calculating measurements, but I cannot wrap my head around love.

So, I don't.

I won't.

I can't.

Everyone would lose.

It would kill me.

Love isn't everlasting. It's built on conditions and promises and . . . and it ends in failure. I'd rather fail her now than later. She has less to lose.

I never should've started this to begin with.

"We were doomed from the start," I say, a lump building in my throat.

Part of me hopes she argues and tells me I'm full of shit. Instead, she nods.

"You're right. I think you focused so much on what could go wrong that you made it happen." She wipes at the corner of her eye. "I just wish you could see what everyone else sees in you. But I can't do that for you. No one can. You have to make the effort to do it, and until you do, you're not going to move forward relationally in life."

"Ave . . ."

Panic fills me up from head to toe as I watch her put together the string of words I know is coming. I've always known they would come because that's what happens in these sorts of things. Someone sees the other's flaws and runs. You can't blame a person for wanting to get out from under a burden that's not theirs to carry, and I don't blame her.

Even if it means she'll walk away.

Even if it means I'll never be the same.

"I'm sorry, Penn," she says. "I promised myself when I got here that I would only get involved with someone that wanted me. You don't. You want the idea of me. You're not willing to hold me or love me or value me in a way that's anything more than a friend you're fucking."

Her words are salt in an already open wound. "Avery, please. That's not true."

"Please what? It is true." She pauses to give me time to come up with a response. When I fail, she gives me a sad smile. "You deserve to be happy. I deserve that too."

The air swirls around us like the final credits are playing. I want to find the remote control and press "Pause" or "Stop" and end this from happening. But the longer I watch the resolution in her eyes, I know the end is going to come whether I want it or not.

"Avery! Where did you go?" Matt calls out.

She tries to smile as she backs toward the door. "I have to go."

And she walks out of the room . . . and out of my life.

All I can do is watch her go.

CHAPTER TWENTY-EIGHT

Avery

It's my fault," I say.

Harper sits on the chair across the room with a frown. "As much as I like Penn, Avery, this isn't your fault."

"No, it is. I let myself get in way too deep." I shove a cookie in my mouth. "In my defense," I say, spraying crumbs everywhere, "it was entirely too easy. A custom-built trap."

"I imagine it was easy. And in your defense, you did resist him longer than anyone ever has."

I cringe. Maybe I should have taken more notice of how it would feel to know that we were a short fling. I bet I should've contemplated how it's going to feel seeing him be *friends* with someone else.

"What good did that do me? Actually, I think that's the reason it turned out this way. If I would've just slept with him that first night and gotten it over with, he would've moved on, and I wouldn't have all these memories of him now to deal with."

I pull my legs up on the couch and try to sweet-talk my brain into putting a mental block on Penn. It would be nice going forward if every color of blue, all things construction, and anything remotely dealing with fish and kisses didn't take me right back to him.

"Maybe he just needs some time," Harper says.

"Well, he can have all the time in the world that he wants, but I'm not waiting on him to figure it out." I shake my head and toss another cookie in my mouth. "I've spent my whole life in this state of limbo, waiting to see what I can do next because of someone else's problems. I couldn't go to camp in junior high because Oakley wanted us to take a trip to Mexico instead. I couldn't leave her alone. I missed my prom because Dad checked himself into a rehab in Utah and no one knew, so Mom hauled us up there to pretend we were having a family weekend skiing to throw off the paparazzi. Oh, and how can I forget the two years I wasted with Dawson when he swore he was going to take things seriously with me as soon as his film debuted. Spoiler: he lied."

I grab another cookie and inspect it. "This is my favorite brand because the chocolate chips are usually the perfect mixture of bitter and sweet. I can't even taste them right now. I just plow through them because I know I like them and hope the routine of it all brings me some comfort." I drop the cookie and look at Harper. "That's sad, huh?"

"It's not sad." She pauses. "Okay, it is kind of sad, but it's normal."

We laugh, a welcome break from the frustration of the day. I lay my head on the back of the couch and say a prayer of thanks that I'm here with her going through this instead of being in LA by myself.

"What are you going to do?" she asks.

"I'm going to eat this bag of cookies that will only make things worse. Then I might see if you have any rum around here because I might as well go all in. Then, depending on how well the rum stays down, I might get a bath or go to bed or, hell, Harper, I might end up having a karaoke night in your living room and sing sad love songs. Time will tell."

She patiently lets me vent. There's no rush to get to whatever she wants to do, no glossing over what I'm saying and then telling me why I'm wrong. She just lets me feel the things I want to feel, or have to feel, and stays present.

I owe her. Because the longer she allows herself to be a sounding board, the more I can work this out. It gets it out of my soul and lets me hear my feelings out loud. It helps.

"Regardless," I say, "I will wake up tomorrow and get dressed and go to work and have lunch, and I'll be fine. I'm well equipped to deal with rejection. It would be a forte of mine if those kinds of things were braggable qualities."

"I wasn't there, so let me start off by saying that. But it doesn't sound like he all-out rejected you."

"No, I'm sorry. He just embarrassed me repeatedly by acting like I was one of his . . . what does Matt call it? His harem?" I snap down on a cookie out of frustration. "You know what it is, I think? I think that what makes me the angriest about this, and maybe the most hurt, is that he's acting like there are two of him. The Penn that wants me, that's so sweet and gentle and kind. And then there's the Penn that's so afraid of feeling that way that he's an asshole and he doesn't even know it. If he were just one or the other—either one of them—I could handle it."

"I'm so sorry, sweet pea."

The bolt of sadness that comes and goes hits me again, and I set the cookies down. I'll never be able to replace the way it felt to be alone with him with all the cookies in the world. But the highs of those times aren't worth the hit to my self-worth and confidence from the lows of the times in public.

I've been given a list of ways to act while out and about since I was a little girl: *don't do this, don't do that, always be polite in case a story is written, even if you're having the worst, most human day, because we can't hurt Mom*. I can't go through a period again of walking on eggshells because someone else is messed up.

Tears hit my eyes as I think of his warm hugs and silly grin and the way he'd nuzzle his face in my hair. And how he'd listen to me and tell me stories and open up about his life. He'd text me throughout the night when I'd stay at Harper's, like we were teenagers.

How he's the realest, deepest, most vulnerable man I've ever met.

"I feel weak saying this"—I sniffle—"but I really liked him."

Harper gets to her feet and sits by me. She pulls me close. The contact dissolves the wall that was holding back the majority of my tears, and they begin to fall.

My hair sticks to my cheeks. My lips start to swell. I'm a hot mess and I know it, and I don't care, because falling apart and having someone care is freeing and needed.

I get it out—the sadness and the pain and the feeling of rejection. When I pull back, I know my anger lies within myself.

"I'm my own worst heart-keeper," I say, brushing my hair out of my face.

Harper looks at me with the deepest concern. "That's why we give our hearts to the people we can trust with them, sweet pea."

"But how do you know? I mean, clearly you probably don't know since you've been married so many times." I fight a grin as I watch those words sink in.

"Touché, Avery. Touché." She laughs before taking a cookie. Sinking back on the couch beside me, she nibbles on the dessert. "I think these are stale."

"Good. I was afraid I was losing my cookie connection."

I take another, anyway, and fall back into the cushions. We chomp away, both lost in our thoughts. I forget that I'd even asked a question when Harper sits back up.

"Okay," she says. "Here's how you know: you trust the person that doesn't give up."

"You just go with the most persistent? No offense, but that doesn't sound like solid advice."

"Hear me out." She tosses the last half of the cookie on the end table. "Everyone makes mistakes. It's human nature. I screw up, you screw up. We all do, but that doesn't make someone a villain because they don't know what they want right off the bat. Heck, sometimes it takes the eighth or eighteenth try to get it right, if they ever do. We're all just trying our best."

"So we're all screwed up, so pick the less screwy one?"

"No," she says. "The people worth giving your heart to are the ones that keep coming back and trying to do better. You can't hold out for the one that's perfect because you'll never find it. Think about that—the people you've known in your life that look like they have everything figured out. Do they?"

She's right. I know it immediately. I've seen so many people that aesthetically appear completely together. You imagine their pantry has those cute little tubs with stickers labeling every bin and that all the clothes in their washer and dryer were just put in there an hour ago, not maybe a week.

Those people are always the worst when you peel them back. It always looks good because they've spent special effort to try to hide the truth from the world.

"At least the mess-ups are being honest," Harper points out. "Those are the people you can trust. The people being *real.*" She pats my leg and lets that thought dangle in the air.

I don't want to think about it. I don't want to think about anything, really. No amount of tossing this back and forth is going to fix anything.

"You know what," I tell Harper. "If you don't mind, I'm kind of over talking right now. I think I need to just mull it over myself."

"Got ya. I'm going to run you a bath and hope you decide to skip the rum tonight. I know that's not what your best girlfriends are supposed to say, but I want you to keep a clear head about things."

"Thank you. Honestly."

We get to our feet before Harper pulls me into a hug. It's a warm, motherly embrace, and I'm so thankful for it.

"You're going to figure this out," she says. "Whether it's with Penn or not isn't in your control. He has to sort himself out. All you can do is be ready to identify whether someone is qualified to love you when they come into the picture." She gives me a satisfied smile and disappears through the doorway.

I hear the pipes squeak in the wall before the sound of water filters through the air.

Penn's face takes over my mind as that reminds me of him and Dogwood Lake and our time there. I can almost smell his cologne and feel his touch. Tears fill my eyes again as I fight my heart not to squeeze so tight.

He felt right. Being with him felt so good.

If everything that's supposed to work out does in the end, why does this feel like the end of the road for us? Because I know that Harper is right. You trust the person who doesn't give up. And, at the moment, the man who gave up is Penn.

That breaks my heart.

CHAPTER TWENTY-NINE

Penn

"Fuck it."

I sit back down for the three hundredth time since I got up an hour ago. I get ready for work with the intention of going and then end up right back here when I realize I shouldn't.

I can't.

My house is so quiet. Eerily quiet, even for this early. It's as if it refuses to talk to me until I get my shit together.

It was a long night. Miserable, actually. Not checking on her killed me, but I think it would make matters worse—for both of us.

My head goes into my hands. Everything is spiraling harder and harder, and I keep screwing up worse and worse. I can't even find one thing to focus on to fix or how to cope with any of this.

I don't know what to do.

And my typical solution at figuring out what to do—by ignoring it—isn't working.

I tug at my hair. The back of my neck is so tight that I wonder if it's possible for it to snap from the strain. If I pull hard enough, can I actually pull my head off?

It feels like it's possible . . . and like it might not be that bad of a thing to happen.

When I let go, my head drops farther before I lift it up. It feels like a watermelon, all heavy and lopsided.

The clock on the wall tells me I should've been at work an hour ago. Matt's probably cussing me, trying to figure out how to smooth it over with Meredith, and I'm sorry for that. I hate putting him in that position, but I can't show up there today.

Not and see Avery.

"I wish I could just make this all go away," I mumble. But even if I could, I don't know what part of it I'd make vanish.

The time I spent with Avery has been the highlight of my life. It's been the easiest to be me, the most inspiring on many levels. I've looked forward to every day more since I met her than I even did when I was on spring break in Florida that time.

And that was a damn good time.

Still, the parties and girls and free-flowing alcohol with not a care in the world don't even come close to sitting on the couch with her while watching a movie.

The events of yesterday have gone through my mind so many times that they're starting to blur. It's beginning to seem like I wasn't even there. Maybe I dreamed it. But if I did, I wouldn't be alone right now with this hole in my chest. If I did, I wouldn't be able to see Avery's face as she walked away from me, over and over again. The disappointment in her eyes. The pain. The resolution.

Because of me. *The fuckup. The boy who'd never amount to anything,* as my dad both told and showed me year after year.

Boom! Boom! Boom!

The knock on the door is so loud that I wonder if my house is on fire and someone is trying to let me know. I spring to my feet and pull it open with the full expectation to see men in red outfits with reflective tape.

Instead, I get a guy with a scowl and narrowed eyes.

"What the fuck are you doing?" Matt asks.

"Good morning to you too."

I leave the door open and turn back to the living room. As expected, the door slams shut, and his heavy steps follow me down the hall.

"Thanks for calling me this morning and telling me you aren't coming in," he says. "That was a super fun conversation with Meredith."

"I'm sorry."

"You are sorry. A sorry son of a bitch, and I mean that in every way."

I spin around to see Matt *pissed*. In all the years I've ever known him, basically my entire life, I've seen him at this level of angry only a couple of times. Matt just goes with the flow. He doesn't get worked up about things.

He's worked up now.

"What the fuck is wrong with you?" I ask.

"What the fuck is wrong with *me*?" He laughs, but there's nothing funny about it. "It's what's wrong with you, Etling."

"Oh, great." I fall back on the couch and hope that a black hole exchanged places with it while I was gone and I'll just fall into the abyss. I land on the cushions. "Let's hear it."

He paces the room. "You consistently shoot yourself in the foot. You refuse to see your potential. You think somehow it's okay to walk away from people that actually might like your stupid, dumb ass."

"This isn't the pep talk I was hoping you'd come with."

I think steam comes out of his ears.

"Why did you think I'd come with a pep talk in the first place, considering you never even called me?" He squeezes his fists together. "And this isn't even about work. This is about your willingness to get me up in the middle of the night to ask me to help you get your truck unstuck from a giant pit of mud you had no business fucking with at two in the morning, but you can't call me because you just fucked up the best thing that ever happened to you."

His words hurt. They sting as they make their intended target. But what hurts worse is the disappointment in Matt's face.

"I had to hear it from Jake," Matt growls. "I had to hear what went down yesterday from fucking Jake." He almost spits the words.

"Jake doesn't even know—"

"Nah, he said you and Avery went off to discuss it on your own, and that when she came out, she was crying and just left. And that you didn't go after her." He shakes his head. "So I bet I can figure out what happened."

I can barely swallow. Hell, I can barely breathe. To hear it put like that, so cleanly, so without the reasons behind it, sounds so harsh.

"Even Jake can't figure you out, man," Matt says. "When you didn't show up today, he was like, 'You better go check on your boy because he's all the way fucked up.'"

"Well, I am, all right?" I say, getting to my feet. "I am fucked up. It's not like you didn't know that."

"I didn't. I never once in my life thought you were this stupid."

"I can't do it, Matt. I can't . . ." I shake my head. There are too many thoughts and pieces of conversations and emotions swirling in my brain to make sense of any of it. "I'm trying to be who I am, but I can't be who she wants me to be."

"She wants you to be you."

"I am being me."

He stills, squaring his shoulders to mine. I've never actually fought Matt, but if I did, I think it would be a hell of a fight. He's farmer-boy strong and has that gene where he's a teddy bear until he's a grizzly. I'm not sure what he'd be today. I don't want to risk it, because I feel pretty damn weak.

"You're going to fail at the best thing that you've ever tried, and it's because you quit." Matt's tone is low, his eyes boring into mine. "How pussified is that, Penn?"

"I didn't quit," I say as calmly as I can. "She quit me."

My voice breaks on the last word, and I hiccup it back. I don't cry, and I won't cry now. Not in front of Matt. Not unless I'm in the shower and can pretend it's the hot water or that I got soap in my eye.

"She quit you because you won't really try. Why would she keep fucking with you? Why would she waste her time falling in love with you when you have the biggest damn wall right in front of you that you keep building higher and higher to keep her out? She's not an idiot. *You are.*"

"She wasn't falling in love with me."

He grins. "She probably was."

I wipe my face with the back of my hand, my jaw dropping so I can breathe. My heart beats so fast I think I might pass out.

She was falling in love with me? Why would she do that? Girls like her fall in love with guys like Matt. Or Jake. Or Dane.

Not me.

"You're going to have to wake up and see what's happening here," Matt says. He's lost the sharpness to his tone, and I'm thankful for that. "You're a good guy. You're just afraid you're gonna ruin everything because your parents drilled that into you. And while we're broaching that topic, let's point out that their problems had nothing to do with you either."

There must be smoke in the air after all, because the corners of my eyes fill with fluid.

"I know you think that loving someone makes you vulnerable. And you're right, it does. And I'll tell you another secret—*you will* fuck up with Avery or whoever you fall in love with someday because you fuck up everything. *We all do.*"

I want to tell him the only person I'd ever fall in love with is Avery. That I'm not capable of being in love, but if I were, there's not a chance it would be anyone else. She was tailor-made for me. I just can't do it.

"You'll forget your anniversary and maybe her birthday, and there will be nights you show up to Mucker's and forget what she wants to order. It happens. Being in a relationship with someone doesn't mean you promise to get it all right, Penn. It means you decided she's worth you trying to get it right more times than not. It's . . ." He searches for the words. "It's a safety net, an agreement that you do your best and hope it works out."

"But my best is shit." I turn around and dry my eyes with the edge of my shirt. "My mom didn't love me more than she loved my dad, who was, maybe, the worst person I've ever known. And my dad only loved me until I didn't do what he wanted me to do, and look where that ended up."

"Even with you doing the right thing." He grins softly. "Don't you see? You still loved your mom, even though you had every right to walk away from her for not protecting you from your dad. And you did the right thing with him too. You made the hardest choices a boy can make, choices most men fail at." His smile grows wider. "You were the first one at the hospital when I broke my spleen—because I fell off a kiddie ladder, I know. You don't have to say it."

I can't help but grin.

"And you gave up your vacation for Dane's family. Who does that?"

"I didn't really have a choice there, pal."

"We all have a choice. We have choices every day. And what you do with Avery, or what you don't do, is your choice too."

I sit back down. My insides are calmer—more jittery than volatile like they were for the last twenty-four hours or so. I put my head in my hands and try to focus on breathing.

I miss her. I miss her laugh and her smile and trying to find ways to elicit those responses. I miss the way I feel because of her. Capable. Worthy.

Loved?

My bed was so cold last night. My heart even icier. It's like there's a gaping void I can't fill and it's threatening to suck me in.

"You need to trust yourself," Matt says. "You need to trust her."

"But why?" I look up at my best friend. "I heard her talking to Jake. She wants to get married someday. Have kids. Have this charmed little life—"

"And she wants those things, and she's spending time with you. What does that tell you?"

"I don't know."

"Maybe she sees so much good in you that she'd potentially hook herself to you for the rest of her life. She's not dumb, Penn. She's almost thirty. She knows what she wants, and if she couldn't see having a life with you, she'd walk away."

"She did," I deadpan.

"No. *You did.*"

My chest feels like there's a band stretching across it to keep me from breathing. I don't want to think about what Matt is saying in case he's right. He's usually right, the cocksucker. And if he's right this time, that makes me a bastard, and I don't want to be that. Not to her. I don't want her thinking that about me.

She told me what she wanted. She wants something long term, and I told her that wasn't me. Yet . . . yet she held my hand and took the risk to follow me to the lake. She held my hand in public when other people saw us together, even though her life has always been about what people see and think of her.

She wasn't afraid to be with me, despite my flaws. *I* dropped her hand. *I* called her my friend. *I* refused to stake a claim, as Matt said.

I did quit her. Even before she was mine to quit.

Fuckkk.

I get to my feet. "Is she at the old library?"

"No. The official line is that Harper needs her to cut hair during the day, so she'll be painting at night. The real line is that she doesn't want to see you." He pauses. "And I'm not guessing. Harper told me at the café."

I close my eyes and sigh.

I hate myself for this. I hate that my shit is causing her more work and is messing up her life. That's the last thing I wanted.

"We better get over there then," I say. "So we can be out of there before she gets there."

Matt looks surprised for a brief second before it's replaced with more disappointment. He heads toward the door. "You're an idiot."

"You're going to be a good dad someday," I tell him as he steps outside. "You can shame someone with the best of them."

He rolls his eyes and shuts the door behind him.

I'm left alone in my all-too-quiet house. The only things I can hear are Matt's words pummeling me.

I grab my wallet off the counter and head down the hallway. When I reach my bedroom, I peek in. The covers are still a mess from when Avery and I lay there the night before last. I couldn't get in bed last night. I tried, but it was too cold and reminded me too much of her.

I close the door and start back down the hallway. Droplets of paint speckle the floor, and I'm reminded of Avery.

I might have to build that cabin . . . and leave this all behind.

CHAPTER THIRTY

Penn

"I remember the days when pulling in here seemed fun."

I sit in my truck and stare at the door to the old library. I have zero motivation to go in. If I didn't need the money or care that Matt would have to finish it on his own, I'd just quit and be a hermit who lives in a tent by the lake.

There's a lot that's appealing about that.

Unfortunately for me, I kind of like Matt. And indoor plumbing. So I get out of my truck and start toward the building.

Every step feels like a mile. When I spot Jake's car next to Matt's in the parking lot, the march feels like the path to a painful and frustrating day.

Jake. I'm going to have to apologize to that motherfucker, and I don't want to. Not just because this is technically Dane's project and I don't have the right, or desire, to do him any harm, but I was also out of line. All that bullshit yesterday was mine, and I handled it like a baby.

A baby who just lost its favorite pacifier, but a baby nonetheless.

I'm not proud as I walk inside. I wouldn't say I'm enthusiastic about seeing Jake first or that heading his way is something I'm eager about doing. But if I do the hard stuff first, maybe I can wallow in self-pity the rest of the day. Dane taught me that: do the hard stuff first.

This is definitely hard.

I spot Jake in the corner with a hammer in his hand. He doesn't look smug or mad as I approach him. Instead, he meets me in the middle with his hand out. I shake it tentatively and make sure I keep my right foot back in case I need to toss a spur-of-the-moment punch.

"Good to see you today," he says. "I almost called you last night but decided you probably had your hands full."

"Mostly." I force a swallow. "I wanted to talk to you about yesterday . . ."

"There's no need." He smiles genuinely, throwing me off a bit. "Look, I understand you more than you think I probably do."

"How do you figure?"

"You're a good-looking guy. Everyone likes you. You work your ass off, and you're damn good at it. You have a great life."

I did.

His lips twist as if he's fighting back a smile. "And then this woman walks into your life and totally upends it all. We've all been there."

I laugh—a single, solitary "Ha!" that makes Jake laugh out loud.

"If I made things worse for you yesterday, I apologize," he says.

"Nah. I made them worse for me. And I want to say I'm sorry for acting like a kid. Shouldn't have happened. Not here, anyway."

He angles his body so he can study Avery's mural. The sketch is starting to take shape. Little bits of color are popped here and there, and if you can look past that, the intricacies of her design really come to life.

A thimble for the old factory that used to employ most of the town is hidden in the tree. A medicine bottle with "Bernie's" written on the label is tucked into the pocket of a man walking down a street. Headstones in the form of crosses line the bottom-right corner, just under the dogwood tree anchoring that spot. I'm guessing it's to honor those who fought for our country.

"She doesn't miss a thing," I say as I spot the beginnings of an old man and a young boy near the edges of a lake.

It's me and my grandfather. I know it is. The dice in the boy's hand give it away.

Seeing that makes me want to cry.

"I acted like an asshole yesterday," I say. "I hope you won't let that reflect on Dane or Matt. They're seriously way more professional than me."

Jake chuckles, squeezing my shoulder. "Nah, I let asshole-ish behavior fall on the shoulders of the asshole."

I grin. "Fair enough. Kinda harsh, the way you put it, but I get it."

We exchange a smile.

Maybe this guy isn't so bad.

"Can I give you some advice?" he asks.

My shoulders tense because more advice is the last thing I want. "To be honest, I've had enough advice for one day," I say.

"Okay. Forget that I asked because I'm giving it to you, anyway."

"Fabulous."

He takes a deep breath. After studying me for a few seconds, he nods. "Go get her."

My head falls back as I groan.

"Maybe you're not worth the kindness you'd have to show yourself to do that. Fine. I'll give you that. You *were* a dick yesterday," he says.

Maybe I was wrong. Maybe he's a jerk, after all.

"But . . . she is." He waits until I look at him before he continues. "She's a ten in every category. And I can say that because you two are 'just friends,' right?"

"You know, I'm really struggling with whether I like you or not."

He bursts out laughing, catching Matt's attention. Matt gives me a curious look, but I wave him off.

"Here's the truth, Penn: you two aren't 'just friends.' I can tell by how she looks at you and the way you behaved yesterday, because while it was utterly ridiculous, it was out of passion. And that," he says, pointing a finger at me, "is how I know."

"Aren't you missing a golf game or something?"

I was joking, but he looks at his watch.

"Shit. I am. I need to get out of here," he says. "But I'll leave you with this: imagine how you feel right now and then how you'll feel when you see her with someone else. Then consider how much you love her and know that no one else will ever be able to love her like that."

Love her? What?

What's he talking about?

"See ya, Matt," he calls across the room. Then he gives me the biggest "I'm right and you can suck it" face I've ever seen a person make.

Fucker.

I watch him walk out the side door, the one he came in yesterday with Avery.

Love her? Is that what this is?

"Yup." Matt sticks the end of a screwdriver in my side.

"Yup, what? And that hurt, by the way," I say, rubbing my ribs.

"Ah, that hurt? Imagine if it was a sawhorse after you dropped four feet."

I roll my eyes.

"I was yupping what you were just wondering," he says.

"You don't know what I was wondering."

"Oh, I bet I do."

I cross my arms over my chest. "Fine. What am I thinking right now?"

"That you hate me."

"Maybe you are good at this."

He snorts, smacking the end of the tool against his palm. "You do love her."

I turn away from him.

I'm not even sure what that means. If I love her, wouldn't that mean I'd be chasing after her with my tongue wagging, like Dane did Neely? Or that I'm being a yes-man, like my mom was to my dad? Or coddling her like she's dipped in gold, like Meredith does those damn dogs?

What does love even mean? How the hell am I supposed to know?

"You let her walk away," Matt says simply. "You did it because you thought you'd fail her."

"Because I would."

"And you let her go because you didn't want to do that to her. *Because you love her.*"

I don't want to hurt her. I don't want to fail her. I don't want to make her anything other than happy every day of her life.

My head spins. Everything seems to be going fast, swirling like a tornado inside me. Over the top of the ruckus, against the hiss of the wind, I hear her laugh.

I'm fucked.

I think I'm in love.

"I've said all I can say," Matt says. "If you want to ruin your life, that's up to you. But you have about an hour to get it figured out and get in here and actually help me, or I'm calling Dane and having him come. He was up all night with a sick Neely and a sick Mia. So if he comes . . . God be with you."

Matt leaves me standing in front of the mural. My gaze instantly goes to the sketch of the lake, and my grandfather's voice comes back to me.

"You'll be okay. You're strong," he said. *"But you'll need this spot. Trust me."*

"But what if I can't get here? Then what?"

He grinned. *"Then you think about me, and I'll help you."*

"What do I do?" I ask the half-finished sketch. "What do I do now?"

The answer comes to me slowly—in pieces. Colors. Feelings.

There isn't a voice that tells me how to go about things because that would be too easy, but I know it all the same.

I glance over my shoulder at Matt.

He has my back no matter what. Even when I'm a dick or not particularly helpful, or when I forget to order the mushrooms on his pizza, he's still there.

That time I miscalculated on a job and cost Dane $700? He forgave me.

When I broke Neely's favorite cookie jar, she let me come back.

And even when I give Claire tons of shit, she still likes me.

No matter how many times I mess up, my friends are still there. We figure it out. And I don't even worry about it too much, because I know they love me.

Maybe Avery could love me too.

"Thanks, Grandpa," I whisper as I turn away from the sketch. "Matt, I'm gonna need more than an hour."

I rip a piece of cardboard off the paint box in front of me and jog to my truck.

"And tell your brother I'm going to need a vacation!"

CHAPTER THIRTY-ONE

Avery

"You're awfully quiet today," Lorene says.

I give her the best smile I can. "I know. I'm sorry. Long night."

"Oh, I remember those days," she says wistfully. "What I wouldn't give to be young again. Getting old is hard. Your brain is the same as it always was, but your body just won't work anymore."

"You get around pretty good, though." Harper looks at me over Lorene's hair. "There are days when I feel like you get around better than me."

"I do," Lorene says. "But I'm not going to if I keep pretending I'm not almost a hundred years old."

I press on the small of my back. It's tight from sleeping on the couch last night, or trying to. I didn't even go to bed. Having slept in Penn's for the last few nights, I didn't want to imagine him behind me. Or on top of me. Or whispering in my ear when he thinks I'm asleep.

"I feel like crap, and I'm not even thirty," I say.

Yawning, I inspect the speaker in my hand. I found it in the last box of my things I hadn't unpacked. It's not as heavy as the other one, and I figure some double-sided tape will keep it on the wall.

Fuck studs.

All of them.

I took the long route to work this morning so I wouldn't have to go by the turnoff for the library. I don't want to see Penn for a while. It'll take some strategizing, and I'll probably starve to death since I'll have to avoid the café and Mucker's, but I can do it. Here and Harper's house will be my safe places for now.

My eyes look bloodshot in the mirror as I turn to the ladder. I'm embarrassed and have blamed it on allergies to Lorene and a man named Gary Rambis, who was my first customer of the day. He was adorable, asking me for tips on proposing to a woman. I gave him my best advice and tried not to cry.

He tipped me twenty dollars and told me to take care of myself. I'll have to find him when I'm emotionally stable again and thank him for being so kind.

That might take a while.

"Thirty is still young," Lorene says. "Enjoy it. Don't waste a minute of it. If I had back the minutes of my life that I wasted worrying about silly things or about things that never happened, I could've lived a whole other life."

"This life is enough to keep me busy," I say, cutting four strips of tape.

There's something about the silence that makes me look at her. She's eyeing me in the way only a woman of nearly ten decades can. It's a look of wisdom and experience, but also of concern.

"A busy life means a full life," she says.

"Well, right now, I'd rather it be more full of fun, happy things than what I'm dealing with."

"Let me tell you something," she says, scooting around in her chair. "Some of my best memories in life started out as some of the worst. I was distraught at times, just devastated by different things. But if I think back to it now, I wonder if that's what it took to push me the other way so I'd go where I was supposed to be heading."

I nod but have to look away. My eyes burn with tears I refuse to let fall.

She's right. The pain of my life in Los Angeles pushed me here. Despite everything that's happened with Penn, this is where I belong. This is where my soul is supposed to be. I'm more accepted here in a month than I ever was on the West Coast, and I finally know what it feels like to have real family and even friends. Matt and Claire have been so kind to me, and Jake even called to check on me this morning.

Even Penn. The man who loved me more than any man ever has. He just won't accept it.

If I have to hurt like this to find a greater happiness someday, I can make peace with that. I just hope it hurries.

I take the tape and the speaker and climb the ladder. I remember the last time I climbed a ladder in here and had a speaker bracket in my hand. Penn came through the door and ended up catching me.

I fight back the burn in my chest as I lay each strip of tape along an edge of the speaker.

"Hey, Harper," I say, trying to distract myself. "Did I tell you Meredith offered me another job?"

"No. She did? That's great."

"I'm excited." I toss the extra tape to the floor. "It's the animal sanctuary next, but she has all sorts of ideas. I think she's going to keep me busy for a while."

"Great news, sweet pea."

"It really is. Getting to do this every day is a dream."

The door chimes ring and my head whips around. The air moves in a way it only does when one thing happens: Penn's here.

The burn in my chest grows hotter, so hot that I think I might catch fire. I'm afraid to turn around. I'm afraid not to.

My fingers tremble around the cord in my hand as Lorene says hello. I don't know what he says back, but I feel the ripple of his voice through my body. It lands right on my heart.

Damn it.

"Hey," he says.

I look down. He's standing at the base of the ladder. His eyes display an anxiety I haven't seen in them before. I hate it because it makes me want to hold him. But friends don't hold friends like that.

"Why are you here?" My words are caught on a load of emotion.

He takes a deep breath. "I'm here because you're not at the library."

"I'm not at the library to avoid you."

"I know."

My jaw sets. This is hard enough without him shoving it in my face. Maybe we can't be friends until I figure this out.

"Please go," I say, turning back to the wall.

He doesn't. He stands there like I didn't say a word. The longer he watches me fix the last bit of tape to the speaker, the madder I get.

I slam the speaker to the wall. It rattles a little basket of fake flowers that Harper has just above the magazine rack. I let go, praying the speaker holds. It does.

"Interesting way of doing that," he says.

"No one asked you."

Lorene and Harper choose this moment to stop chatting. Of course they're listening. I'd listen too. But I've had enough public embarrassment to last me a few days.

"Will you leave?" I ask.

"No."

"Then please move so I can get down from here."

"I'm glad you got a new ladder."

"Move."

"No."

His face is impassive. It's only his eyes that show what he's feeling, and if I had to guess, I'd venture to say he's feeling about as happy as I am right now. The problem is he won't admit it. Or fix it.

"I'm not doing this with you in front of people," I say.

He stands tall. "Actually, that's a great idea."

"Then move."

"No, we're doing this right here."

"Penn," I warn. "Move, damn it."

He takes a deep breath. The apprehension in his usually confident persona makes me nervous. I have no idea what he's going to say. I don't know if I should even care.

"I messed up," he says softly. "I messed up in a bunch of ways, and none of them were your fault."

My nose burns like I'm going to cry. I grip the top of the ladder and squeeze, hoping it'll distract me enough to not make a fool of myself.

"You scared the shit out of me," he says, his voice tinged with disbelief.

A bundle of emotion begins to creep up my throat. I do my best to block it out, to force it back to where it came from. I have to stand my ground. It's now or never.

"I'm going to scare the shit out of you if you don't move so I can get down," I say with all the force I can muster.

"I'm not moving until you listen to me. If I let you down, you'll run off or something, and I want you to hear me."

"What if I don't want to hear you?"

"Listen to him, honey," Lorene says. "If for nothing else, do it so I can think about this for the next week."

My cheeks heat as I stand at the center of everyone's attention. I don't want to do this, especially here, but it's apparent I don't have a choice in the matter without throwing a tantrum.

"Make it quick then," I tell Penn.

He wastes no time.

"I was wrong." He looks me dead in the eye. "I got scared. I thought not putting a label on things would protect what we had together."

"But 'friends' was a label."

"I know." He gulps. "And by not being honest with you, or myself, I couldn't protect anything. I stood to lose it all. And I did. I lost everything. I lost you."

I can't take the sadness in his face. My heart hurts for the man I know has struggled with feeling loved and feeling love. This is new to him. Heck, it's new to me because I've never felt anything like this either.

"I was afraid I couldn't be what you want," he says. "I heard you talking about marriage and kids, and that's like light-years ahead of me. I'm just figuring out how to be here, where I am."

"I want marriage and kids *someday*, Penn. Not today. Not tomorrow. Not next year, even."

"But your babies would be so beautiful," Harper says. When we look at her, she gasps. "I'm sorry. I said that out loud, didn't I?"

"Yeah, you did," I say. "Shh."

I turn back to Penn. He's biting his bottom lip as he waits for me to continue.

There's no shield up, no poise to jump in and correct someone's opinion of the two of us. Just a man trying . . . and isn't that all I can ask?

Maybe. But I also need him to understand where I am. And maybe, too, I need to be honest with myself about where, exactly, my thoughts are now.

"I want to create a life with someone," I tell him softly. "To figure out what I want and what they want and give and take. And bake two desserts for the football games on Sundays because I like cheesecake and he likes brownies. I want that. Arguing late at night because we both are passionate about something. Kissing until morning because we love each other that much. I want to know someone is there to catch me when I fall. Long walks around town and lazy afternoons at the lake. That's all I want."

He clears his throat. The sound is heavy and snotty, and his eyes blur.

"And you could be that guy, Penn," I say, my voice cracking. "You caught me that night at the lake. You were the first person to see and hear me. I left here thinking that there was hope because you existed. I held on to that all these years."

I notice that his right hand, the one with the gorgeous tattoos, is behind his back. I wonder if that's why he hasn't reached for me or if it's because he doesn't want to. If I'm still misreading this. Maybe I still have too much hope.

"You caught me in here when I almost fell—"

"And I'll keep catching you if you let me." His left hand runs across his face. "I'm sorry I embarrassed you. And I'm sorry for acting like a child. And I'm sorry for not being the man you may have thought I was." He takes a step forward. "But I'll try to be him. I'll listen and pay attention and—"

"I just want you to be you." I reach out and touch the side of his face. "Genuine and funny and handsome and kind. I don't want perfect."

He blinks, a smirk on his cheeks. "But I'm close to perfect, right?"

I kick at him, which makes him laugh. It's music to my ears.

"I made you something," he says. There's a flush to his cheeks that hits me right in the heart.

His arm comes out from behind his back. He hands me a piece of cardboard. I take it and turn it over, and the tears flow down my cheeks.

In colored markers, a mural has been drawn. What I'm assuming is Dogwood Lake is colored in blue. And a pair of dice—both fives. And a paintbrush and a set of lips. There are an orange circle and a yellow circle that intersect, making a big red heart. I'm guessing those are our auras.

The brightest yellow happy face I've ever seen is tucked in the upper-right-hand corner, and a bag of chips sits along the bottom with some ants marching out. There's a bag of pretzels on top of an airplane, and a dog that I think doesn't actually refer to an animal.

Then the fucker put a heart in the bottom corner.

That's the last thing I see before the tears get to be too much. I wipe them away only to have them fill up again.

"I was looking at your sketch this morning," he said. "The detail was insane. It's so good, Ave."

I smile as my nickname rolls off his tongue.

The tears slow. He's so handsome, even blurred, with his unshaven face and unkempt hair. I wonder if he had the night I had last night.

"I thought I could make you a mural of my own, to try to show you what you mean to me." He grins shyly. "I'm trying to talk to you in your language."

"Just talking to me in any language helps," I say with a laugh. "But this is amazing, Penn. Thank you."

"It's markers on cardboard," he deadpans.

"It's perfect." I hold it to my chest. "Now will you move?"

"Not yet."

He takes another breath and glances at Harper. My heartbeat thumps wildly as she smiles back at him.

"I'm proud that you would want a guy like me."

"I don't want a guy like you. I want *you*." My voice cracks as tears fill my eyes.

His smile stretches across both cheeks, hitting the corners of his eyes. "If you will give me another chance, I'll be honored to tell everyone I know and see that I am yours and that you are mine. You can label it whatever you want." His forehead mars. "I only have two requests."

I sigh, dropping my shoulders, and Harper and Lorene both exhale. We all laugh as Penn looks at the floor, grinning softly.

"But you were doing so well," I tease.

He looks up, his eyes full of mischief. "First, you have to accept that I'm going to mess up and be patient with me. I'm trying. I'll need help, but I'll get there. Eventually."

"You know, Penn—I never thought you had it figured out to start with."

He laughs. "And second: the only label I don't want is, like, the married kind. I'm not ready for that."

I laugh, tugging his sketch to my heart. I take in this beautiful, brave man in front of me.

What the future holds for us, I don't know. Hopefully it works out, but there are no guarantees. There were no assurances when I came here, either, and it's the best decision I've ever made.

Besides the one to give Penn my heart. Because whether he knows it or not, he's the best thing that's ever happened to me.

"Deal," I tell him.

He beams. "Want to jump and I'll catch you to prove I mean what I say?"

I smile at him. Someday he'll realize he doesn't have to do all the work. The onus isn't on him—it's on us. It'll take us both, working together, to make things work. He'll get there someday.

"Nope," I say. "But you can hold my hand, and we can do it together."

He grins, taking my palm in his and guiding me down the steps. I don't make it down all the way before he wraps me up in his arms. He pulls me into his chest, burying his head in my hair. His Saint Christopher's medal presses against my cheek as I let myself nuzzle him.

It's then, in that moment, that I know: Dogwood Lane isn't where I belong. I was wrong.

This isn't the place that my soul has searched for my whole life.

He is.

EPILOGUE

Avery

Two weeks later

"Rocket Razzle?"

Alexis stands next to the table, a pen and notepad in her hands. She waits on me to give her my order as our friends, *my* friends, chatter around us.

Penn sits next to me with his hand on my thigh. He's always touching me. I'm not sure he even notices it. Sometimes it's just his knee against mine under a table, and sometimes his shoulder bumps mine or he pokes me as he walks by. I think he needs that connection, so I don't shoo his hand away, even though it's too humid tonight to touch anyone.

Even him.

"Yes, definitely the Rocket Razzle," I say.

She nods as she scribbles her note and heads back inside the restaurant.

I sit in my seat and look around the table. Dane and Neely are at the other end with Mia sitting at the head. She's such a pretty little girl, especially with paint in her hair from helping me with the mural this evening.

The library project has expanded into almost a community affair. Once news broke about what Meredith was doing, everyone wanted to do their part. It's amazing to watch a town rally like they have. All it took was someone with enough willpower and spirit to make it happen. She said we are going to talk about the animal rescue project next weekend when we go to Nashville for our girls' night out with Haley.

Trevor sits next to Dane and gazes adoringly across the table at Haley. I've never seen someone as happy as she is. No matter what is going on, she's ready to jump in and help with a smile on her face. Right now, the smile is because of one of Claire's jokes.

"Um, Claire," I say, nodding toward the end of the table. "There are little ears here."

"Oh, shit." She clamps a hand over her mouth. "Sorry, Mia."

Mia doesn't look up. She just bops her head around as she flips through the pages of a book.

Dane laughs. "She has those ear things in and is listening to music."

"Good idea," Claire says. "I'm going to get some of those for the next time I have too many Razzles and end up staying with Penn and Avery." She looks at us and smiles wickedly. "You two are *loud*."

Penn shrugs, totally taking that as a compliment.

My first instinct is to blush. But when Penn squeezes my knee, I realize I don't have to be embarrassed. It's true.

We *are* loud. The entire house is loud when we're together, and that's more often than not. He's hinted about me moving in, but I think it's a little too soon. Yet I stay there every night, so it's probably for naught.

"I'm sorry," I tell Claire. "If you were dealing with eight inches, you'd be loud too."

The table erupts, some of them laughing, others telling me not to encourage Penn's antics. Penn, on the other hand, wraps his arms around my shoulders and drags me into his chest.

He nuzzles his head into my hair. His chest bounces as he laughs. A kiss is pressed on the top of my head before he rests his chin there.

"I love you," he says, still laughing.

My entire body stills.

Matt whips his head to us. Claire looks our way, too, thinking she heard what she did but not being sure.

I heard it. And even if he didn't quite mean it—even if he just said it in a way that I say it to Claire or Harper—he said it.

My heart swells so big I think it might burst. A grin splits my cheeks as I try to contain my reaction to something that's not entirely embarrassing.

"Did you just tell her you love her?" Matt blurts out. "Holy shit."

"He did, didn't he?" Claire's jaw hits the table as the rest of our friends angle themselves so they can see the unbelievable.

"Um, yeah," Penn says, pulling me tighter. "I did. Got a problem with it?"

I don't.

Wrapping my hands around his arms, which are crisscrossed over my chest, I hold on to him for dear life. The jellyfish looks up at me. I think back to what he said, about how the jellyfish is a reminder to follow his instincts. And how, even then, he had the wherewithal to wrap it around the dice.

Maybe he knew back then we were fated to be together.

I squeeze him tighter.

Neely smiles, holding a french fry dipped in ranch dressing in the air. "Did we just witness his first declaration of love?"

"What makes you think it's his first?" I ask. Although it is. And they all know it.

"Because he said it and then his eyes looked like giant saucers," Matt says. "And I'm around you two every day, and I would've heard it by now."

"So what?" Penn says. His chest rises and falls hurriedly. "I love her. I do. And the last time I pussied out of using certain language, she left. So, whatever. I love her. I love you, Avery."

I twist so I'm facing him. My heart is about three sizes bigger than it was before his admission, and I'm not sure I won't burst.

His face in my hands, my eyes glued to his; I let them do all the talking before I say anything.

"I love you," I whisper.

He grins. "Um, you're gonna need to say it louder for the peanut gallery over there, or they'll ride my ass that you didn't say it back."

"I don't care what they think."

"Me either, really, but humor me?" He looks over my head. "She said it back. She loves me."

"I love him," I shout.

The table erupts again, everyone commenting on and discussing our love. They'd apparently ruled out this kind of thing ever happening with Penn.

I'm happy they were wrong.

"It took you two long enough," Claire says. "It took you guys longer to admit you're boyfriend and girlfriend than it does Haley to pick a wedding date. Could you hurry up, please?"

"We have a lot to figure out," Haley says. "And he still wants wedding cake. I want wedding doughnuts. Big challenges to overcome."

"If you'll just marry me, you can have whatever you want." Trevor looks at her over his beer. "Just marry me."

"Hey," Matt says, clearing his throat. "You could have it at the inn."

"And why would we do that?" Haley asks.

"Because I kind of agreed to buy it on a contract from Lorene today."

"You did not!" Haley squeals.

The table breaks out into a loud chatter as everyone celebrates Matt. Penn and I offer our congratulations before sinking back into our own little corner of the table.

Penn sways back and forth with me in his arms. I close my eyes and wonder how I got so lucky. A couple of months ago, I was in Los Angeles, hating life. One quick decision to move across the country with no game plan changed everything.

It gave me a life. A life full of laughter and happiness and bursts of creativity. It gave me friends who care about me and a community that feels good to be a part of.

It gave me Penn.

He leans forward and presses his lips to my ear. "One of these days, I'll ask you that."

"What?"

"I'll ask you to marry me. One day. Not today, but it will happen. I want you to know that."

I turn around to look at him. "I'm in no rush."

"I know. But I always want you to know where I stand." He presses a sweet, simple kiss to my lips. When he pulls back, his eyes shine. "I love you, Avery."

"I love you too. Even if you are trouble."

ACKNOWLEDGMENTS

It takes a village to write a book. I'd like to thank a few special people who loved, supported, and cheered me on through this process.

First and foremost, I'd like to thank God for His blessings and the ability to do what I love.

There aren't enough words in the English language to express my gratitude for my husband. Saul, you are the best thing that ever happened to me. I'll never know how I got so lucky to meet you when I was merely a child, but it's the biggest blessing I've ever received. I love you. Forever.

My children, the four sticky, ornery, beautiful faces that I get up in the morning for, sacrifice so much when I'm writing. Alexander, Aristotle, Achilles, and Ajax, you are the best stories I've ever written. Everything I do is for you. You make me prouder than any book ever will.

Growing up, my parents always told me I could do anything. I believed them. Thank you, Mom and Dad, for instilling in me a belief that I could move mountains. I love you both.

I also would like to extend many thanks to my in-laws, Peggy and Rob. You two are such a blessing. Thank you for loving me like your own. Your excitement and encouragement over my career warms my heart.

Kari March is the most creative person I know. Thank you, Kari, for getting behind all my ideas and mock-ups and sorting through my rambling visions. The day I met you changed my life. I hope you know that.

Tiffany Remy and Kim Cermak keep the wheels turning. You two make everything possible. Thank you for your support, kindness, patience, and figuring out what I mean when I'm going a million miles an hour. Your friendship is priceless.

There are so many things I could say to Carleen Riffle, but none of them would come close to explaining all she is to me. You're simply one of the strongest, most brilliant, and most thoughtful women I know. You amaze me every day. I'm honored you work with me again and again, even if you did infect me with your rambling disease. Ha! Team Mess, always.

Thanks to Marion Archer for having my back in so many ways, and to Becca Mysoor for being my sunshine.

Huge love to Mandi Beck for random check-ins, the best stickers, and for being the person I can always count on to answer the phone when no one else will. You're the realest of the real, my friend. There's no one else like you.

S.L. Scott is the kind of friend who will drive across town and sit in your lucky parking lot—the one that she's always in when you get great ideas. Thank you for being a rock in my foundation.

Jen Costa and Susan Rayner have been with me from the beginning. Their consistent friendship and sweet camaraderie keep me afloat, even on the bad days. I hit the lottery with you two.

Ebbie Moresco, Kaitie Reister, and Stephanie Gibson are the women behind the scenes who keep everything going. Your input and dedication to my groups don't go unnoticed. You're brilliant and kind, and I adore and respect you so much.

Big thanks to Joe's Italian Foods. Your pesto basically fueled the writing of this book.

Sincere gratitude to the bloggers who continue to show up and shout loud about my books. You're the real MVPs. Thank you for all you do.

And to my readers: thank you for choosing to pick up my books. I appreciate and acknowledge you.

ABOUT THE AUTHOR

Adriana Locke is the *USA Today* bestselling author of the Gibson Boys series and *Tumble* and *Tangle* in the Dogwood Lane series. She lives and breathes books. After years of slightly obsessive relationships with the flawed bad boys created by other authors, Adriana created her own. She resides in the Midwest with her husband, sons, two dogs, two cats, and a bird. She spends a large amount of time playing with her kids, drinking coffee, and cooking. You can find her outside if the weather's nice, and there's always a piece of candy in her pocket. Besides cinnamon gummy bears, boxing, and random quotes, her next favorite thing is chatting with readers. She'd love to hear from you! Find out more at www.adrianalocke.com.